## ZOMBIE JAMBOREE

The zombies walked in . . . Well, they didn't walk actually—they danced. And a queer, stilted, stiff-legged sort of shuffle it was—but when the dead dance, you don't ask them to be graceful. In fact, you don't ask them anything. You run.

Which most of the courtiers and ladies did, with a single unified scream. They pushed away from the tables and backed up, hands out to ward off the macabre things . . . Then the music caught their attention.

It was a jangly sort of sound that had a beat that kept thumping where you didn't expect it to, a lighthearted, carefree sort of melody that made you want to dance . . .

Magnus was deciding that it really wasn't all that bad, once you got used to it. In fact, if they weren't so stiff-jointed and dry-looking, he might not have been able to tell the zombies from living people at first. They wore winding-sheets draped for modesty and their skin had darkened—but their empty eye sockets were alive with sparks of light, and they grinned with delight, not rigor mortis.

"Calypso," Rod was saying. "It's definitely calypso."

*Ace Books by Christopher Stasheff*

A WIZARD IN BEDLAM

*The Warlock Series*

# THE WARLOCK ROCK

## CHRISTOPHER STASHEFF

ACE BOOKS, NEW YORK

This book is an Ace original edition,
and has never been previously published.

THE WARLOCK ROCK

An Ace Book / published by arrangement with
the author

PRINTING HISTORY
Ace edition / September 1990

ISBN: 0-441-87313-8

Ace Books are published by The Berkley Publishing Group,
200 Madison Avenue, New York, New York 10016.
The name "ACE" and the "A" logo
are trademarks belonging to Charter Communications, Inc.

PRINTED IN THE UNITED STATES OF AMERICA

10  9  8  7  6  5  4  3  2  1

With thanks to
Ms. Ginjer Buchanan
for all her help with this book,
in all its incarnations.

# THE WARLOCK ROCK

# 1

"Praise Heaven!" Cordelia sighed. She may have been overdoing the sigh a little, but Alain had managed to sneak back to their table to join them, and he was very handsome, in addition to being a crown prince. Cordelia was fourteen, and noticing such things with great interest these days. "Praise Heaven that Mama hath given it to the Lord Abbot!"

"Given what?" Prince Alain watched the High Table, where the Gallowglass children's mother was slipping off a thick chain that held a massive pendant.

She was thirty feet away, for the children sat at a side table, and the Great Hall was seventy-five feet long by fifty wide, which may not be gigantic, but was big enough for the ceiling and the corners to be lost in shadow when the Hall was lit only by torches along the walls, and candles on the tables—and, of course, the great fireplace in the north wall. In the centers of the walls, though, there was enough light to make the lions and dragons on the tapestries seem to jump out at you, and the knights in their shining armor seemed much brighter, and the damsels much fairer, than they ever could by daylight.

But Lady Gwendolyn Gallowglass seemed the fairest of all—at least, to her children's eyes—as she held out the pendant to the Lord Abbot. As he took it, Lady Gallowglass flipped the cover open, and the grown-ups all gasped. Small wonder; even from ten yards' distance, Alain could see the glow of the stone. "What is it?"

"'Tis a circuit . . . ouch!" Geoffrey Gallowglass swore, grasping at his shin.

"'Tis a rock that Father hath made," his sister Cordelia explained to Alain.

"Say rather, 'found' or 'cut'," said Diarmid, Alain's little brother. "A man doth not 'make' a rock."

"Speak of what thou knowest, sprat!" Alain scolded, and Gregory, the littlest Gallowglass, said helpfully, "Papa doth. Thou canst, too, if thou dost mix the right potion. Make a brine so salty it doth become thick, then hang a twine in it—and in some days, thou wilt see rocks of salt growing on it."

Diarmid stared; if Gregory said it, it had to be true.

Geoffrey managed to get his mind off his shin long enough to think of revenge. He glared at Cordelia, and was just starting to speak when something jolted him back. It was his older brother Magnus, hauling him aside to whisper frantically in his ear.

"Salt rocks, but not rough," Cordelia agreed. "They are faceted as sweetly as the finest jewel."

Alain frowned. "And thy father thus made that blue stone?"

"Aye," said little Gregory, "though 'twas a good deal more of a coil in the brewing."

"Certes," said Alain. "'Tis a jewel, after all, not a lump of salt."

"Yet it seems," said Cordelia, "that it was not what he meant it to be."

Geoffrey returned to the table, sulky but silent. Magnus sat down beside him.

"What did he mean to make?" Diarmid asked.

"An amulet," said Cordelia, "that would give any who wore it magical powers."

Alain could only stare.

"Havoc!" Diarmid said instantly. "There would be no law, no order! Every man's hand would be turned against his neighbor!"

"Thou dost see to the heart of it," Gregory said, impressed. "Still, friend, if *all* were witches, would not the world remain as it is? The strong would rule, the good folk would obey."

Diarmid furrowed his brow, trying to find the flaw.

"'Tis of no matter." Magnus waved the point away. "Papa's rock did not what he wished; when he bade a plowman wear it and seek to work magic, naught did hap. 'Tis what it *did* when Papa wore it himself, that was the trouble."

"What trouble?" Diarmid asked; and,

"What did it do?" Alain demanded.

"He set it in a circlet," said Cordelia, "and wore it on his forehead whiles he tried to uproot a sapling that was growing too near the house."

"Could not thy father do that without the jewel?" Diarmid asked.

"Aye, so he gave it only the merest thought—but naught did hap. So he thought harder, then as hard as he could— and still the tree stood."

Alain stared. "The stone locked up his magic?"

"Nay," said Geoffrey, coming alive at last, "for when he thought his hardest, the sky grew dark."

"Dost thou remember that sudden rain that did drench us a fortnight agone?" Gregory asked.

"It was a totally new psi power," Rod Gallowglass explained, "new to me, anyway. I mean, I'd heard of rainmakers before, and I still think it's just another form of telekinesis. . . ."

"But it was not the form thou didst wish at the moment." The Abbot set the stone down on the table and took his hands from it.

"That *is* the point," Rod agreed. "Of course, I took it off right away and came inside—and I made sure I put it in the safest place I could think of, before I went to dry off."

Father Boquilva glanced at Gwen, but forbore to ask what that "safest place" had been. "Then other than making the locket to hold it, thou hast done naught with it since?"

"Nothing," Rod said firmly, "and Gwen was very careful with her magic while we considered what to do."

"And what hast thou decided?" Queen Catharine asked.

"That I won't try any more experiments," Rod answered.

"Wise, until we are sure what thou hast wrought." The Abbot closed the locket's cover gingerly. Father Boquilva watched him, looking rather pale and a little green around the gills.

"Then," Gwen said, "we did concur that we should ask thee to take it to thy monks at the monastery, who make a practice of investigating such things, that they may decide if it is a thing of no use—or ill use alone."

Rod nodded. "If it's more trouble than benefit, please destroy it. Only don't tell me you did," he said as an afterthought. "I was rather proud of it. . . ."

"It is indeed an immense accomplishment." The Abbot picked up the amulet—warily, by the chain—and slipped it into a pocket hidden inside his robe. "We shall do as thou dost ask—and my monks will use all possible care, I assure thee. By good fortune, I've little enough of the Power myself, so it should be safe with me as I take it back to the monastery. Which I will do straightaway"—he turned to the King—"if thou wilt lend me some few knights and men-at-arms to ward me as I ride."

"That will I, and right gladly," Tuan returned.

That was when the zombies walked in.

Well, they didn't walk, actually—they danced. And a queer, stilted, stiff-legged sort of shuffle it was—but when the dead dance, you don't ask them to be graceful. In fact, you don't ask them anything. You run.

Which most of the courtiers and ladies did, with a single unified scream. They pushed away from the tables and backed up, hands out to ward off the macabre things. Tables crashed over, platters and ewers fell bouncing, and men

shoved their wives and sweethearts behind them, pulling
out their swords and daggers with that sick sort of look that
said they knew it wouldn't do any good. Magnus pushed his
two little brothers and his sister behind him, of course, but
Geoffrey ducked back out in an instant, his sword drawn
also, and Cordelia dodged around to his left—only to jar
into the back of Alain, who was insisting on being protec-
tive, too. By way of saving face, she caught Diarmid and
Gregory to her and spat, "Lean aside! I must see!"

"Look, but meddle not." Somehow, her mother was
there, right behind her. Cordelia noticed that Gwen didn't
try to get out in front of her sons—after all, Magnus was
seventeen now, and a young man—but she knew that they
were as well protected as though Gwen had.

Then the music caught her attention.

It was a jangly sort of sound that had a beat that kept
thumping where you didn't expect it to, a lighthearted,
carefree sort of melody that made her want to dance, in spite
of the gruesome pavane before her.

Magnus too was deciding that it really wasn't all that bad,
once you got used to it. In fact, if they weren't so
stiff-jointed and dry-looking, he might not have been able to
tell the zombies from living people at first. They wore
winding-sheets draped for modesty, and their skin had
darkened—but their empty eye sockets were alive with
sparks of light, and they grinned with delight, not rigor
mortis. They clapped and sang, occasionally yelling something all together, though he couldn't make out the words,
and some of them held rocks which they clicked in unison
with that odd, off-beat rhythm.

"Calypso," Rod was telling Tuan. "It's definitely
calypso."

"What?" said Father Boquilva. "The nymph who entranced Ulysses and his crew?"

"No, the form of music. It's from ancient Terra."

"Yet how came it here?" Tuan demanded.

Rod shrugged. "How are they making the music at all? I
don't see any instruments."

The zombies all yelled a word in unison again.

The Abbot frowned. "Now I comprehend what they have said—but it means naught."

"Jamboree!" the zombies cried again.

"It's a sort of a party," Rod explained. "A very big party."

Tuan stepped forward, holding his sword out. "Mayhap Cold Iron . . ."

"No." Rod stayed the king with a hand on his forearm. "Only salt will waken zombies—but you have to put it in their mouths, and make it stay there. Then they'll run back to their graves—but it's very dangerous for anybody who happens to be in the way."

"It matters not," Catharine said, tight-lipped. "They leave."

Leaving they were, in a shuffling procession, clacking their rocks together, snapping their fingers, clapping their hands, chanting the words that the courtiers couldn't understand, punctuated now and again with that shouted word, "Jamboree!"

Their singing faded; finally, they were gone. The whole of the Great Hall stood in silence for a few minutes.

Then ladies collapsed onto benches, sobbing, and their gentlemen turned to comfort them. Cordelia stood rigid, determined not to cry, and Gwen was watching Diarmid and Gregory with concern—but Diarmid was only grave, as he always was, and Gregory was fascinated.

"Come!" Alain cried. "Papa will say what to do!"

But as they approached the High Table, Tuan was saying to the priests, "What was it we spoke of all day? A hodgepodge of hedge-priests, who we thought might become a danger because they praised the life of poverty and chastity?"

Rod nodded. "Somehow they don't seem all that pressing all of a sudden."

"Indeed not." Catharine saw Gwen, and heaved out a sigh that seemed to loosen every joint. "What can it mean, Lady Gallowglass? Whence came they?"

But Gwen could only spread her hands and shake her

head. "From their graves, Majesty. Yet who hath raised them, I cannot say."

"Nor why they sent them here." Tuan began to frown.

"Oh, that is easily said!" Catharine snapped. "They have sent them to afright the Crown and the Court, look you, and even now they dance out through the town, like as not to send the citizens of our capitol screaming in terror."

Tuan turned, snapping his fingers, and a guardsman appeared by his side. "Tell Sir Maris I would have a troop of guards follow those spectres—but stay at a distance, and do naught but watch till they have fled the town."

"Yet if any are hurted in their fright," Catharine said quickly, "aid them."

The guardsman bowed and turned away, but the look on his face said that he was considering a career change.

"Fright is all that would hurt them," Tuan agreed. "Yet a fright of this sort will have the whole land clamoring to the Crown, to banish these fell revenants." He looked up at the Abbot. "And what can the Crown do?"

The Abbot was silent a moment, then said, "I shall consult with my monks."

"Naught, then." Tuan turned back to Catharine. "And the people shall see their monarchs powerless. This is the purpose."

"To hale us down," Catharine said, white-lipped. "Will they never be done? Will they never leave us in peace?"

"Never," Rod said, "for your land and your people are far too important, Your Majesties."

Catharine thawed a little, and there was a glimmer of gratitude in her eyes. She didn't ask to whom she and her people were important; she and her husband had wormed as much of that as they could from the Lord Warlock, and Catharine wasn't sure she wanted to know any more.

But Tuan was another matter. "Who are the 'they' she doth speak of?"

"Why, the ones who raised the zombies," Rod hedged.

"And who did that, Papa?" Gregory asked.

"Nice question." Rod looked down at his youngest,

trying not to let his exasperation show. "Got any ideas, Gregory?"

"A sorcerer," said Diarmid.

"Fair guess." Rod nodded. *"Which* sorcerer?"

Gregory shook his head. "We do not know enough to guess, Papa."

"Then," said Catharine, "I prithee, go learn."

# 2

"Because the Queen said, 'Go learn,' that's why." Rod tightened the cinch on Fess's saddle.

"It seems to me, Rod, that you take virtually any excuse to go on a journey these days." Rod picked up the great black horse's voice through an earphone imbedded in his mastoid process. Of course, he could have heard the robot without it, now that Fess had figured out how to transmit in the family telepathic mode—but the earphone didn't demand any concentration.

"Well, true," Rod conceded, "so long as Their Majesties are paying expenses." He grinned wickedly. "Sometimes even if they're not. But it cuts down on the explanations when it's official."

"Still, you are pursuing a manifestation that resembled walking corpses. Do you truly think it is safe to bring the children along?"

Rod stopped with the saddlebags over his arm and ticked off points on his fingers. "One: There was absolutely no sign of violence from the cold ones. In fact, they seemed remarkably good-natured. Two: None of my children showed much in the way of fear at the sight of them. Three: Do you really think we could get them to stay behind, if we tried?"

"Not unless Gwen did"—the horse sighed—"and she does seem to have her mind set on the expedition."

"And if *she* thinks it's safe enough for them to go, then it's safe."

"I concede the point." Fess sighed, again. "Still, as the children's tutor, I must protest this interruption in their studies."

"Who said anything about stopping the homework? I'm sure you can find time for a lecture or two." Rod slung the saddlebags over Fess's back, led him out of the stable, and turned back to close and bolt the door.

"There is small need for that, Lord Warlock," said a small voice from the tussock of grass beside the building. "We shall ward thy cot and barn well in thine absence."

Rod inclined his head gravely toward the tussock. "I thank you, brownie. Simply a matter of responsible behavior—I shouldn't task you any more than is necessary. Oh, and I left the bowl of milk inside."

"We ha' known of it," the invisible manikin replied. "Godspeed, Lord Warlock."

"I thank you, Wee Folk," Rod called out, then turned away to join his wife and children, where they waited with their packs.

Gwen looked askance at him, then turned to watch the children. Rod didn't need to read her mind to know she was wondering about the wisdom of letting Fess try to lecture about mathematics when the children had clearly decided they were on holiday. For his part, Rod was beginning to think it wasn't such a hot idea, either, especially from the degree of ruddiness in Geoffrey's countenance.

"Such a deal of parabolas and hyperbolas and tangents!" the boy finally exploded. "What matter *they* to a warrior?"

"They will matter greatly," Fess responded, "if you lay siege to a castle."

Geoffrey stared at him. "How?"

"Excellent question. How do you aim a catapult, Geoffrey?"

"Thou dost point it at the castle, and loose!" The boy spread his hands.

"And if the rock falls short of the wall?"

Geoffrey expanded, delighted to talk about something he knew. "Thou dost bring the catapult closer."

"But the castle's archers will make pincushions of your men if you come too close," Fess pointed out.

"Why, then," Geoffrey said, disgusted, "one doth make a stronger catapult."

"Good enough. But let us say that you make it too strong, and the rock sails over the castle wall and into the bailey."

" 'Twill do *some* damage. . . ."

"But it will not breach the wall. You could tilt it, though."

"Catapults do not tilt." Geoffrey scowled, suspecting a trick.

"Then you must invent one that does."

"Wherefore?" Geoffrey protested. "What good would it do?"

"Why not make a catapult, and show them?" Rod suggested.

Whatever Fess's answer was, it was drowned out by Geoffrey's cheer. He and Gregory set about gathering sticks and creepers, and in ten minutes' time had lashed together a serviceable imitation of a catapult, while Cordelia and Magnus watched with indulgent smiles, trying not to look interested.

Fess said, with resignation, "Load the catapult, Geoffrey."

"Aye, Fess!" The boy snatched a three-inch pebble from the ground, placing it into the cup at the end of the catapult's throwing arm.

"Aim it at that large oak tree at the side of the road ahead," Fess instructed.

" 'Tis the thickest for a rod's walk." Magnus grinned. "An thou canst not hit that, brother, I shall have to fetch thee an oliphant."

Geoffrey gave him a black glare, but before he could speak, Fess said, "I did not ask for your input, Magnus. Is your aim complete, Geoffrey?"

"Aye, Fess."

"Loose, then."

Geoffrey pushed the 'trigger,' and the arm slammed forward. The pebble shot up into the air.

"Notice that the path of the stone is a curve, children. In fact, if you watch closely, you will see that it is a curve with which you are familiar."

"Why, so 'tis," Geoffrey agreed. " 'Tis like to the path of an arrow, when the archer doth shoot at a distant target."

"It is indeed—and it is also a parabola. With the proper mathematics, one can calculate from the elevation, the angle, the length of the catapult's arm, and the tensile strength of its rope spring, exactly where that arc will end."

"And therefore where the rock will strike!" Geoffrey cried, his eyes lighting.

"Odd teaching method," Rod murmured to Gwen, "but for him, it works."

Gwen shook her head in exasperation. "He will learn naught if it bears not on the waging of war."

The stone smacked into the tree, and a reedy, distant voice said distinctly, "Ouch!"

The children stood stock-still, staring.

Then they turned to one another, all talking at once.

"Didst thou say 'ouch'?"

"Nay, I did but watch. Didst thou?"

"I never say 'ouch'!"

"I did not. Didst thou say 'ouch'?"

"Nay, for nothing struck me."

"Children!" Gwen said sternly, and they stilled on the instant, turning toward her. "Now—who did say 'ouch'?"

"The rock did," Gregory answered.

"That is impossible," Fess assured them. "Rocks cannot talk. They are inanimate."

"In Gramarye, Fess, aught can do anything," Magnus reminded him.

Uncertainty underscored the robot's response, "You imply that the pebble in question is a false stone?"

"I do not, Fess. As thou hast taught us," Cordelia reminded, "*we* do not imply—*thou* dost infer."

"I must admit your accuracy," Fess acknowledged. "The rock must have said 'ouch'."

Rod was amazed at Fess's progress. "Time was when that would have given you a seizure."

The children gave a cry of delight and shot off toward the stone.

"Stay back, children," Fess said, but they had already pelted across the stableyard to the tree. Fess boosted his amplification. "Stay back! We must assume it is dangerous, since we do not know what it is."

Gwen frowned. "That is not needful, Fess."

"But advisable," Rod qualified, "and he has given an order."

Geoffrey reached out a forefinger.

Gwen sighed, and called, *Geoffrey! No!*

Admittedly, she gave the call telepathically, which may have been why the boy yanked his finger back and gave her a wounded look. "It cannot hurt me, Mama."

"You cannot know that, any more than I can." Fess came up behind them and lowered his head, searching for a fallen stick. He found one and picked it up in his teeth. "No matter what it is, it can do far less damage to my body than to yours, since I am made of steel, and you are only made of flesh. Since it is apparently necessary to test this item, you must stand back."

The children took a small step away.

"Giant step," Fess commanded.

The children sighed and complied.

"Three," Fess ordered.

"There is no need," Cordelia huffed, but they did as he said, then held their breaths as Fess reached forward slowly.

In the silence, they became aware of faint strains of music, melodious, but very repetitious, and with a heavy bass rhythm.

Magnus lifted his head, looking about him. "Whence cometh that sound?"

"From the stone," Fess answered.

They stared at the rock and strained their ears. Sure enough, it was giving off music.

" 'Tis a most strange stone," Gregory breathed.

"Then it requires most careful handling." Very gently, Fess prodded the stone with the stick.

It giggled.

"It lives," Gregory gasped, eyes wide.

Rod and Gwen both stared. "What thing is this?" Gwen asked.

" 'Tis not dangerous, at the least." Geoffrey straightened up, relaxing.

"It would seem not." Reluctantly, Fess added, "Very well, children. You may touch it."

They gave a minor cheer as Geoffrey stepped up, knelt, and prodded the stone with a forefinger.

"Stop that!" It giggled.

The children gawked. "It talks!"

"Of a certainty I talk," the pebble said. "Dost not thou?"

"Well . . . certes, I do," Gregory answered, "yet I am not a rock."

"Of course not," the pebble told him. "Thou art too soft."

"As art thou." Geoffrey picked up the stone and squeezed it. " 'Tis a soft rock."

They all stared, startled. In the silence, they could hear the faint, endlessly repeating melody again, its strong bass chords thrumming.

"Cordelia," Fess said, "please stop nodding your head."

"I did not move it," she replied.

Gwen frowned. "Nay, daughter, thou didst."

Cordelia turned to her in surprise, and Fess interjected, "You simply were not aware of it."

"Put me down," the stone protested. "Thou dost tickle."

"Give it me." Cordelia held out her hand, and Geoffrey gave her the pebble. The rock giggled again. She stroked it with a forefinger, and the giggling turned into a purr.

"Oh, 'tis delightful!" She stroked it again. "As though 'twere moss!"

"Moss." Gwen lifted her head. "Certes, my children. It must be a thing of witch-moss."

Witch-moss was a type of fungus exclusive to Gramarye. It was telepathically sensitive; if a projective telepath thought at it, the witch-moss would take the form and color of anything the telepath visualized. It could even gain the power of speech and the ability to reproduce.

Magnus looked down at the stone, frowning. " 'Tis true—it must needs be of witch-moss. An it were aught else, how could it exist?"

"What doth it here?" Geoffrey demanded.

"I make music," the rock answered.

"What is the purpose of it?"

" 'Tis but entertainment," the rock assured him.

"An odd word is that. Where hast thou got it?"

"Why," said the rock, " 'twas ever within me, sin that I was made."

"If 'tis witch-moss, one must needs have crafted it." Gwen tilted her head, eyeing the stone. "Who made thee, rock?"

"Another rock," the stone answered.

Gregory looked up at Gwen, startled. "How could another rock have made it?"

"Oh, silly!" Cordelia said in her loftiest manner. "How do mothers and fathers make children?"

Gregory just stared blankly at her, but Fess said, "I doubt it would be quite the same process, Cordelia. After all, the stone referred to only one other rock."

"Then 'tis a babe," Cordelia crowed with delight. "Oh! 'Tis darling! I am half a mind to take thee home with me, as a pet!"

"Do not dream of it," Gwen said instantly. "I've trials enough without music that will not stop in my house."

"It will stop when 'tis indoors." Cordelia turned to the rock. "Thou canst cease making music, canst thou not?"

"Nay," the rock answered. "I am filled with melody; it must come out."

"Art thou never empty, then?" Gregory asked.

"Never," the stone answered firmly. "The music doth but grow and grow inside me, until I feel that I . . . must . . . burst!" It bounced out of Cordelia's hand. She gave a wordless cry and grabbed for it, but Magnus caught her wrist. "Let me *be!*" she snapped, instantly furious. "I must have . . ." Then her eyes widened, and she stopped, staring, for the rock was rotating on the ground in front of them, hissing over the gauzy, iridescent film that coated the dead leaves under it. Just as suddenly, it stopped.

"How did it know when to turn, and when to stop?" Gregory whispered.

"It has responded to light," Fess pointed out. "Note that it now lies in a sunbeam. It is nearly noon; I believe you will find that it oriented itself by the angle of the sun above the horizon."

Rod stiffened. What Gramarye esper could know about solar cells?

"Would it not rather orient at sunrise or sunset?" Magnus asked.

"No, because at noon, the sun is at its zenith, and its angle above the horizon indicates position north or south. The stone has positioned itself relative to the pole."

"It doth swell," Geoffrey breathed.

They all stared. Sure enough, the stone was growing bigger.

"Back, children!" Gwen ordered, and, "Down!" Rod snapped.

Without demur, they all leaped back and hit the dirt.

"Wherefore, Papa?" Cordelia called.

"Because," Rod answered, "I've known things like rocks that fly apart hard enough to kill people!"

They all wormed back further, Geoffrey, Magnus, and Cordelia hiding behind trees, Gregory ducking behind his parents. Then they peeked out as the rock swelled and swelled, bloating up to twice its original size. It began to tremble and shrink in the middle, pinching in until it looked as though someone had tied a piece of string around it, and kept on shrinking until, with a bang and a metallic crash, it split apart, two pieces flying off into the air.

The children stared, stupefied, but Fess saw a perfectly good demonstration going to waste. "Notice its path as it cuts through the air, children! What is its form?"

"Oh, a parabola," Geoffrey said in disgust.

"We must follow it!" Cordelia leaped to her feet and set off.

"Now, wait a minute," Rod said.

The youth brigade halted in the act of setting forth, then turned back to eye their father with trepidation. "Thou dost intend summat," Magnus accused.

"May I offer an idea for consideration?" Fess asked.

"Which is?" Rod asked.

"Consider: This is presumably the same mechanism that brought the rock here to this location in the first place."

"Certes!" Magnus cried. "*That* is its meaning, in saying another rock made it!"

"Precisely, Magnus. There was one rock, but there are now two. It has reproduced itself."

"Yet with only one parent!" Cordelia said.

"Indeed. This form of reproducing by splitting is called 'fission.'"

"Yet why did it swell and burst?" Cordelia frowned. "What occasioned it?"

"The sun reaching the zenith no doubt triggered it. As to how it swelled, did you notice where it landed when you dropped it?"

Four pairs of eyes darted to the soft rock, and the gauzy sheen beneath it. The patch of iridescence had shrunk to a half-inch circle around the stone. "It did land in witch-moss," Cordelia breathed, "and did absorb it all."

Rod and Gwen exchanged glances.

"Precisely. Let us hypothesize that it swelled so rapidly because it had only just landed in more witch-moss, and noon was almost upon it."

"Why hypothesize?" Geoffrey demanded. "'Tis plain and clear!"

"Many things are plain and clear until we count on them, and they fail to happen. If you wish to be sure you have guessed rightly, Geoffrey, you must create the same conditions and see if they cause the same result."

"Why, this is the scientific method of which thou hast taught us!" Magnus cried. "We first observed and gathered information, then we sought to reason out what that information signified, and now we have stated an hypothesis!"

"Thou hast sneaked a lesson upon us, Fess," Cordelia accused.

"Of course; we are still within school hours."

"Keep it up, Metal Mentor," Rod breathed.

"If you insist. I now propose that we test the hypothesis we have formulated."

"Thou dost mean we should experiment," Gregory translated.

Geoffrey glared at him. "Showoff!"

"Wast not thou, with thy catapult?" Gregory retorted.

"Yes!"

"How can we experiment, Fess?" Magnus asked. "Seek another soft rock, and set it in a patch of witch-moss?"

"Yes, and come to look at it shortly before noon tomorrow, to see if it has grown," Fess answered.

"Well enough!" Geoffrey clapped his hands, delighted by the prospect of action. "Let us follow the rock!"

"We could," Rod said thoughtfully, "or we could go in the opposite direction."

Geoffrey halted and turned back, frowning. "Wherefore?"

"Why would a captain do such a thing, son, if he saw a scout ride toward him?"

Geoffrey gazed off into space. "Why—to seek out the army from which the scout rode!"

"And if we do backtrack the rock, we may find its parent?" Cordelia asked, eyes lighting.

"We may indeed," Fess said, "and we can use it for our experiment."

"And in seeking it," Geoffrey asserted, "we will perform

*another* experiment—one that will determine whence the rock came!"

"What a wonderful insight, Geoffrey! Really, there are times when you delight me! You have hit the precise point—that we may as well perform two experiments at once, thus answering two questions for the price of one! Come, children—let us see if we have guessed rightly as to the rock's source!"

Cordelia, Gregory, and Magnus gave a shout and followed Fess away from the musical rock. Geoffrey followed more slowly, flushed with pleasure at Fess's compliment, but somehow feeling he'd been manipulated.

As his parents knew very well he had, and by a master. "I have never truly known Fess's worth as a teacher," Gwen said softly as they followed the children.

"Neither have I," Rod admitted, "and I was his student."

# 3

The Gallowglasses set off cautiously, Fess following behind. They walked awhile in silence. Then Magnus spoke.

"Yet how could a stone make music? 'Tis not in the nature of the substance; rock is hard and unfeeling."

"'Tis equally unnatural for stones to be soft, then," Cordelia reminded.

"Not for a stone made of witch-moss," Geoffrey snorted.

"Aye. What is *not* in the nature of witch-moss?" Gregory asked.

Gwen smiled, amused. "Why not ask what *is* in its nature?"

"Everything and nothing," Rod answered. "Right, Fess?"

"That is correct," the robot replied. "Of itself, the fungus had no properties other than color, texture, composition, mass, and the ability to respond to projected thought. Its 'nature' is entirely potential."

"I comprehend how it may be crafted; I have done it." Cordelia frowned. "Yet how can it keep the aspects I give it, when I am far from it?"

Rod shrugged. "Dunno—but it can. If I'm guessing right, the first elves were made of witch-moss by people who didn't know they were doing it—grandmothers, maybe, who were projective telepaths but unaware of it, and who liked to tell stories to their grandchildren. But the nearest growth of witch-moss picked up the stories, too, and turned into the characters the story was about."

"Dost say the Puck is a thing of witch-moss?"

"Not where he can hear it—but he probably is."

"Yet whosoever crafted him must be five centuries in his grave!" Magnus protested. "How can the Puck endure?"

"I should think he is sustained by the beliefs of the people all about him," Fess put in. "One might say that, on Gramarye, the supernatural exists in a climate of belief."

"Thou dost mean that other folk with the power to send out their thoughts do sustain him?" Magnus nodded slowly. "I can credit that; yet how then can he think?"

"*Doth* he truly think?" Gregory asked.

Fess shuddered. "That is a philosophical question which I would rather not broach at the moment, Gregory." In fact, he didn't intend to broach it for about ten more years. "For the moment, suffice it to say that Puck, and all other elves, do indeed exhibit all the symptoms of actual thought."

"An it doth waddle and quack, can it be a hen?" Geoffrey muttered.

"A what?" Cordelia asked.

"A hen! A hen!"

"Do not clear thy throat; thou shalt injure thy voice. . . ."

"Are they so real that they can even, um"—Magnus glanced at his sister and blushed— "have babes?"

"I had little difficulty accepting the notion," Fess replied, "once I accepted the existence of witch-moss. It is only a question of whether the crafter makes an elf of witch-moss himself, or does it by one remove."

"And if we do credit an elf's thinking," Gwen mused, "wherefore should we not credit a stone's making of music?"

"But there are no tales of singing stones, Mama!" Geoffrey protested.

"What difference does it make?" Rod countered. "If the people of this land believe in magic, they probably believe in anything anyone can imagine."

"Yet a true rock could not make music?" Gregory asked anxiously.

"Not a *true* rock," Fess said slowly, "though it could conduct vibrations, and resonate with them . . ."

"Then a rock could be made to convey music!"

"In a manner of speaking—but it could not make music itself. However, a person could make a substance that looks exactly like stone."

"Thou dost speak of molecular circuits," Magnus said, relieved to be back on the solid ground of physics.

"I do. You have all seen the ring your father wears; the jewel contains a molecular circuit, and the setting contains others."

"Can it make music?"

"Your father's ring? No—but it can 'hear' music, and send it to the receiver behind his ear. Still, one could build a circuit of that size that *would* create simple music—and that is certainly all that is at issue here."

"And 'twould look just like stone?"

"It could," Fess confirmed, and Rod explained, "In a way, such circuits *are* stones, since they're usually made of silicon—but they're very carefully made rocks."

"Ah!" Magnus looked up, finally connecting ideas. " 'Tis that which thou didst research, by making the amulet thou didst give Mama!"

"And that she very prudently gave the Abbot. Yes."

Cordelia looked up at the robot-horse, a mischievous twinkle in her eye. "Art thou pleased with the fruit of thy teaching, Fess?"

"I cannot deny it, Cordelia—the boy turned out remarkably well, in spite of it all. He not only absorbed the information, but also learned how to think, which is a different matter entirely, though related. He even began to enjoy learning, and eventually found it to be so great a source of pleasure that he seeks new information purely as recreation now."

Rod tried not to blush.

Geoffrey shuddered. "How could one *enjoy* learning?"

That saved him. "Believe it or not, son, it can happen."

"I have seen you reading of the famous generals of the past, Geoffrey," Fess pointed out. "In fact, when you learn that even peacemaking is an extension of the same root purpose as warfare, you will find that virtually *any* information is enjoyable."

"Pray Heaven I never do!" Geoffrey exclaimed.

"Yet if thou dost take such pleasure in learning, Papa, wherefore dost thou so seldom seek new knowledge?" Cordelia asked.

"Not *that* seldom," Rod protested. "I've always found time to read the odd book or two."

"And some of them are very odd indeed," Gwen added.

"As for research," Fess said, "it is simply that he rarely has adequate time for such pleasures."

"He hath found such time *this* year," Cordelia pointed out.

"Yeah, and it's been such a relief." Rod grinned, stretching. "Gramarye seems to have been struck by a wave of peace for the past dozen months or so. When your mother politely hinted that I was becoming something of an encumbrance around the house . . ."

"Oh, I *do* remember thy discussing that Papa had not been to the castle for some time. . . ."

"That was the occasion, yes. So I went down into the spaceship, and passed some time quite pleasantly in the laboratory, which is small but spacious. . . ."

"Wilt thou *never* show us where it is?" Geoffrey demanded.

Gregory said nothing; he had already deduced the spaceship's location, but he didn't dare try to visit it.

"It would be of small interest to you, Geoffrey, since it has only minimal armament," Fess said, while Rod was still trying to think up a tactful answer. "The laboratory is adequate for a broad range of research, however, and your father settled down to see if he could grow a molecular circuit that could function as a psionic transceiver."

"All right, so it wasn't a complete success," Rod said quickly, to forestall criticism. "Still, it should have *some* worth, as a transducer. In fact, I would have experimented with it myself, if only . . ." He broke off, glancing at Fess.

"There is no need to hide it from them," Gwen said, "sin that 'tis where it shall be safe."

"What? what?" Magnus asked in concern. "Hath it a property thou hast not told us of?"

"More of a side effect than a property," Rod hedged. "It's not just that it shifts one form of psi energy into another, see—it also turns the esper's power back on its source."

"Thou dost say that an I were to wear it, and seek to lift a stone with my thoughts, I would instead find *myself* lifted?" Gregory asked, wide-eyed.

"We can move ourselves already," Geoffrey scoffed.

"*I* cannot," Cordelia pointed out.

"You wouldn't want to," Rod assured her. "The thought-impulse picks up energy from its surroundings, and comes back at you about ten times stronger."

Gregory stared. "Thou dost say that my own thoughts would come back to me more strongly than I sent them forth?"

"Oh! What a wondrous device!" Geoffrey cried. "I could move mountains with it; I could make walls to tumble!"

"Sure," Rod said sourly, "if we could figure out which power converts into telekinesis—and if it would hit the wall. But it doesn't—it hits you."

"If you sought to break a castle wall, Geoffrey," Fess explained, "that purpose would turn back on you, and it is *yourself* who would be broken."

That brought Geoffrey up short. "Mayhap I should not wish it," he said slowly.

"Only 'mayhap'?" Cordelia said aghast, watching him out of the corner of her eye.

"But there is worse to tell." Fess's voice was flat and toneless. "That tenfold thought would still be projected out of you again, and the wall would return it to your mind, multiplied by another ten. . . ."

"An hundred times stronger!" Cordelia breathed.

"Exactly. And the hundredfold signal would push out, to be returned multiplied by ten yet again."

"A thousandfold." Geoffrey was definitely beginning to see the horror of it.

"Yes, Geoffrey; we call such a phenomenon a 'feedback loop.' And, being uncontrolled . . ."

"It would burn out his mind," Magnus whispered.

"It would, if you did not cease pushing out your thoughts almost instantly. Fortunately, your father knows what feedback is, and ceased the experiment as soon as he felt his own mental power turning back on him. Even so, he had a raging headache, and I kept a close watch on him for twenty-four hours, fearing brain damage."

"That was when he failed to come home!" Geoffrey exclaimed.

"No *wonder* thou wast so distraught," Cordelia said to Gwen.

"I was quite concerned," Gwen admitted, "though Fess sought to reassure me."

"I immediately informed her that he was well, but would rest within the spaceship for the night. He had connected me to its systems, as he does whenever he goes there, so I was able to monitor his condition closely through his sickbed. But he recovered, with no sign of brain damage."

"Did he ever dare use it again?"

"I dislike that glint in your eye, Geoffrey. Please give over *any* thought of using the device; it is simply too powerful."

"But is it truly safe where it is?" Gregory asked.

"The friars of St. Vidicon of Cathode have sifted such matters five hundred years," Gwen assured them.

"And five centuries of research into psionic affairs should give them a certain competence," Rod pointed out. "In fact, Brother Al assured me they were the best in the Terran Sphere, even better than the scholars on Terra."

"If *they* cannot handle it safely," Fess said, "no one

can—and they will have the good sense to know that at once."

"Then they may destroy it?" Gregory sounded so disappointed that Fess interpreted it as a danger signal, but his programming wouldn't allow him to lie. "I cannot be certain, Gregory, for your father asked them not to tell him if they did so."

"I was kinda proud of it," Rod admitted.

"So," Fess said, "they may liquidate it—or they may yet use it as a research tool. We simply do not know."

"Yet we *can* know that we will never have it out from there," Geoffrey said, disgusted.

"Quite so, Geoffrey." Fess was relieved to see his most tenacious student finally let go of the notion. "Destroyed or intact, it has gone where it will be safe."

Geoffrey suddenly lurched, tripping over something among the dry leaves. "Ouch!"

They were all suddenly still, for there had been a very odd echo to his word.

In the silence, they heard music.

" 'Tis louder," Gregory observed.

"And with a stronger fundament." Geoffrey's head began jerking backward and forward in time to the beat.

"Geoffrey," Fess commanded, "hold still!"

The boy looked up at him, hurt. "I did not move, Fess."

"Yet thou didst," Gregory assured him, and turned to Fess, wide-eyed. "What insidious thing is this, Fess, that doth make one's body to move without his own awareness?"

"It is rock music, Gregory," Fess answered. "Come, look where Geoffrey tripped."

They turned back a step and pushed aside the leaves. Sure enough, there it lay, the twin of the first rock they had found.

"We were right!" Cordelia cried, clenching her fists and hopping with delight. "Oh! Hath our experiment succeeded, Fess?"

"It has, Cordelia; our hypothesis is validated. Now, gather more data."

"Well enough!" Cordelia knelt and picked up the rock. It chuckled. "Oh!" she said, surprised. " 'Tis harder!"

"Yet still doth yield." Geoffrey poked the rock with a finger, and it fairly howled with laughter.

"Let me! Let me!" Gregory dropped down to probe the stone, and it laughed so hard it coughed—right on the beat, of course. "Leave off!" it wheezed between coughs. "Oh! I shall die of tickling!"

Cordelia dropped it and rubbed her hands on her skirt.

"Art thou alive, then?" Gregory asked.

"Aye; no fossil form am I." The rock chuckled. "Oh! I have not laughed so since last I split!"

"Last?" Magnus looked up. "Thou dost halve oft, then?"

"Have off what? . . . Oh!" The rock chortled. "Aye, foolish lad! Whene'er I increase far enough!"

"Didst thou divide today?"

"Divide today into what? Oh! Morn and afternoon, of course! Nay, I did not—the sun did that."

"Whose son? Oh! Thou dost speak of the orb in the sky! Yet didst thou split when it rose to its highest?"

"Aye, lad, every day I have! 'Tis fertile land here, midst the leaves! And I do take my leave whene'er I may!"

"Dost thou never work, then?"

"Nay, I exist but to make music! A bonny life it is!"

"So long as there is witch-moss by for thou to roll into," Cordelia returned. "Yet wherefore art thou hardened?"

"Why, for that I've aged. All things must needs grow hard as they grow old."

"Not *every* thing," Rod said quickly, with a glance at Gwen.

"It is not entirely true," Fess agreed. "Still, I must admit that is the common progression."

"Yet an it hath progressed as its progenitor did . . ." Magnus stood, gazing thoughtfully off into the trees.

"Aye." Gregory pointed. "Yon doth continue the vector we did tread, brother!"

"Another hypothesis?" Fess was ever alert for the sounds of learning.

"Nay, further evidence for the one we've tested. An we

backtrack farther on this vector, Fess, we should discover the parent of this parent rock."

Fess nodded judiciously. "That is a warranted extrapolation, boys. Yet time grows short; let us send the spy-eye." The pommel of his saddle sprang up, and a metal egg rose out of it.

"Fun!" Cordelia cried, and the children crowded around Fess's withers, where a section of his hide slid up to expose a video screen that glowed to life, showing a bird's-eye view of the immediate area. They could see Fess's head, neck, and back with their own four heads clustered around, growing smaller in the screen and swinging off to the left.

"I did not know of this," Gwen told Rod.

"Never thought to tell you," he admitted. "Remind me to dig up his specifications chart for you one of these days."

The rock increased the volume of its music, miffed at being so suddenly ignored.

"Cordelia," Gwen said, "cease tapping thy foot."

Cordelia glowered, but stopped.

On the screen, greenery streamed past faster and faster as the spy-eye shot toward the west. Then, suddenly, it slowed to a halt.

"Three hundred meters," Fess said, "the same distance we have come from the first stone. Here is the audio, children."

From the grille below the screen music blared, faster than that in the air around them, and with a heavier beat. The music from the speaker jarred with the music around them, out of phase; the children winced, and Fess turned it down. "There is another music rock nearby, of a certainty. Let the eye descend, Fess."

The leaves on the screen seemed to swim upward, past the edges of the frame and out, until the brown of fallen leaves filled the screen. The brush swelled until the children could see the outlines of each stick and branch.

" 'Tis there!" Geoffrey cried.

"Directly where we said 'twould be," Magnus said, with pride.

" 'Tis a darker gray." Cordelia pursed her lips. "Would it be harder, Fess?"

"Since this stone is harder than the first we found, and since it maintains that hardness comes with age, I should say the prospect is likely, Cordelia. Can you make any other inferences?"

The children were silent, startled by the question. Then Magnus said slowly, "Thou dost mean that an we seek farther in this direction, we shall discover more rocks."

"That does seem likely."

"And then the farther away they are, the harder they will be?" Geoffrey asked.

"I would presume so, though the spy-eye cannot test it."

"Yet it can see if they are there. Send it farther"— Magnus eyed the angle of the sunlight that streamed through gaps in the trees—" farther west, Fess."

The scene on the screen shrank as the spy-eye rose, then shot into a blur as it swept away.

"Hypothesis: that the farther west we go, the more rocks we shall find, at an interval of approximately three hundred meters," Fess postulated, "and that each rock shall be harder, though we cannot test it. . . ."

"And darker!" Cordelia cried.

"And with louder and more driving music!" Gregory added.

"Harder, darker, and with more raucous music," Fess summarized. "Why do we extrapolate so?"

"Why, because the farther west we go, the older the rocks must be!" Magnus said triumphantly.

"A warranted inference, Magnus! Yet that insight should yield one more."

The children were silent, staring at the screen.

"I would I had had such a tutor," Gwen murmured.

"Why, that the first rocks . . . must have come from the west country," Magnus said slowly.

"Excellent, Magnus! And what does that, in its own turn, tell us?"

"That the crafter who sent out the first rock must be also in the west," Gregory breathed. "I had forgot that there must needs have been a person who did make the first of these rocks."

The scene steadied on the screen, and there it lay, neatly centered, a dark gray rock. Fess turned up the speaker, and twining music with a hard, quick beat boomed out at them. They winced, and the sound dwindled quickly. "Hypothesis validated," Fess said, with a trace of smugness.

"I could use this form of thought to discover an enemy's camp," Geoffrey whispered.

"It is a powerful tool," Fess agreed.

"Yet this is not the only hypothesis involved," Gregory said, his little face puckered in thought.

"Indeed?" There was an undertone of anticipation in Fess's voice.

"We have tracked the trail of this one rock," Gregory said, "yet wherefore should the crafter have made but one?"

His brothers and sister stared at him, startled, and Rod and Gwen shared a proud glance.

Then Cordelia said slowly, "Aye, 'tis unlikely. E'en an he did it solely for the pleasure of it, would he not have made many, to delight in his own prowess?"

"That is possible." Fess carefully said nothing of the plague of songbirds that had struck the area around the Gallowglass house earlier that spring. "But how could we answer that question?"

"An there were other rocks," Magnus said slowly, "they would have split and flown three hundred meters at a time, even as these did."

"That is sensible, if we assume such rocks were identical to the ones we have already found."

Magnus shrugged, irritated. "There is scant reason to think aught else. They should therefore be each at a distance north or south from each of these we've found, but at an equal distance east and west."

"Why, how is that?" Geoffrey demanded.

"Oh, see, brother!" Magnus said, exasperated. He caught up a twig and dropped down to sweep dead leaves aside, exposing bare earth, and scratched with the twig. "An the rocks begin from the crafter, there in the west—let this dot stand for him—then the rocks we've found sprang from him three hundred meters at a time, here . . . here . . . here . . . and so forth." He made a series of dots moving farther and farther east. "Yet if another stone so split, and sent forth offspring, 'twould be either hard by each of these—and we know 'tis not, for we'd have seen them—or at some little distance, here . . . here . . . here. . . ." He punched another line of dots, moving farther north as they moved east. Then he froze, staring down at his own diagram.

So did his parents.

Slowly, Gregory reached in with another twig and punched another line of holes south of the original line, moving farther south as they moved east, then another line south of that, and another, and another. . . .

" 'Tis a set of circles," Cordelia breathed.

"With a common center," Geoffrey agreed.

"The term for such circles is 'concentric,' " Fess explained.

Magnus looked thoughtfully at Fess. "There is no reason why this could not have happed, Fess."

"I agree," the robot said softly. "Let us send the spy-eye searching north and south—though as you have noted, children, it must search in an arc, not a straight north-south line."

"Yet how shall it know *how* sharp a curve that arc must have?" Geoffrey asked.

"Why, by the distance from the center of the circle, brother!" Magnus crowed. "Dost thou not remember that the circumference is equal to *pi* times the diameter?"

Geoffrey glared at him.

"But in this case, we do not know exactly where the center is," Fess reminded him.

Magnus looked startled for a second, then had the grace to look abashed.

"Fortunately, the rocks we seek send forth sound," Fess added. "I shall turn amplification up to maximum, children. If the spy-eye comes near a rock, we shall know by its music."

The children waited in breathless silence, trying to ignore the droning of the stone behind them.

A tinny, clattering sound came from the screen.

" 'Tis there!" Geoffrey said.

"We shall proceed in the direction of maximal increase of signal," Fess told them. On the screen, the scene swooped down and around, and steadied on . . .

"Another rock!" Magnus cried, and Cordelia clapped her hands. Gregory only smiled up at the screen, his eyes glowing.

The rock lay in the center of the frame, medium gray, and heavily thumping under its cascade of metallic notes.

"Seek again," Magnus urged.

"Seeking," Fess answered, and the picture blurred once more. The children held their breath as one sound dwindled and another grew, then . . .

" 'Tis there!" Magnus pointed, and the other children cheered.

The rock lay in the center of the screen, almost identical to the last two, both in appearance and sound.

As the sound slackened, Gregory piped, "Fess—canst thou determine an arc from three points?"

The robot was silent for a beat, then said, "If we assume it is an arc, Geoffrey, yes."

"Then do so, please! And show us it on a map of Gramarye."

Rod stared, amazed, as he realized what the boy was getting at.

"Remember," Fess said slowly, "that this is only an hypothesis."

"Hypothesis! Hypothesis!" Geoffrey protested. "Doth one hypothesis lead ever to another?"

"Yes, Geoffrey. That is how human knowledge progresses."

The screen flickered, and the children found themselves staring at an overhead view of the Isle of Gramarye. Then a circle appeared over it, cutting through the western corner of Romanov, down along the western edge of Tudor and the western corners of Runnymede and Stuart, to intersect the

Florin River in the middle of the Forest Gellorn, and on through the western corner of Loguire to cut Borgia in half from north to south.

The children stared at the screen.

Then Magnus asked, in a hushed whisper, "Where is its center, Fess?"

"Where radii meet," the robot answered, and a large red dot appeared at the western edge of Gloucester.

"The center of the rock music is on the West Coast," Gregory breathed.

"The *hypothetical* center," Fess reminded them, "and the word is 'western,' not 'west.' It is an adjective."

"Oh, what matter?" Geoffrey grumbled. " 'Tis the location of the crafter we do seek. Is he on the coast or not?"

"Remember, we are making several assumptions that may prove false," Fess cautioned. "We really must have more data before we can claim our hypothesis is sufficiently well validated to rank as a theory."

"And a theory is a statement of fact?" Magnus asked.

"Yes, Magnus, with the understanding that such a statement may later prove to be only part of a larger pattern. Do not make the error, as so many do, of saying 'theory ' when they really mean 'hypothesis.' "

"Then let us hypothesize further." Geoffrey folded his arms, frowning at the screen. "Let us ask what will hap if we are right, and this development of rock music doth proceed without hindrance."

"A valid question," Fess said slowly, while Geoffrey's brothers and sister (not to mention his parents) stared at him in surprise. "Extrapolate."

"This arc of thine will expand, at the rate of three hundred yards a day."

"Why, then, we may calculate how long it hath taken to come this far east," Gregory said, eyes lighting.

"How shall we do that, Gregory?"

"Divide the distance from the western coastline by three hundred yards!"

The answer appeared on the screen in blue characters.

"Two years and three-quarters?" Magnus stared. "How is't we've not heard of this sooner?"

" 'Tis but entertainment," the rock behind him answered. Magnus gave it an irritated glance. Fess said, "It is probably correct, Magnus. No one thought the phenomenon worth reporting; all thought it too trivial."

"How long shall it be ere the whole country is filled with soft rocks?" Geoffrey asked.

"Good question," Rod murmured.

"Extrapolating at the current rate of three hundred yards per day, and assuming no change?"

"Aye, aye!" Geoffrey said impatiently. "How long ere the rival army doth conquer us, Fess?"

The robot was silent a moment, then said, "I would prefer you not think of these rocks as an enemy army, Geoffrey. . . ."

"Any pattern may be enemy action, Fess!"

"Nay!" Gregory looked up, alarmed. "Any pattern may have a meaning, but that meaning need not be hostile!"

"Tend to knowledge, brother, and let me tend to arms. A sentry doth not cause a war. How long, Fess?"

"Four years and a month, Geoffrey"—the robot sighed—"and allow me to congratulate you on correct use of the scientific method."

Geoffrey leaped in the air, shaking his fists with a howl of triumph.

Piqued, the music-rock boosted its volume.

"I question, however, the purpose for which you have used it," the robot said. "Still, I must applaud the alacrity with which you have learned the day's lesson."

"*I* have learned . . . ?" Geoffrey gaped at the robot. "Fess! Thou didst not tell me 'twas *school!*"

"We were still within school hours, Geoffrey. But it is so no longer; my clock shows 1500 hours. School is out for the day."

The children cheered, turned about, and plowed into the forest, heading west.

Rod stared after them, startled. "What do they think they're doing?"

"Children! Come back!" Gwen called.

"Fess did but now say school was out." Cordelia turned back, puzzled. "We are free to do as we wish, are we not?"

"Well, aye," Gwen conceded. "Yet what is't thou dost seek to do?"

"Why, to test our hypothesis," Magnus said.

"We must needs seek the information," Gregory explained. "Fess hath said we have not yet enough."

"Come to think of it, he did," Rod said slowly.

"It was not intended as an imperative, though," Fess protested.

"Is not that what we came to do?" Geoffrey demanded.

"Not quite," Rod said, as much to straighten out his own confusion as theirs. "We're supposed to be finding out who's sending zombies into Runnymede, trying to scare the taxpayers!"

Geoffrey cocked his head to one side. "And where shall we seek to learn that?"

Rod opened his mouth, and stalled.

"Here, at least, there is a clear path to follow," Gregory pointed out, "and the two phenomena are as likely to be related as not."

"There is a tempting refutation of logic in that. . . ." Fess said.

"Yeah—it comes down to: when you don't know where to look, one direction is as good as another." Rod threw his hands up. "So, okay! Why *not* go west?"

The young ones cheered, and charged into the woods.

# 4

"Do I suppose it, or doth the music gain in loudness?" Geoffrey frowned at the echoing forest.

"You have used the precise term," Fess told him. "The volume of sound can be measured as a signal, and its 'gain' is its increase. Yes, the gain has decidedly increased."

"Doth this show that folk around about believe in it more?" Cordelia asked.

Rod stopped stock-still, struck by the idea. "Not a bad idea, Delia. The music's been around this neighborhood for at least seventy-eight hours; the local peasants must have heard it. They sure wouldn't doubt their own ears. Yes, they'd believe in the music-rocks more strongly."

"There are a greater number of rocks, too," Gregory noted.

"That would certainly increase the overall ambience," Fess agreed.

"Especially," said Gwen, "if thou art between two rocks."

"Yet how can one not be, when there are so many?" Magnus asked.

The trees opened out into a large clearing, and the children stared at the sight that met their eyes. "Fess," asked Magnus, "what is that slanted slab of rock that doth stand upright on its edge?"

"The angle," Fess said slowly, "is that of the sun at midday. Can you not tell me?"

"It is a gnomon—the 'hand' of a sundial, that doth cast its shadow on the number of the hour of the day."

Fess nodded with satisfaction. "You *did* know it."

"Then there should be numbers on the ground about it," Gregory said.

"Why, so there are!" Cordelia said, astonished. "Yet they are so huge that I did not recognize them. And made of flowers! Oh! How pretty!"

"Why, thank you," someone said.

"Not thee, horseface," Geoffrey said, glancing up with absent-minded scorn, then back at the huge sundial—and spun about, eyes wide and staring. " 'Tis a rocking horse!"

"That *talks?*" Rod asked, amazed.

"Certes I do talk. Dost not thou?"

"I have heard that aforetime," Magnus muttered.

"Small wonder, son," Gwen assured him. "It, too, must needs be made of witch-moss."

"The ingenuity of these psionic crafters astounds me," Fess murmured.

The horse rocked gently in time to the music of the rocks—or was the music coming from the toy itself?

"What dost thou here?" Cordelia skipped up to the horse, hands behind her back. Her brothers glanced at one another; they knew her techniques.

"I do seek to grow," answered the rocking horse. "Dost not thou?"

"Aye, yet I did not know a thing of wood could gain."

"Why, a tree doth, and 'tis a thing of wood. Wherefore may not I?"

"For that thou dost lack roots," Gregory answered reasonably.

"Thou dost, also. Yet I have arcs of wood beneath mine

hooves, which can gain nourishment from the grass I rock on. The more I rock, the more I grow."

Gwen glanced down at his rockers. "Small wonder; thou dost rock upon a patch of witch-moss."

"I think he may also gain from the beliefs of the latent projectives around him," Fess murmured.

"Didst thou not tell me that nigh onto all the folk of Gramarye may be latent witch-folk of one sort or another?" Magnus asked.

"'Espers,' son," Rod corrected. "You're old enough to use the more technical term, now."

"Yes, I did say exactly that," Fess confirmed. "I have calculated such a saturation, based on the assumed propor- tion of the original colonists who had latent psionic powers. That is, however, only an assumption. We would need to check the character-profiles of all of them most carefully, to determine whether or not there is any basis for that assumption."

Gregory's eyes lost focus in a particularly dreamy look.

"The things of witch-moss grow," Magnus pointed out. "That is evidence of a sort for thy conjecture."

"Yes, but scarcely conclusive. I would not yet develop it as an hypothesis."

"What wilt thou be when thou art grown?" Cordelia asked the oversized toy.

"A rock horse," the equine answered.

Geoffrey frowned. "If that is what thou wouldst wish to become, then what wouldst thou term thyself now?"

"Oh, I am but a hobby," the rocking horse answered. "When I am grown, I shall be a career rocker!"

"Thou shalt career about on only two rockers?"

"Nay! Regard my fetlocks!"

The family looked, and saw large, brightly painted wheels attached just above the arcs of wood.

"I had thought them mere decoration," Gregory said.

"Nay, they are more. The more I rock, the more I grow; and the more I grow, the wider grow my wheels, till they shall touch the ground as I rock forward, shooting me farther and faster along my way; and the rear pair shall likewise touch and scoot me as I rock back. Thus shall I rock and roll about, full-grown and strong, and fit to pull full many a gig!"

"A small carriage? 'Twould be pleasant to ride in such a chaise," Gregory said wistfully.

"It will take time for thee to grow so big," Cordelia warned the horse.

"Not so long as thou dost think—for as I go about this dial, I shall make the time go faster for me!"

Magnus looked quizzically at Fess. "He cannot truly make time speed, can he?"

"No, Magnus, but he can create such an illusion for himself—and will perhaps extend it to the people he meets."

"And he shall gain strength from their belief! So that for him, time *will* seem to go faster, and he shall grow the greater!"

"All rockers are in a rush to grow up," the horse informed them, "and therefore do I rock without ceasing, day and night."

"Yet they would seek to remain also things of childhood," Gregory pointed out, "as thou art."

"What a wondrous thing, to be a child grown!" Cordelia exclaimed in tones of wonder.

Rod shuddered.

"It will indeed," the horse agreed, "and therefore do I rock around the clock."

Fess exclaimed, "Full-grown human beings, with the independence and abilities of adults, but the minds and emotions of children? What a chaotic vision!"

Magnus stiffened. "Chaotic? Fess . . . do I detect outsiders' hands in this?"

"Maybe you do, son," Rod said slowly. "Maybe you do."

"Develop the inspiration," Fess suggested, "and see if you can formulate an hypothesis."

Magnus was silent, deep in thought.

"I hesitate to offer a notion," Cordelia said, with that bashful manner of hers that almost guaranteed the other person would ask—and the rocking horse was no exception.

"What thought hast thou in mind?"

"Why, that thou couldst go more quickly an thou didst not depend upon these arcs of wood for travel, but did use thine hooves."

"What!" the horse cried, appalled. "Wouldst thou have me be off my rocker? For shame, damsel!"

" 'Twas not well counselled," Geoffrey agreed. "What chance would he have against a full-grown horse?"

"Why, most excellent chance! Is not thy companion just such a one as I, yet full-grown?"

The children grew wide-eyed, then turned slowly to Fess.

"In what sense do you mean that?" the robot asked carefully.

"Why, thou art no more real than I—only a model of a horse, and just as much a thing of crafting as I am! Yet thou hast grown, as I do strive to!"

"We are both artificial," Fess admitted, "yet there the similarity ends. My 'brain' is a computer, and yours is only a recorded pattern of responses imposed on you by the mind that engendered you."

"Fess," Magnus said, voice hollow with dread, "hast thou not but now described a program?"

The great black horse was silent, immobile. Then he said, "That description is a horrendous oversimplification, Magnus."

"Yet the point is well taken," Gregory pointed out. "Do witch-moss crafters impose some form of program on their witch-moss toys?"

"Toys!" the rocking horse snorted, insulted. "I am no toy, but a thing of great moment!"

"Of many moments, an thou dost hold to a clock," Geoffrey said, eyeing the sundial.

"Nay, such a hobbyhorse as thou wouldst be far more than a toy—thou wouldst be a boon companion." Gregory pouted. "Where wast thou when I did yearn for thee, three years agone?"

The rocking horse stared at him, taken aback.

"Peace, brother," Magnus assured him. "We all did wish for such a companion in our nurseries."

"Save Cordelia!"

"Save thyself an thou dost say so!" Cordelia retorted. "I did ride Magnus's hobby more than he did himself!"

"It need not be a broom for her to ride it," Magnus agreed, "though that last doth come more naturally to her."

Cordelia stuck out her tongue at him.

"Why," the rocking horse said slowly, "an thou dost wish my company, I am glad to give it. Wouldst thou ride me?"

"Oh, aye!" Gregory leaped up onto the horse's back. Startled, it rocked back with a wild and musical neigh, rearing, and Gregory howled with joy.

"Gregory!" Gwen cried, alarmed. "Do not . . ." But she held her tongue as she gazed at the little boy swooping and ducking along the great arc of the sundial, swatting at the rocking horse's flanks with his hat and whooping with glee.

"Let him be, dear," Rod murmured, smiling.

"Do not tell him not to, Mama," Cordelia pleaded. "We see no danger."

"Aye." Gwen relented. "He doth so seldom have the chance to behave as the child he is!"

"That had occurred to me," Fess admitted.

"He hath almost never behaved as babes rightly should," Geoffrey said stiffly, his body taut and his face a granite mask. Magnus saw, and started to reach out toward his younger brother, then hesitated and took his hand away. "I am sure the rocking horse will allow us all rides an we should wish it."

"Oh, aye!" Cordelia exclaimed, eyes alight, but Geoffrey snorted. "And foolish *thou* shouldst look, brother—a youth of seventeen, on a child's plaything! Nay, surely we who have grown past the nursery must be generous in allowing the lad this play."

Cordelia turned to him, startled. Then she saw the look on his face, and her own expression saddened.

So did her mother's.

"Dost thou not agree, Delia?" Geoffrey ground out.

"Oh, aye!" she said quickly. " 'Tis even as thou dost say, Geoffrey! Nay, let the babe play."

"And let him have some moment of childhood that is his alone," Rod murmured.

Cordelia looked at him in surprise. Then her face brightened a little, into a tremulous smile. "Aye, Papa. He hath ever played in our shadows, hath he not?"

"His clothes were once mine," Geoffrey agreed, "and I, at least, had a toy arbalest and catapult, which he disdained. Nay, let him be."

Gregory finished the circuit and sprang off the horse, cheeks flushed and eyes bright. He whirled about, doffing his cap and bowing low to the hobby. "I thank thee, good horse! Ne'er shall I forget this ride!"

"Thou art welcome," the horse answered, bowing forward on its rockers. "Nay, come here again, and thou shalt once more ride."

"Oh! May I?"

"Mayhap on the way home," Gwen answered. "Yet now, I think, we must needs be on our way, Gregory."

"Cannot the rocking horse come?" Gregory asked, crestfallen.

"Nay, though it doth warm mine heart to know thou dost wish it," the rocking horse answered. "Yet I must needs rock here on my dial, or I'll not grow. Wouldst thou deny me that?"

"No," Gregory said, as though it were pulled out of him. "Yet I shall miss thee, good horse."

"And I thee," the horse answered, and for a moment, its music swelled up, slower and sadder than it had been.

"It must let thee go thy way." Cordelia laid a hand upon Gregory's shoulder. "And thou must let it grow."

"Indeed I must." Gregory turned away, following his siblings and Fess with lowered gaze. Cordelia's eyes misted. But Gregory turned back and called to the horse, "Shall I see thee when thou art grown?"

"I doubt it not," the horse cried, rocking away on its arc.

"Belike I shall be transformed into a great spring-steed—yet I will know thee."

"And I thee," Gregory returned. "Till then!" He waved once, then turned away, catching his sister's hand as he straightened up, squared his shoulders, and lifted his chin. "Come Delia! For I must let it rock!"

She squeezed his hand and followed a half-pace behind, hoping he would not see the tenderness in her smile.

Gwen blinked several times, caught Rod's hand, and followed.

# 5

"This deal of sound could become a great nuisance."
Gregory winced at the raucous noise around him. As they
walked ahead through the trees, it dwindled behind them;
but before it had faded, the music of the next rock wafted
toward them on a truant breeze.

"It is not terribly loud yet, Gregory," Fess suggested. "It
is not truly the volume that irritates you."

"Cordelia," Rod said, "stop nodding."

"Mayhap." Gregory looked distinctly unhappy. "Yet the
coarseness of it doth jar upon mine ear."

"Even so, son," Gwen agreed.

"It is the timbre, the quality of the sound, that bothers
you, is it not?" Fess asked Gregory.

"Cordelia," Rod said, "stop bobbing!"

"The quality?" Gregory frowned, listening to the music
for a minute. "Aye, 'tis summat of the sort. 'Tis harsh; an
'twere less so, that fall of notes might be a ripple, whereas
now, 'tis a grating."

"Perhaps it is the rhythm of the bass, the low notes, that
bothers you."

"Magnus!" Rod snapped. "Can't you walk without tapping your toes?"

"Mayhap." Gregory cocked his head to the side, listening. "Aye, for each third beat hath stress when it should not. . . . Fess!" Gregory's eyes widened. "It doth no longer grate upon mine ear!"

"I had hoped that would occur."

"Yet how hast thou . . . Oh! When I do begin to analyze it, the music doth cease to irritate, and doth fascinate! Or if not it, at the least its composition!"

"Precisely, Gregory. There are few irritants that cannot become a source of pleasure, if you make them objects of study."

"Fess! It hath become greatly louder!" Magnus called.

"It has." The robot-horse's head lifted. "What causes that?"

The path widened suddenly, and they stepped past the last trees into a broad meadow with a stream running through it; but on the other side of the stream was a churning mass.

"Well, then, what have we here?" Geoffrey growled.

"Naught but a pack of children." Magnus looked up, frowning, then stared. "A pack of *children?*"

" 'Tis the bairns of three villages, at the least!" Gwen exclaimed.

"Each beast comes in its own manner of grouping," Gregory said. "Sheep come in flocks, as do birds—and lions come in prides. Yet 'tis wolves do come in packs, brother."

"Then what do children come in?" Geoffrey demanded.

"Schools," Gregory answered.

Geoffrey turned away with a shudder. "Scour thy mouth, brother! An thou dost wish to be fish, thou mayest go thine own way!"

"I do not seek to gain on such a scale," Gregory protested.

"Whatever their aggregate, we must discover their purpose." Magnus jumped into the air and wafted over the stream toward the mob of children. "Come, my sibs! Let us probe!"

Rod started to call him back, alarmed, but found Gwen's hand on his arm. "There is no danger, and we must discover wherefore these children are gathered here."

Rod subsided, nodding. "You're right. Let the younger generation take care of its own."

Cordelia, Geoffrey, and Gregory swooped up to follow Magnus with yelps of delight.

"However," Rod said, "I'd like to hedge my bets. Fess, you don't suppose that you . . ."

"Certainly, Rod." The great black horse backed up from the riverbank a little, then bounded into a full charge, accelerating to a hundred miles per hour in fifty feet, and sprang into the air, arcing high over the water to come thudding down ten feet past the opposite bank. Not that he needed to fear wetting, of course—his horse-body had been built with watertight seams. But jumping was faster, and the river *was* muddy, and it would have been so tedious to have had to clean all that sediment out of his artificial horsehair.

Still, the children *could* have waited.

"I see a boat." Gwen pointed downstream.

Rod looked up and nodded. "Careful, dear. It gets soggy, over there." He offered his arm; they began picking their way through the cattails.

By the time Fess caught up, the Gallowglass children had landed and were prowling around the edges of the mob, staring, fascinated, for the crowd of children was in constant motion, pulsing like some huge amoeba. On closer inspection, the pack proved to be composed of smaller groups, each doing something different—skipping, dancing, tossing a ball—but each child was making every single movement to the beat of the music that twined all about them, throbbing and swooping.

"What hath set them to moving all together so?" Cordelia wondered, nodding her head in time to the beat.

"In truth, I could not say," Geoffrey answered, his hand beating time.

"Why, then, let us ask them." Magnus reached out to tap a six-year-old on the shoulder. The child looked up, nodding to the beat, but his eyes didn't quite seem to focus.

After a moment, he turned away and, on the downbeat, tossed a ball to another six-year-old ten feet away.

"Hold! I would speak with thee!" Magnus cried, tapping him again; but the child only looked up once more with unseeing eyes.

"What dost thou?"

Magnus looked up to see a ten-year-old step up behind the smaller child. "I do but seek to speak with him."

The ten-year-old shrugged, head and shoulders bobbing, and spoke with the beat. "He is young, and hath not yet caught the trick of speech."

"Trick of speech?" Geoffrey was puzzled. "Why, how is this? A child hath learned that much by the time he is two!"

"But not the knack of speech in time," the nodding boy answered. "He cannot therefore speak, till he hath caught the rhyme."

"There may be rhyme to thee, but no reason! Nay, then, do *thou* tell us—how dost thou come to all move together so?"

"Together?" The boy frowned, looking about him. "We do not move together. I move as I wish, and they as they wish!"

"Yet thou dost all make thy movements of a piece, at the same instant!"

"Why, how else can one move?" the boy asked, surprised.

"I do not understand."

"Then thou art dimwitted," a twelve-year-old said, stepping up. "Cease to pester my brother, and let him return to his jackstraws."

The children watched, astonished, as the ten-year-old knelt down in three separate, rhythmical stages, picked up the jackstraws on one beat, settled them on another, and dropped them on a third.

"Can he not move between beats?"

"What beats?" the twelve-year-old countered.

Geoffrey's face darkened. "Dost thou seek to mock me?"

The other boy's face hardened. "Have it as thou wilt."

Geoffrey's arm twitched, but didn't swing—only because

Magnus had hold of it. "He doth not realize there are beats to the music about him."

Geoffrey was totally dumbfounded. "Dost thou not hear the music?"

"Aye! Why else would we have come?"

"But is not the music everywhere?"

The boy shook his head—in time to the beat. But his attention wandered, and so did he. Geoffrey leaped forward to catch him, but so did Magnus, catching Geoffrey. A twelve-year-old girl stepped in front of him, smiling. "What seekest thou?"

Her smile was radiant, and for a moment, Geoffrey was motionless, gazing at her.

Then Cordelia giggled, and he flushed and said, "We did but ask the lad if this music is not everywhere."

"Oh, nay!" The girl laughed. "Our grown folk did gather up all the rocks, and hurl them hither! They cannot abide these sounds!"

"I cannot blame them," Gregory muttered, but Geoffrey said, "They do not come hither?"

"Nay—and therefore may we here do whatsoe'er we please."

"They allow thee?"

The girl shrugged, her attention drifting. "We did not ask. . . ." She remembered her purpose and turned back to Geoffrey. "Wilt thou dance?" He shrank back, horrified, and she gave him a strange look, then shrugged again. "Thou art so offbeat." She danced away, her whole body bobbing with the rhythm.

"So then—they have come to the music, with no care for their parents." Geoffrey frowned, watching the children, head nodding.

"And the music doth make them to move." Magnus looked out over the crowd. "There's none here older than twelve, from the look of them—and none younger than ten could pause long enough to talk."

"I have watched the two a-tossing of the ball," Cordelia told him. "They have never ceased their game for a moment."

"The younger they are, the more firmly the pulsing of the low notes doth seize them," Magnus said. "Yet why cannot the oldest comprehend our questions?"

"Who could think with this sound beating at one's ears?" Gregory answered.

"Come!" A fourteen-year-old boy leaped forward and caught Cordelia's hand. "Dance with me!"

She gave a shriek, and her brothers yelled and leaped after her—but the crowd closed around her on the beat, and the boys slammed into bodies, bodies that rotated on one beat and punched at them on the next. Magnus shoved Gregory behind him and blocked, but Geoffrey had the sense to counterpunch on the offbeat, and his fist slammed home. His opponent's head snapped back and he fell; his comrades weren't able to move aside until the next beat, so he landed slowly, staring up at Geoffrey in amazement. "How didst thou that?"

" 'Tis almost as though the time between beats doth not exist for them," Gregory exclaimed.

"Why, then, betwixt beats, we can wend betwixt bodies! Come, brothers!" Magnus nodded his head. "One, AND two AND three, NOW!"

They shoved through and saw Cordelia dancing, her whole body bobbing and weaving, a delighted smile on her face and a glazed look in her eyes as she stared at the boy who had pulled her in.

"Is he handsome?" Gregory asked, with interest.

"As lads go, I suppose," Geoffrey grudged, "though he cannot be much of a boy if he doth wish to dance with a lass."

"Alas!" a pretty blond twelve-year-old girl cried, catching his hand. "Wilt thou not dance with me?"

Geoffrey recoiled as though a snake had bitten him. The girl flushed, hurt, and Gregory tried to smooth it over by asking quickly, "Dost thou not mind this great press of bodies about thee?"

"Nay." The girl beamed. "Wherefore should I? 'Tis but entertainment." She eyed Geoffrey with a slow smile, but he recovered, straightening, his lip curling. The girl saw and pouted for a beat, shrugged on the next, and whirled away on the third.

The boys stared at their dancing sister in the wrapping of music.

"There are words to it!" Gregory said, wide-eyed.

They listened, and heard the twanging music form into phrases:

> *Chew bop, chew bop!*
> *Bee bee yum hop!*
> *Yum chew sip sop,*
> *Boy and girl drop!*

"What arrant nonsense!" Gregory shivered with distaste.

"What is its meaning?" Geoffrey wondered.

"Naught, I hope," Magnus scowled. "Come, brothers! We must haul our sister out from here."

"Yet how?"

"Catch her arms and fly."

"They will seek to prevent us," Gregory warned.

"I depend upon it." Geoffrey clenched a fist, his eyes glittering. "On the 'and,' brothers!"

"One AND two AND," Magnus counted. "To HER left NOW, catch HER arm AND rise AND fly NOW!"

He and Geoffrey shot off the ground with Gregory trailing behind. Cordelia disappeared so suddenly that her partner looked about for her, at a loss—to left and to right, but not up above.

She writhed and twisted in their hands. "OH! Do LET me GO now! THOU foul KILLjoys!"

"Sister, wake!" Magnus cried, but she kept twisting until Gregory swooped up before her, beating time with his hands, then clapped suddenly under her nose on the offbeat. Cordelia's head snapped up, her eyes wide, startled. "OH! What . . ."

"Thou wert ensnared," her littlest brother informed her.

"I was not." She blushed and looked away. "I did only . . . attempt to . . ."

"Study the phenomenon from within, perhaps?"

All looked down, startled, to see Fess looking up at them from the edge of the crowd.

Cordelia couldn't fib with his plastic optics on her. "Nay, I was caught," she admitted grudgingly. "But, oh! It doth take such a hold of one!"

"I do not doubt it," Fess said. "There is entirely too high a concentration of rock music in this meadow. Come away, children, so that we can hear one another talk."

He turned and trotted away. The boys exchanged a glance, nodded, and swooped off after him.

After about fifty feet, Magnus looked up, alarmed, and circled back to accompany his sister. "What kept thee?"

"My broomstick," Cordelia reminded him. "Thou couldst have waited, Magnus! 'Twas but a second's work to leap upon it—yet in that time, thou wast an hundred feet ahead."

"My apologies," Magnus said ruefully.

*Down,* Gwen's voice commanded inside their heads.

They looked down, surprised, to see their parents climbing out of a skiff and onto the bank. *Aye, Mama,* Magnus thought back at her, and all four children landed neatly in front of Rod and Gwen.

"What hast thou learned?" she asked.

Cordelia blushed, and Magnus was just starting to answer, when a sizzling sound made them all turn and look up.

Sudden heat seared, and a muted roaring swelled in volume and rose in pitch. "Hit the dirt!" Rod yelled and leaped aside, knocking his children down like bowling pins as a huge mass of flame shot by overhead and plummeted away in front of them, its roar fading and dropping in pitch.

"Children! Are you well?"

"Aye, Mama," Cordelia answered shakily, and her brothers chorused after her. "What is *that?*" Magnus cried.

"The Doppler effect," Fess answered obligingly. "As the object approached, its sound rose in pitch, and as it went away . . ."

"No, not the sound!" Rob said. "The object! What was it?"

"Why, do none of you recognize it? You have seen enough of them in your lifetimes, I know."

"Wilt thou *tell* us!"

"Why," said Gwen, "it was a fireball, such as witches and warlocks throw at one another! You have seen them ere now."

"It *was* a fireball." Cordelia stared off at the trail of smoke.

"*That?* 'Twas as much a fireball as a hillock is a mountain!"

"The difference is merely a matter of scale," Fess pointed out.

"A scale of that much difference must come from a whale!"

"The whale is no fish, thou ninny!"

"Nay, but *thou* wilt be, and thou dost call me a . . ."

"Quiet!" Rod snapped. "Here comes another one!"

"Two more!"

"Three!"

They stood rooted to the spot, staring at the huge spheres of flame that roared toward them. "They truly are great balls of fire," Gregory marvelled.

Fess's head snapped up. "But their elevation is significantly lower than that of the first! Flee! Fly! Or you will be seared for certain! *Go!*"

The family leaped into the air, the boys shooting away over the meadow, Gwen and Cordelia swooping away on their broomsticks. Rod brought up the rear.

But the fireballs swooped faster.

"To the sides!" Gwen called. "Out of their pathway!"

They veered sideways, Cordelia and Gregory to the left with their mother, Magnus and Geoffrey to the right with their father—but the outside fireballs only sheared off after them.

"The menace comes with purpose!" Fess cried. "Up! See if you can rise above it!"

The family made a full-scale try at transcendence, swooping up into the sky so fast their stomachs thought they'd been forgotten—but the fireballs swooped up after them.

"They have our measure!" Magnus cried in despair. "How can we evade them?"

"I see a river!" Rod called. "Dive, kids! With as deep a breath as you can, then hold it! Maybe the fireballs will stay away from the water!"

As one, the children gulped air and stooped, barrelling downward like lead weights from the Tower of Pisa, and shot into the water as though they were holding a splash contest, with Rod and Gwen right behind.

The outside fireballs veered back toward the center one, and the three of them shot by overhead. Fess knew he had to be mistaken; the noise of their passage couldn't truly have had an undertone of disappointment. "They have passed! You may come up!"

Four waterspouts erupted with four children inside them, exhaling explosively and gulping air like landed fish. They fell back into the water with cries of relief. Rod and Gwen followed with a little more dignity.

"They were chasing us!" Now that the crisis was over, Geoffrey could afford to be angry. "They truly did chase us!"

"Go rebuke them, then, brother," Magnus said, disgusted.

"Who could have set them on us?" Gregory wondered.

The four young Gallowglasses were silent, staring at one another.

"We do have a few enemies," Fess admitted.

"And these fireballs, like the rocks, have sprung from one of them!" Geoffrey slapped the water. "Did I not say 'twas an enemy behind it?"

"We do not know that, and . . . *Out of the water!*"

"Wherefore?" Geoffrey asked, peering around him. "I see naught to fear."

"Aye," Magnus agreed. "There is naught but those four bumps on the water's surface."

"Those four bumps approach," Cordelia said nervously,

"and there is a log on our other side that doth likewise come nearer!"

"Out!" Gwen snapped, and gave them a head start with telekinesis as Fess explained, "Those are no logs, but giant amphibians! And they are hungry! Quickly, children! Out of the water!"

The family shot out like pellets from a blowpipe, looking rather bedraggled; the ladies' brooms were definitely not at their best with soggy straw. The collection of bumps and the log shot toward each other, slammed together, and climbed halfway out of the water, following them in a crescendo of flashing teeth and writhing serpentine bodies. But the huge jaws snapped shut a good yard short of anyone's heels, and the two great lizards fell back on top of each other and lay glaring up at the children.

"Don't just sit there like a bump on a log," the bottom one grumbled, "go get them!"

"I didn't come equipped with wings, fishface!"

*"Fishface?* Who do you think you're calling fishface, snaketail?"

"What are they, Fess?" Cordelia stared down at them fearfully.

"Why, I do know them!" Magnus said, staring too. "Thou didst show them me in my bestiary—though we have never seen them here, and I had thought them but myths! They are crocodiles from Terra!"

"Very good, Magnus!" Rod said, impressed.

"However," said Fess, "only one is a crocodile. The other is an alligator."

"How canst thou tell?" Gregory demanded.

"The alligator's snout is more rounded at the tip; the crocodile's is more pointed. There are other differences, but those are the most obvious ones."

"They got away," the crocodile groused, glowering up at the children.

"Inflation does it," the alligator answered. "Everything's going up these days—even food."

"Well, it was a nice try." The crocodile sighed, turning away.

"Probably sour children anyway." The alligator turned away, too.

"Well! Such audacity!" Cordelia exclaimed, jamming her fists onto her hips. "I'll have thee know I am quite *mmfftfptl!*" The last bit of pronunciation was occasioned by the clapping of Magnus's hand over her mouth as he hissed in her ear, "Wilt thou be still! The last we should wish would be to have them think thee sweet and tender!"

Cordelia gave him a murderous glare over the top of his wrist, but held her tongue.

"I'm gonna go hunt up some mud guppies," the crocodile grumped.

"Yeah." The alligator turned away. "Me for some crayfish."

"They'll do in a pinch," the croc agreed. "See you later, alligator."

"With a smile, crocodile."

They swam away, disappearing into the muddy waters of the river.

"Well! Praise Heaven we have survived that!" Cordelia watched the two reptiles depart, still miffed. "How dare they call me sour!"

"Thou wouldst not wish them to know thee better, sister," Magnus assured her.

"Come," said Gwen, "let us be on our way, and quickly—I do not wish to give them time to think again."

# 6

They hadn't gone far, though, when Cordelia stopped, staring down at the grass. "What things are these?"

"Let me see!" Geoffrey jumped over to her, and Gregory twisted his way in between them. Gwen looked up, interested, and stepped over.

An insect was toiling its way through the long grass, but with such intensity of purpose that Geoffrey said, "Can it be a warrior bug?"

"Not properly a bug." Fess's great head hung over them. "It is truly a beetle, children. It is strange, though."

Rod looked up, alert. "In what way?"

"I had thought they were extinct."

"What?" asked Gregory.

"This particular variety of insect. It is a scarab, such as were represented in ancient Egyptian art."

"Here is another," Magnus called, ten feet away. "It doth move . . . why, toward Papa!"

"Toward me?" Rod looked down—and saw another scarab struggling through the grass. "Hey, I've got one, too! Only it's heading toward you!"

56

"Toward *me?*" Magnus stared.

Cordelia clapped her hands. "Belike they seek one another!"

"Nay," said Gwen. "They move toward the fairy ring."

They all looked up and saw, midway between Rod and Magnus, a flattened circle of grass—and in the center of it, a larger-than-average rock, thrumming away.

Rod frowned. "What's this? Are the Wee Folk helping out on rock distribution now?"

"Oh, nay!" Gwen said, with a mock glare at him. "Thou dost know the Wee Folk dance in circles, and leave rings behind them—but here all is flattened, not the circumference only!"

"What hath made it?" Gregory wondered.

"Perhaps the rock itself," Fess said slowly. He moved closer, being careful not to step on the scarab, and lowered his head toward the circle. "Yes, it is a small depression, a sort of natural bowl. If the rock landed with enough momentum, it might have rolled around and around the circle until . . ."

A scarab struggled out of the grass on the far side, teetered on the brink, and tumbled into the depression.

"Oh!" Cordelia clapped her hands. "There is a fourth!"

"Ours doth arrive now, too," Gregory noted.

Magnus came up to the bowl a step at a time, eyes on the ground. "Mine doth approach."

"Mine, too." Rod was only a step away from the rim. "They're all attracted to the rock."

"Even *scarabs?*" Gwen exclaimed.

Gregory was peering closely. "They are oddly colored, Mama—a slate gray. One would almost think they were, themselves, stone to the core."

Rod frowned. "Then the question arises, were the beetles attracted by rock, or made by rock?"

"It is immaterial—they only seek their own kind," Fess pointed out. "But the question is academic. What *is* pertinent is that they are all moving toward the rock."

The four scarabs converged on the stone, reached out with their antennae, and all touched rock at the same moment—then, frozen, they glittered, glimmered, and all changed color.

"Why, they have become silver!" Cordelia stared.

"Hath the rock transformed them, then?" Geoffrey asked.

"Or have they transformed the rock!" Gregory pointed. "Hark!"

The stone glistened, twinkled—and its music metamorphosed into lilting, soaring melody. At its bass, though, the beat went on.

"What wonder is this?" Gregory breathed.

Magnus frowned. "The stone is a thing of witch-moss—which is to say, it is imagination made concrete. Are these beetles also but things of whimsy?"

"Whatever their source, they have purpose!" Cordelia pointed. "See where they go!"

The four scarabs had joined together and turned away. With determination, they struggled out to reach the world.

Gregory leaped up. "We must follow them. Do not ask me why I know, but I do!"

"They trend west by south." Geoffrey pursued the scarabs attentively.

"Cordelia," Gwen said, "leave off thy dancing, and follow."

"They have touched another rock!" Geoffrey cried.

Lilting music ascended.

"They toil onward!" Magnus kept pace, following the silver scarabs with avid interest.

Behind them, the first rock split with a gunshot crack.

"Duck!" Rod shouted, and his offspring hit the ground. The stone sailed over their heads. Almost instantly, more of the lilting music rose.

"It hath conveyed its strains to other rocks," Magnus murmured.

But Rod was rising, looking toward the northwest. "Its better half is making music, too."

Cordelia said, incensed, "Why dost thou say 'better'? What music could be more melodious than this?"

"The stuff its brother is making." Rod went after the

other rock. He stood a moment, listening, then said, "Its music is richer, fuller."

"Let me see." Gwen came over, then lifted her head, amazed. "Why, it is—and there is summat of an under-song with it!"

"More and more!" Magnus called from farther across the meadow. "They leave a broadening swath of music behind them!"

"Leave them be, and come this way!" Rod called. "Whatever they're doing, it can't be as important as the progress this rock is making!"

Cordelia clouded up, chin firming. "Nay! I will not leave them! I will follow wheresoe'er they go!"

Rod spun to her, taken aback by her sudden rebellion.

"There is much of interest in them, Papa," Magnus said, stepping into the breach. "Whatsoe'er hath seized this land, these scarabs may well spread to encompass all."

"They are important," Gregory asserted, staring intently up at his father. "We *must* follow them, Papa!"

Geoffrey said nothing; he only had eyes for the silver scarabs.

Rod reddened, anger rising. He was alarmed at his own emotion and strove to hold it down; but he also felt righteous indignation at his children's refusal to obey.

Gwen touched his arm, murmuring, "It is time to let them go awhile."

Rod stilled.

Fess said, "It is not as though they have never been apart from you."

Rod found his voice—without shouting. "Yes, but they didn't exactly get high marks for obedience that time."

"Mayhap they did not," Gwen said, "but the Crown might have toppled without their meddling."

Rod stood still.

"I kept them safe," Fess murmured, "though I will admit the margin of safety was narrow at times."

Rod lifted his eyes, gazing at his eldest two over a widening gap. For a moment, he was afraid to let them drift away—but he knew Gwen was right. "Okay. You kids follow the scarabs, and we'll follow the rock's progress."

Cordelia relaxed, beaming. "Oh, Papa!"

"But you'll stay together!"

"Oh, aye!"

"I shall not let them stray from my sight," Magnus promised.

"I'll hold you to it." Rod looked up at Fess. "You'll make sure they stay safe?"

"Certainly, Rod."

Cordelia looked disappointed, but Gregory cried, "Oh, good! Fess will be by us!" and Geoffrey cheered.

"All right, then." Rod turned away. "You'll take the low road, and we'll take the high." He managed a smile as he turned back to wave. "Be careful, huh?"

"Oh, aye, Papa!"

"Godspeed, Mama!"

"God be with you!"

"God be," was all Geoffrey managed, before he was off trailing his quarry.

Rod sighed and turned away. "Hope we're making the right decision."

"Be assured, husband." Gwen clasped his arm. "If aught miscarries, we can be with them right swiftly."

"Yes—and Fess can call even if *they* don't want to." Rod nodded. "Okay, darling. I'll try not to worry."

At their feet, the stone cracked with the sound of a gunshot, and its pieces went flying.

"Follow the northern shard," Gwen suggested.

Rod nodded, and off they went after the progressive rock.

# 7

As they moved after the scarabs, Magnus asked his sister, "I ken how that music did fascinate those children—yet how can it have gained so thorough a hold on thee?"

"Thou canst not know till thou hast begun to dance to it." Cordelia shuddered. "Do not ask, brother—but when thou hast begun to move thine whole body to its rhythms willingly, it doth seem quite natural to continue."

"'Tis a foul twisting of all that's right in the use of one's body," Geoffrey said, disgusted. "Thy limbs should ever move with purpose, one set forth by thy mind and made effective by practice; they should not twitch to some sound that doth but pass by thy brain."

"'Tis horrid to see children so young become victim to it." Magnus had to clasp his dagger to keep his hand from trembling. "I might credit it in one of mine own age, though I would still deplore it. Yet in children!"

"Aye, grandfather of seventeen," Cordelia said, with full sarcasm. After all, she *was* almost as tall as he, at the moment.

But Gregory said only, "How can mere music have absorbed them so completely?"

"How can it have become so much louder?" Geoffrey retorted. "I can comprehend how it can induce bodies to move, for I do feel mine own limbs respond to the beat of the music, almost as to mine heartbeat. . . ."

"Thine heartbeat! Thou hast it!"

"Why, I should hope I do, else would I be dead." Geoffrey frowned. "How is this, little brother?"

"Thy body is accustomed to doing all to the beat of thine heart! In truth, dost thou not gauge the strength of thy feelings by its speed? Thus when the music doth pulse, thy limbs do respond!"

"A most excellent notion, brother," Magnus agreed. "Yet the music's beat is not my heart's—unless it should by some happenstance beat with a very odd rhythm."

"Such as a comely lass passing near," Cordelia said sweetly.

Magnus gave her a dark look, but Gregory said, "Ah, but 'tis therefore that thy limbs do move to the music! For an 'twere but thine heartbeat, look you, thy limbs would be as much in accord as they ever were!"

"Gregory may have a point," Fess said slowly. "There are certain natural rhythms to the body's functions; the heartbeat is only one of them. And, as Geoffrey points out, once the music becomes too loud to truly ignore, the body naturally tends to respond."

"I wot no physician would countenance such a notion," Magnus muttered.

"Yes, but I am not a physician," Fess noted. "And I must stress, Magnus, that the idea we are discussing is only conjecture at the moment; it is not yet sufficently detailed to even be termed an hypothesis."

"Yet what *hath* made the music so much louder?" Geoffrey demanded.

"Why, the grown folk, brother," Cordelia explained. "When they threw so many stones together, there was more music in one place!"

"That would suffice for that one field, sister," Geoffrey answered, "yet it doth not explain the greater loudness all around us."

Cordelia stopped, casting about her. "Why, it *hath* grown! I *do* hear it all round! How is't I had not noticed that sooner, Fess?"

The robot started to reply, but a sudden cry belted from farther down the woodland path, around the bend. "Ho!" followed by a "Ha!" all in the woodwind timbre of adolescent boys' voices, repeating and repeating. "Ho! Ha! Ho! Ha!" Then, above their rhythm, came girls' voices, chanting:

*I sought for love, and love sought me,*
*And found me there beneath a tree.*
*Touch and kiss and soft caress*
*Taught me of sweet love's duress.*

*Loving whispers, sweet love's moan.*
*Say I'll never be alone.*
*Lip to lip, and heart to heart,*
*Seek to cling, and never part!*

"What manner of song is *that?*" Geoffrey asked, goggle-eyed.

Cordelia's nose wrinkled. "Oh! 'Tis vile! Is love naught but the press of bodies?"

"Yet who doth sing it?" Magnus asked, frowning.

Round the bend of the path they came, a chain of thirteen- and fourteen-year-olds, linked by clasped hands, their feet stamping out the pattern of a dance, their bodies and heads tossing in time to the music.

The Gallowglasses stared, astounded.

"What comes?" Geoffrey demanded.

Then the line of youths and maidens was upon them, twining them into their cordon as the Gallowglasses lurched staggering from one to another.

"Oh, come, or thou wilt never stand," a pretty maiden said, laughing. "Thou must dance or fall!"

"Must I truly?" Magnus muttered.

"I do not *wish* to dance!" Geoffrey snapped.

"Then leap aside," a hulking boy behind him retorted

lightly. "Yet what ails thee, that thou dost not wish to step?"

"What ails *thee,* that thou *dost* wish it?"

But the boy didn't even seem to hear him; he had turned his head to gaze into the eyes of the girl behind him.

"What manner of music is this, that doth order thy feet?" Gregory gasped, hurrying to keep up.

"Why, 'tis *our* music!" the girl next to him answered. "Its strains are woven solely for folk of our age!"

"Canst thou not control thine own feet?"

"Wherefore?" The girl laughed. "I do love what they do!"

"Brace thyself against it!" Cordelia enjoined her. "Thou must needs be thine own master!"

The girl looked at her as though she were some sort of monster. "What manner of lass art thou, to not wish another to guide thee?"

"Mine own! A lass who will not be a chattel! Dost thou not see this throbbing sound doth rob thee of thy self?"

"Nay! How could it?" said another girl, also laughing. " 'Tis but entertainment!"

"Who hath told thee that?" Cordelia demanded furiously.

"Why, the very rocks do cry it!"

"The throbbing of it is wondrous!" a third girl said, eyes glowing. "It doth beat within thy blood; it doth set thy whole body to humming!"

Cordelia's eyes widened in horror. "Assuredly thou dost not believe the foul lie its words do sing!"

The first girl frowned at her. "What lie is that?"

"There is no lie in them, but truth!" said another girl farther down the line. She was a little taller than the others, buxom, and very pretty. She smiled at Magnus, eyelids drooping. "Dost thou not hear the wonder of them? Love!"

Magnus's eyes were fixed on her, fascinated, but he mustered the strength to answer, " 'Tis not love those words do speak of, but the hot, unbridled passion of the body's lust."

"What difference?" the girl asked, puzzled. Then she

smiled again and leaned backward, and her lips seemed to grow fuller as her face swayed close to Magnus's. "Wherefore dost thou not dance? Doth not our company please thee?"

"Nay," Magnus managed, but he knew he lied.

She knew it, too. "My name is Lalaina. Wilt thou not tread the measure with us?"

"There is no measure, nor no rule, in that which thou dost seek." But Magnus's feet began to fall into step with hers, and his gaze was riveted to her face.

"Wherefore should there be?" Lalaina breathed. "We are young, in the season of joy! An we do not take our pleasures now, when shall we?"

"Dance," the boy behind him commanded, "or step aside! For we would raise the boughs with our singing, and thou dost bind us to the earth!"

"Canst thou not dance?" jeered another boy, Magnus's own size.

"Thou canst not be our friend an thou dost not tread the welkin with us," said a third, grinning.

Lalaina swayed a little further back, and let her lips brush Magnus's. He jolted to a stop, electrified, and the dancers rocked to a halt with him. All stood watching him, lips smiling, holding their breaths, poised. . . .

Then Cordelia screeched. "Thou hussies! Thou vile, grasping Liliths! Wouldst thou then drag him down with thee?"

"Aye," answered one tall girl, "with all my heart."

"And body." Lalaina gazed deeply into Magnus's eyes.

"He cannot wish to dance with them," Geoffrey cried, appalled.

"He doth hang in the balance." Gregory twisted away from the girl holding his hand and dove toward his big brother. "Magnus! Wake thee! They do weave a spell, they do enchant thee!"

"Why, 'tis no enchantment," a boy scoffed. "'Tis but entertainment."

"Thou heartless wretches!" Cordelia stormed. "Dost thou think a woman's naught but a plaything?"

"Believe them not!" Gregory shouted to Magnus. "They do seek to ensorcel thee, to draw thee into the self-same maelstrom of droning and stamping as they are caught in!"

"Give in to it," a boy coaxed. "Thou wilt not believe the pleasure of it, the heady giddy feeling!"

"Hold fast!" Gregory reached up to thump his big brother's arm. "Thou art thine own man, not some mindless puppet!"

"The music is great, the music is all!" another boy countered. "Submerge thyself in it; let it roll over thee! Then reach to find another's hand, to touch, to stroke!"

"Thou knowest right from wrong!" Gregory insisted. "Thou hast so often told me of it! 'Tis wrong, thou didst say, to let another think for thee! How much more wrong must it be, then, to let mere music make thee mindless?"

"Aye." Magnus's face hardened and, with a huge effort, he squeezed his eyes shut, shook his head, and turned away from Lalaina. "I am my own man still."

"Then thou art not ours!" the hulking youth cried. "Avaunt thee! Get thee hence!"

"Didst thou say we are *naught* but things of play?" taunted a girl not much older than Cordelia. "What more should we wish to be? Thou art but jealous for that thou hast so little of thine own!"

"What I have *is* mine own!" Cordelia answered hotly. "What! Wouldst thou give thyselves to boys who see thee as naught but toys?"

A long, scandalized gasp raked along the line of dancers. Then the girls' faces hardened, and they stepped forward.

"What a foul mouth thou hast!" a smaller boy snapped at Gregory. "We must stop it for thee!" And he caught up a fistful of dirt.

"Stand away!" Geoffrey leaped in front of his little brother, glaring. "Thou shalt not touch him!"

"Then we shall bury *thee!*" the hulking youth cried and, with a roar, several of the boys leaped at Geoffrey.

"Thou hast spoke too much now," Lalaina grated, glaring at Cordelia. "Have at thee, wench!"

Magnus leaped up beside his brothers, catching two of the boys by their collars and hurling them at the hulking youth, while Geoffrey dispatched the third with a left jab and a quick right cross.

"Thoul't not touch my brothers whilst I can stand!" snapped Magnus.

"Why, then, we shall hale thee down!" the hulking youth bellowed. "Out upon him, lads!"

With a roar, the boys all leaped at Magnus.

With one unified scream, the girls leaped on Cordelia.

"Repel them!" Magnus shouted, catching his brothers' hands, and Gregory caught Cordelia's. Their faces turned to stone with strain, and the air about them glimmered a split second before the girls and boys fell upon them with the howl of a wolf-pack . . .

. . . and slammed into an invisible wall.

They bounced back, crashing to the ground with howls of surprise and fright—but Lalaina screeched, "They are witches!"

"Then we should fly," Magnus grated, tight-lipped. "Away, my sibs!"

And the word ran through the mob like a trace of gunpowder: "Witches! Witches! Witches!"

"Then we shall burn them!" cried the hulking boy, and the crowd answered with a roar.

But the Gallowglasses had already disappeared down the woodland path and around the bend, so the pursuing mob careened into a great black horse, with a *bong* like a boxful of bolts in a belfry. They recoiled, yammering and clamoring, and ducked under, around, and over as the great horse danced about, maneuvering to make it harder for them—but they all twisted past somehow, and sprang after their quarry, howling in full voice.

"We must go aloft," Magnus panted.

"There is no space!" Cordelia answered, tears in her eyes. "There are too many branches, all too low!"

The pack rounded the bend, saw them, and burst into wild yelling.

Then out of the roadside brush sprang slavering jaws with furious barking, red-rimmed eyes above and sharp claws below, leaping and growling and snapping, and the mob screeched to a halt in sheer shock with howls of panic.

"Throw!" Cordelia cried. Her brothers skidded to a stop, whirled about to look, and every loose stick around leaped up spinning to shoot whirling at the mob. The pack stood for a second, wavering; then the first stick struck, and they turned about with a woeful yell, fleeing in panic.

Magnus and Geoffrey stood tense, unbelieving, but Cordelia and Gregory collapsed with a sigh. "I shall never trust a crowd of folk again," Gregory croaked.

"Nor ever did, I wot," Geoffrey answered. "Mayhap thou hadst the right of it, small brother."

The dog turned and came up to them, wagging its tail. It was a tall, rangy beast with long ears, drooping eyes, and jowls; but the eyes were all friendliness now, and guileless. It sat down in front of Geoffrey, cocked its head to the side, and barked.

In spite of himself, the third Gallowglass began to grin.

"And who art thou, who hast come so timely to help us?" Magnus stepped forward, still wary, but opening his mind to the dog's.

The dog barked again, and both boys read its feelings. "It did like us the moment it saw us," Gregory said, grinning widely now. "What! Wouldst thou be my friend?"

The dog barked and wagged its tail.

"Mama will never allow it," Cordelia warned.

"Wouldst thou sleep in the stables?" Magnus asked.

The dog nodded, panting and still wagging its tail.

"There is another tenant in that room," Gregory reminded.

Right on cue, the great black horse came round the bend toward the children.

Cordelia scrambled to her feet. "Do they rally, Fess?"

"They do not," the horse told her. "In fact, as soon as you were out of sight, they seemed to forget you; and when they had calmed for a minute or two, they began to dance again. They have gone on their way, and one would think they had never seen you."

"Praise Heaven for that!" Cordelia sighed. "Mayhap this nepenthe of music hath its uses!"

"But how did you rout them, children? I trust you did no irreparable harm. . . ."

"We only threw sticks," Magnus assured him, "few of which struck. But the greatest work was done by this stalwart." Gingerly, he placed a hand on the dog's head. "He sprang upon them so suddenly that the surprise itself did rout them."

"Then he is a friend in deed." Fess came closer, and the dog stretched its nose up at him, sniffing. Then it sneezed, and stared up at him indignantly.

"There is no deceiving a large nasal cavity." The horse sighed. "He knows I am no true equine."

"Can I take him home, Fess?" Geoffrey asked.

The robot horse stood immobile for a moment, then said, "You may *bring* him, Geoffrey—but whether you may *keep* him is for your parents to say."

The dog's tail beat the ground furiously.

"Papa could not turn away a valiant ally," Geoffrey protested.

"I suspect you may be right—though I refuse to commit myself on the issue. Bid him stay here, and he may join us when we return home."

Geoffrey dropped to one knee, holding the dog by the sides of its head and staring into its eyes. The animal panted up at him eagerly. Concentrating, Geoffrey projected into the dog's mind a picture of him watching the four children and the horse walking away, and the dog shut his mouth, staring. Then Geoffrey made the picture darken into night, then lighten with dawn, fill to midday, and darken to night again; then, on the second dawn, the children and the horse came in sight again. The dream-Geoffrey reached down to pet the dog, and the final picture showed the four children, the horse, and the dog walking away together.

The dog whined, and Geoffrey read in his mind a succession of pictures of him leaping and snapping at five wolves until he drove them away, while the four children cowered behind the horse; of the dog barking furiously at a band of robbers, who turned tail and ran; and of the dog taking on a huge bear single-handed, biting and clawing and howling until finally the bear lay dead, and the children crowded around with petting and cries of admiration.

"Brother," Geoffrey said, "he doth . . ."

"I have seen; he doth wish to protect us from all the hazards of the forest, for he doth believe himself to be twenty times more powerful than any canine could be." Magnus knelt down beside the beast, shaking his head sadly. "Thou canst not do such great deeds, for thou art nothing but a hound, dog. And we may not take thee with us now, for we know not to what we go, and cannot halt for another member of our party."

The animal's head drooped, and his tail flopped still.

"Nay, 'tis not so bad as that," Geoffrey protested, rubbing the dog's head and scratching behind its ears. "Thou art a most wonderful beast indeed, and I do long to have thee for my companion all the years of my youth!"

The dog lifted its head with a hopeful look.

"Canst thou not bide here in patience?" Geoffrey asked. "Then, when we return, we shall take thee to our home. Wilt thou so serve me?"

The dog stared up at him. Then its mouth lolled open again, and its tail beat the earth a few times.

"Stout fellow!" Geoffrey tousled its ears and jumped to his feet. "Bide in readiness, then, and thou shalt yet be a stable-dog. . . . An thou wilt, Fess?" With trepidation, he looked up at the horse.

"I would be honored to share my stable with so faithful a companion, Geoffrey—but you understand that the decision must still remain with your parents."

"Oh, surely, Fess! Yet an thou wilt permit him the stable, I do not think Mama will object!"

"Come, then." Cordelia had been watching the whole affair with ill-concealed impatience. "The West awaits."

"Aye! I will come gladly!" Geoffrey turned and strode away, turning back to wave goodbye only twice as he and his brothers and sister moved away down the path with Fess behind them. He didn't even hear Cordelia muttering under her breath, something about a great, smelly, slobbering beast.

# 8

The forest thinned; the trees became fewer and more slender. The ground began to rise and, as the sun rose to mid-morning, the children found themselves in an upland moor. Wind tossed their hair, and the wide-open view lifted their hearts. "Oh!" Cordelia cried. "I could dance!"

"Please do not," Fess said quickly. Even here, strains of repetitive music rose from rocks all about them.

Magnus looked about, his brow furrowed. "I see no springs or ponds, Fess."

"You will find very few," the robot confirmed. "Open water is rare on a moor. When we do find some, we must fill waterskins."

"And if we do not?"

"Then we shall not turn back," Fess said, with decision, "until we do."

"Do we not chance fate, Fess?"

"With ordinary children, yes. But you can fly; when you begin to grow thirsty, we shall go aloft."

Cordelia swallowed. "I have thirst now."

"That is only because we have been discussing the issue, Cordelia."

"I might flit to the stream we camped by last night," Gregory suggested.

Fess lifted his head. "Of course! I continually fail to correlate the full range of your powers with current circumstances."

"Thou doth mean thou dost ever forget what we can do."

"Not 'forget,'" Fess demurred.

"'Tis only that he doth not wish to acknowledge it," Geoffrey muttered to Magnus, but Big Brother shushed him.

Fess affected not to have heard. "Then there is little peril from thirst, since you can fetch water whenever you wish. However, there are bogs, children. Be careful to remain on the path; those patches of soft earth could swallow a child whole."

"Not with *thee* by us, Fess," Gregory piped.

"Yet Mama would be wroth at so much mud on thy clothes," Cordelia pointed out. "Mind thy steps, brother."

Gregory's lower lip jutted in a pout, but he followed as they set off up the path, two abreast, Geoffrey and Cordelia in the lead, Fess following behind.

They crested the top of a rise and found a huge boulder blocking the path. On top of it glowed a pair of girls' shoes, electric blue.

Cordelia let out a cry of delight and ran to the rocky pedestal. "Oh! They are so beauteous!" She caught up the slippers and held them up in the sunlight. "And so soft."

"Soft?" Gregory asked, wide-eyes. "Are they cloth, sister?"

"Nay, they are leather—but velvet to the touch."

"It is a leather-finish termed suede," Fess explained. "Cordelia! They are not yours!"

"Yet who else's could they be?" Cordelia kicked off her shoes and pushed her toes into the blue slippers. "Surely, if someone left them and went away, they must care not who takes them! And see, they are new from the last!"

"And also from the first." Magnus scowled. "Why do I mistrust them?"

A bass note thrummed especially loudly. Magnus jumped

aside, and saw a new rock landing almost where he'd been. "A plague upon these noisy stones!"

"They *are* a plague." Then Gregory stared at his sister, wounded. "Cordelia! Not thee too!"

Cordelia's feet had begun to step lightly to the music of the rock, her body swaying. "Wherefore not? Ah, now I ken wherefore this music hath so strong a beat—'tis for dancing!"

"I have lost all stomach for the sport," Magnus declared, "since we have seen what others make of it. Give over, Delia! Let us be off!"

"There is no harm in dancing, Magnus," Fess told him. "Let her amuse herself for a few minutes; we assuredly have no pressing schedule."

Magnus looked up at him, startled, and gave the robot a glare that clearly accused him of treachery. Fess only watched Cordelia, though, immobile and patient as a block of iron.

" 'Tis more silly than aught I have seen," Geoffrey snorted, "to dance to strains that go DOO-DOO-DOO." He grunted along with the tune, hopping about in a crude parody of Cordelia's dance. She screeched in outrage. "Thou vile boy! Canst thou not see another's pleasure, without need to lessen it?"

" 'Ware, brother," Magnus cautioned. "Thou dost begin to step quite deftly."

"Oh, aye, and to trip the light fantastic," Geoffrey said, with withering sarcasm. But he forgot to grunt his musical burlesque, and went on dancing. Sure enough, his steps began to be rather neat and nimble, and a slow smile spread across his face.

"Thou dost take as much pleasure in it as I," Cordelia gloated.

Geoffrey jerked to a halt, paling at the insult. "Never! 'Tis a girls' game, that!"

"You will find it pleasant enough when you are grown, Geoffrey," Fess assured him, "even as you will find the company of young women to be one of your greatest delights."

"I could wish not to grow, then!"

"Do not, I prithee," Gregory said quickly, "for wishes have an uncommon way of coming true—in Gramarye."

Geoffrey glowered, but he didn't answer.

"We have passed enough time," Fess said. "Come, Cordelia. Finish your dance; we must resume our journey."

"Oh, thou dost spoil the joy of it," Cordelia complained. "Naetheless, the sun grows low, and I shall go with thee."

"Well, then, come," Magnus repeated. "Cease thy dancing."

"Why, so I do!"

"Oh, dost thou!" Geoffrey grinned. "I could swear thou yet dost hop!"

"Assuredly, thou dost not truly believe thou hast stopped, Cordelia," Gregory added.

"Nay, I do not," Cordelia said, alarmed. "Yet I assure thee, brothers, I do strive to! Nay, be still, my beating feet!"

Fess lifted his head. "The shoes themselves continue to dance! They will not let her stop!"

"How can that be?" Gregory protested. "They are not living things!"

"Perhaps a living being is nearby, to animate them; perhaps they *are* alive, as much as any witch-moss construct is!"

"Shoes of witch-moss!" Magnus said, unbelieving. "Surely they could not endure!"

"They need last only a bit longer than Cordelia's strength, to do their wretched work," Gregory answered. "Come, throw all thy weight upon her toe! Hold still her foot!" And he leaped at Cordelia, both heels slamming down at her feet.

But the slippers skipped aside, even as Cordelia screeched, "Do not step on my blue suede shoes! I could not bear to have them spoiled!"

"Then I shall catch thy body!" Gregory threw his arms around her waist, just as a crow of victory split the moorland and a very large woman leaped out from behind the boulder, whirling a net over her head. Her skirts were full, her face was gaudy with rouge and powder, and her neckline scooped low enough to violate the laws of aesthetics. "Two at one catch!" she cackled. "Eh, I'll have much gold for them!" The net spun high, weights on its border spreading it wide as it swooped down to snare Cordelia, and Gregory with her. "A catch, a catch!" the woman cried, and waddled toward the mound of netting that thrashed and heaved, for Cordelia's body whipped in wild movements, the shoes still beating at the ground in their dance.

Cordelia screamed, and Gregory shouted, "Brothers, aid me!"

Magnus and Geoffrey dove in with a will, Magnus throwing his arms around Cordelia from behind in a bear hug, Geoffrey sailing in at the back of her knees in a perfect tackle. Cordelia slammed down, and Magnus fell with her, but her shoes kept striking about wildly, trying to continue their dance. Geoffrey struggled out from under and yanked at the slippers.

"Leave off! Leave off!" the harridan shrieked, swatting at him. " 'Tis *my* catch!"

"Nay, 'tis my sister!" Geoffrey whirled, scarlet with rage, unleashing a glare at the fat woman. She staggered back screeching, as though a football halfback had slammed into her, and Geoffrey's lip curled as he turned back and with a violent jerk pulled one of the slippers off.

"Ow!" Cordelia cried. "Gently, brother! 'Tis not a block of wood thou dost hold!"

"Pardon, sister, but there's small time for gentleness." Geoffrey yanked the other shoe off.

Another net swooped down around him, gathering all four of them into a churning mass, and the overblown woman howled with glee as she heaved at Magnus, rolling him over Cordelia into a hempen cocoon. "Wouldst thou strike at a woman, then? Vile, unmannered brats! I have thee now!"

"What art thou?" Magnus cried, finally ready for the next danger on the list; but the woman giggled, "Only a poor spinster, lad; and call me Arachne, for I've caught thee in my web!"

Geoffrey managed to draw his dagger with his left hand

and started sawing at the ropes. Magnus realized he had to keep Arachne's attention. " 'Twas thou didst craft these shoes!"

"Nay! I may be wicked in my way, child, yet I'm not a witch! I found the shoes, hard by a music-rock. And well they've served me—for they held this little beauty till my net could settle over her!"

"And what wilt thou do with her?" Magnus tried to sound as though dread were hollowing him.

"Why, sell her, lad, for gold!" Arachne replied. "I know a fine gentleman, who dwells not far off within a cave, and who will come out this night to give me gold for her. I've sold him girls before, and I doubt not he will wish to have her. Nay, I wot that he may give me more gold for each of thee, though thou art lads!"

"*Buy* us?" Geoffrey protested, scandalized. "I shall not be a slave!"

"Nay, thou shalt!" Arachne crowed. "And thou shalt do whatever he doth wish thee to do! Now—wilt thou suffer thyselves to be bound and hobbled, and walk before me? Or must I knock a rock upon thy pate, and drag thee thither?"

"Strike me an thou canst!" Geoffrey cried, surging up out of a long rent in the net with his dagger stabbing out. Arachne shrieked and leaped back. Then she clamped her jaw and lifted a huge, knobby cane, swinging it up.

A great black horse seemed to rise up out of the ground behind her, rearing up.

Geoffrey grinned, and pointed over her shoulder. "Beware!"

"Dost thou think me a bairn, to be caught with so ancient a ruse?" Arachne spat, just before a steel hoof cracked into her head. A stunned look came over her face; then her eyes rolled up, and she slumped to the ground.

"Aye," Geoffrey answered her, then looked up at Fess. "Many thanks, old ruse. How ancient *art* thou?"

"Five hundred thirty-one years, ten months, three days, four hours, and fifty-one minutes, Geoffrey."

"Yet who doth count?" Magnus murmured as he fought his way loose of the net.

"Terran standard, of course," Fess added.

Geoffrey nudged Arachne with a toe. "Mayhap we should bind her?"

"Do, with her own net," Magnus agreed. Geoffrey nodded and knelt to start packaging the harridan while Magnus turned to peel the other net off Cordelia. She sat up with a shaky moan. "I thank thee, brothers. 'Tis long since I have been so frighted."

"She left the shoes as bait for her trap," Gregory informed her.

"I believe I might have guessed that, brother."

Geoffrey shrugged. "Guessed or not, thou wert snared."

"Oh, 'twas I alone, was't?"

"Your brothers were caught because they sought to aid you, Cordelia," Fess reminded her.

She hung her head. "Aye, I know. Oh, brothers! I was so afeard thou wouldst be trapped because of me!"

"Aye, yet 'twas we caught the trapper." Magnus squeezed her around the shoulders. "We could not allow her to harm our fair only sister, could we?"

"Nay!" Geoffrey's brows drew down, hiding his eyes. "None may touch thee whiles we live! For thou art *our* sister!"

"As thou art my brother." Cordelia leaped forward and caught Geoffrey in a bear hug, planting a quick kiss on his cheek. He shrank back with a cry of dismay, but she only beamed at him. "And none shall touch *thee* without my leave!"

If this boded ill for all their future courtships, Fess alone took note of it. However, he only said, "Perhaps it is time to rejoin your parents, children."

They whirled on him, dismayed, erupting into a chorus of frantic denials. "There is no danger, Fess!" "We are more than equal to any peril!" " 'Tis not even twilight yet!" "We have not found the information we seek!"

"I would say we have found ample data," Fess contradicted. "We now need time to sift it, organize it, and deduce its implications."

"Ample, mayhap, yet not complete!" Gregory's chin

jutted. "Wouldst thou have us build hypotheses when we've less than full evidence?"

Fess stood still and silent.

"And there is that other poor lass!" Cordelia said.

The robot-horse's head turned to her. "Which other juvenile female?"

"The one that Arachne hath already sold to the man in the cave! Are we to turn our backs upon her?"

"Nay!" Geoffrey cried. "We must free her!"

"There could be danger there, children," Fess said slowly.

"Pooh! From one mere man, 'gainst four witch-children? Yet an he doth prove more puissant than we expect, thou mayest step in and smite him!"

"Provided I do not have a seizure . . ."

"There's small enough chance of that," Magnus said quickly, ever alert for egos needing bolstering. "Yet there's smaller chance of need of thy strong hoof."

"An thou dost doubt," Gregory suggested, "ask Papa."

Fess heaved a burst of static. "Very well, I shall contact him." He turned toward the northeast, opening his mouth to form a parabolic dish, and shifted to radio frequency. *Rod. Father Warlock—this is Fess. Tutor to progenitor—come in, Rod.*

*Receiving.* Rod's signal was weak; the transmitter imbedded in his maxillary was broadcast, not directional.

*We have encountered a potentially dangerous situation, Rod. It could imperil the children.*

*I doubt it,* Rod answered. *Still, it must be one hell of a situation, to give you pause.*

*No, only hooves.*

*Are you developing a sense of humor? If you are, I'll have to see about having it upgraded.*

*Certainly not. Purely coincidental, I assure you.* Fess was suddenly aware of having been caught in an error, which caused a logic-loop almost equivalent to an emotion. *It was simply a failure to distinguish between homonyms; I experienced a delay in interpreting contextual references. I assure you it will not happen again.*

*Oh, I don't mind. Just be a little more deft, will you?*

Unwittingly, Rod had given Fess a directive. The robot's memory adjusted his program accordingly; Fess would now, obediently, make every pun he could—except the really bad ones, if he could distinguish them. *Executed. Which is how you may wish to treat the woman the children have just vanquished.*

*Oh?* Rod's voice tightened; Fess could almost hear the adrenaline shooting through his veins. *What'd she do to them?*

*She trapped them, and intended to sell them to a man who lives in a cave.*

*Draw her and quarter her.* Fury in Rod's voice, then sudden brooding. *On the other hand, is there anything left to draw?*

*Oh yes, Rod. Your children have been well trained; they avoid serious injury whenever possible, and shy at the thought of killing. She is merely unconscious—and it was myself who struck the blow, not one of them.*

*As long as she's out of commission. So what's the danger?*

*The woman—Arachne, she calls herself—has already sold at least one young girl to this man in the cave.*

*And the kids want to free her? Well, I can't really argue with that. Just make sure there's something left of the man for the bailiffs to bring in, will you?*

*I shall take every precaution, Rod.* Fess sighed. *You are not concerned for the children's safety, then?*

*What, with only one nut to crack? The only problem is that he might get mean enough so that they can't be gentle. If that happens, you knock him out first, okay?*

*As you say, Rod,* Fess acknowledged reluctantly. *Yet there is still the possibility that I might have a seizure before I could intervene.*

*Oh, all right!* Rod sighed. *I'll ask Gwen to call for a contingent of elves to shadow you, unobtrusively. Think that will be enough protection?*

*I had more in mind a command to rejoin you. . . .*

There was a pause. Fess suspected Rod was discussing

the situation with Gwen. When he gave answer, it confirmed the notion.

*No. Categorically. We can't insulate them completely from the world, Fess. If there's evil out there, they've got to learn something about it, firsthand.*

*Perhaps that experience should not be too vivid, Rod.*

*There's no reason to think it will be, from what you've said so far. Especially with you for protection, and a squad of Little People.*

*That should be adequate,* Fess admitted, capitulating. *I do not think they will be able to complete this mission before dark, though.*

*Of course they will, if they fly! Don't let 'em take too long with this slavemaster, okay?*

*Even as you say, Rod. Over and out.*

*Over and out. Good luck, Old Iron.*

Fess turned to the children. "Your parents have no objection—they only ask that you exercise all due caution."

The children cheered.

"Where is the cave?" Geoffrey demanded.

"We must seek that from Arachne's mind," Gregory answered.

The topic of conversation moaned.

"She wakes." Geoffrey dropped to one knee beside the harridan, hand on his dagger. "Speak, monster! Give answer!"

"Not so roughly." Cordelia knelt by the woman's other side. " 'Tis flowers bring bees, not nettles."

"Then beware their stings," Geoffrey growled.

"I shall." Cordelia reached out to pat Arachne's cheek. "Waken, woman! We have questions for thee."

Arachne's eyelids fluttered, then cracked open, squinting painfully.

"Aye, thy head doth ache, doth it not?" Cordelia said, with sympathy. "Yet rejoice—thy pate's not broke, though 'twas a hard hoof that felled thee."

Arachne rolled her head to peer at the great black horse, who was cropping grass for appearance's sake. "Whence came that beast?"

"He was by us throughout. Thou wouldst have seen him an thou hadst paid heed," Geoffrey sneered.

Arachne turned her head to glare at him.

Behind her, Gregory said, "There is no sense of greater room within mine head, nor any sign that she doth hear our thoughts."

Arachne's gaze darted up; she craned her neck, trying to see. "What creature is that, which doth speak of hearing thoughts?"

"'Tis but a small warlock," Cordelia soothed, "my brother."

"Thy brother!" Arachne stared, horrified. "Then thou art . . ."

"A witch." Cordelia nodded. "And thou, we find, art not. Whence, then, didst thou gain the dancing shoes?"

"I have told thee—I found them by a music-rock." White showed all around Arachne's eyes, and Geoffrey nodded, satisfied. *She is too much affrighted to speak falsely.*

*She is terrified,* Cordelia thought, rebuking; and aloud, "How didst thou learn their power?"

"Why, I put them on, and began to dance."

Cordelia glanced at Arachne's large feet. "How couldst thou pull on shoes so small?"

Arachne reddened, embarrassed, but Gregory said, "I doubt me not an they fit their size to the wearer."

Arachne's eyes rolled up again in fear.

Cordelia nodded. "'Tis of a piece with their magic. Yet how didst thou take them off?"

"Why, I tired, and fell," Arachne said, as though it were the most obvious thing in the world.

"She hath not the endurance of youth, I wot," Geoffrey said grimly. "And thou didst then think to use them to trap maidens?"

"Well, young lasses, at least." The old woman frowned. "Such a one came by, donned the shoes, and capered right merrily. When she began to tire, I flung my net and caught her."

"Wherefore? Didst thou know this cave-dwelling gentleman already?"

"Aye, for I'd seen him about of nights, gaunt in the moonlight."

Cordelia wondered what the woman had been doing out in the woods at night.

*Belike she did seek to learn magic,* Magnus's thought answered her, *and, failing, is the more in awe of we who have it.*

*The more sin that we are so young,* Gregory agreed.

"And what had this proud gentleman done, to make thee think he would buy a girl?"

"Why, for that I saw him stalk a lass who dallied in a clearing, to meet a lover. He fell upon her and carried her away to his cave—and thus I learned where he dwelled."

Cordelia felt a chill envelop her back. What manner of man was this, who went out hunting maidens by night?

*'Tis an evil one, certainly.* Geoffrey's thoughts were grim. *He will also be twisted and warped in his soul, I doubt not.*

*We must rid the forest of him,* Magnus agreed.

"What did he to the lass?" Cordelia demanded.

"Naught of great harm that I could see," Arachne answered, "for I went to look the next day, and saw her sitting by the cave-mouth; yet she was drawn and pale."

"And did not seek to escape?" Magnus frowned.

"Nay—so he could not greatly have hurt her, could he?"

"Either that, or he hurt her vastly, yet in her soul, not her body," Magnus said gravely. "What, monster! Thou hast seen what he hath done, and yet thou didst sell a young lass to him?"

"Aye." Arachne's jaw jutted out. "For I saw no great harm, seest thou, and he paid me in gold."

"And gold is worth the vitality of a lass?" Geoffrey spat. "Nay, then! Let us sell thee to the headsman, and take gold for thy pate!"

Arachne's eyes widened in alarm.

"She doth know she hath done wrongly," Gregory pointed out.

"She doth that." Magnus frowned, bending over to glare down at the harridan. "Where lieth his cave, hag?"

"Why, to the west and north, hard by the dark pool before the cliffs," Arachne stammered, shaken by the look on Magnus's face. "Thou . . . thou wilt not seek him out?"

" 'Tis our affair," Geoffrey answered her, "as art thou still, I fear." He looked up at Magnus. "What shall we do with her, brother?"

Arachne cried out in alarm. "Assuredly thou wilt not hurt me!"

"Wherefore not?" Geoffrey retorted. "Wouldst thou have scrupled to hurt my sister?"

"I—I did not know she was a witch!"

"Which is to say, thou didst not know that she could hurt thee." Geoffrey turned away in disgust. "Whate'er we do, brother, 'twill not be excessive."

"Yet *I* scruple to hurt her," Magnus said slowly. "Are we to be no better than she, brother?"

Arachne went limp with relief.

"Shall we take her to the bailiff, then?" Gregory asked.

"Why, what evidence shall we offer of her misdeeds?" Geoffrey demanded.

"Only our word of what she hath said," Magnus said sadly, "and 'tis the word of young ones 'gainst that of a woman grown. Nay, we must seek other justice to which to hand her."

Arachne stiffened again, eyes widening.

Geoffrey frowned. "What justice can that be?"

"Why, that of the land itself." Magnus turned his head and called, "By Oak, Ash and Thorn! An thou canst hear me, proud Robin, please come!"

Arachne stared at him, her foreboding deepening; but Magnus only held his stance, frozen, waiting, and his siblings watched him in silence.

Then leaves parted, and Puck stepped forth. "Wherefore dost thou call me, Warlock's Child?"

"I cry thy justice upon this woman, Robin."

Puck's head swivelled around; he stared at the harridan. Then his eyes narrowed. "Aye, we have seen her aforetime, yet her offenses were never so great as she yearned for them to be. What hath she now done, that thou dost think her worth our concern?"

"She hath stolen a woman-child," Magnus answered, "and sold her for gold to a gentleman who doth dwell in a cave."

Puck's face turned to flint. "We know of him; 'tis a vampire." Slowly, he turned to Arachne. "And thou hast sold him a maiden?"

She looked into the elf's eyes, and screamed.

# 9

For Rod and Gwen, it had been a slow journey, since they had to wait for the rocks to absorb enough witch-moss to split. A few times they cheated by rolling a fragment of stone into the nearest patch of the fungus. The children were well out of sight before they had gone more than a hundred yards.

So the sun was setting as they backtracked a flying stone out of a small woodlot into a meadow. Before them, dimly seen in the dusk, another line of trees loomed.

"We must give the poor wee thing a chance." Gwen nudged the stone toward a crop of grass webbed with fungus.

But Rod heard a sound, and turned back to look. "Gwen . . ."

"Aye, milord?"

"We're, uh . . . being followed."

Gwen turned to look, and stifled a shriek.

It was at least as big as a pony, but it had a long, bushy tail and a shaggy gray coat.

"Grandma, what big teeth you have," Rod murmured.

It was a wolf, dancing toward them on pads the size of platters.

"Fight, or fly?" Gwen readied her broomstick—as a quarterstaff.

"Go, but I think we can stay on the ground." Rod nodded at the huge beast. "It can't go very fast, that way."

The wolf's paws were weaving in the steps of an intricate dance. It was surprisingly graceful, but it took two steps backward for every three forward.

"True," Gwen agreed. "Let us move toward the far wood, my lord, for there may we entrap it, if we see need."

"Good point." Rod moved with her, with quick glances back over his shoulder. "Uh . . . it's not working."

Gwen turned to look, and saw that the wolf had speeded up its dance. It was stepping closer to them with every measure. "Let us walk as swiftly as we may—the wood is better for us."

"Anything you say." Rod was beginning to feel the old, atavistic dread of teeth that go clash in the night. As much to reassure himself as her, he said, "We can wipe it out any time we want to, of course."

"Certes." Gwen frowned. "Yet I am loath to do so, for 'tis a living being, even as we are."

"Living," Rod agreed, "but dangerous to sheep and small peasants. We can't really leave a thing like that around to roam the countryside, Gwen."

"Mayhap it can be tamed," she offered.

Rod shook his head. "Whether it was generated by imagination or genes, it was born to be wild. We're going to have to find some way to pull its teeth."

Those teeth were coming entirely too close. The wolf's tongue lolled out between them, almost in a smile, and the great eyes glowed in the dusk.

"First," Rod said through stiff lips, "I think we'd better go aloft. Ready?"

Something shot over their heads, a flurry of night wings and a long, mournful, echoing call. The stepping wolf howled, dodged aside, then leaped up, jaws snapping, but the giant bird banked away. It came circling back, though, and the dancer had no attention to spare for its erstwhile quarry. The night-spirit cupped its wings and stretched its claws down, landing between the wolf and the humans—an owl eight feet tall, poising wings that seemed to stretch out forever as a shield for the tender ones at its back. Rod saw the gleam of a curved bill the size of his arm, and eyes the size of dinner plates that stared at the predator. A long cry filled the night again.

"*Who-o-o-o-o-o-o,*" the great bird called. "*Who-o-o-o-o!*"

"Doth he mean to threaten?" Gwen asked.

"Threat or comfort, it's music to my ears. But he can't really hold off that wolf, can he?"

The four-footed dancer seemed to have come to the same conclusion. It crouched, snarling, readying itself for a leap.

"*Who!*" the great owl exclaimed with a snap of its wings, and the wolf rocked back, startled for a moment.

Before it could regain its poise, a sonorous gong-roll filled the night, and an awkward figure appeared, flapping long-sleeved arms for balance, teetering in front of the giant owl. It wore a tall, pointed cap painted in spirals of mauve and lavender, interspersed with stars and crescent moons, which also adorned its patchwork robe, five sizes too big. "Here now, here now, what's all this?" the small man said in a peevish tone. He looked up at the great owl through a huge pair of circular spectacles. "What did you call me for, Hoot?"

The night-king gave a hoot, nodding its head toward the wolf. The patchwork wizard turned to peer into the gloaming, adjusting his spectacles. "What's this, what's this? A dancing wolf, you say? Well, let him dance!"

The owl hooted again.

"People?" The wizard looked up at Rod and Gwen, startled. "Oh! Good evening. I am Spinball the wizard."

"Um—pleased to meet you." Rod hoped he wasn't staring too obviously. "I'm Rod Gallowglass, and this is my wife, Gwen."

"The High Warlock?" Spinball straightened, startled. "And the Wonder Witch, too! Why, you have no need of me! You could skin and stuff this animal before it even noticed!"

"Well, yes," Rod admitted, "but we're a little reluctant, you see. I mean, it's just doing what it was born to do, and we hate to end an innocent life if we can avoid it."

Spinball lifted his head, a glint of respect in his eye. "Ah, well. I can understand that. Of course, yes."

"Cannot this beast be tamed?" Gwen asked gently.

"Oh." Spinball knitted his brows. "You haven't much of a knack with beasts, eh? Well, that makes a difference. I'll see what I can do, then." Abruptly, he smiled. "Nice to have a feeling of purpose for a change." Then he spun away to the wolf.

"He is quite nice," Gwen said carefully.

"Definitely," Rod agreed. "Seems to be a bit of a screwball, though."

"Here, now, Dancer," the wizard said. His tone was firm, but gentle. "You really mustn't bother these people."

The wolf growled.

"Oh, yes, I know you're hungry," Spinball said, "but they have a right to live, too, you know. Now, I can understand the occasional sheep, and possibly even a small cow now and then—but human beings are absolutely forbidden!"

The wolf's growl became more ominous.

"No!" Spinball said, with determination. "Absolutely out of the question! Really, you *should* limit yourself to deer and rabbits, you know, with now and then a bit of a boar. Taking livestock always brings hunters with wolfhounds, after all."

At that, the wolf threw back its head and howled. Rod and Gwen stared, amazed—but were even more amazed when the howling began to slide up and down in pitch, then to rise and fall with a definite feeling of structure. Somehow, it seemed to synchronize perfectly with the thrumming beat from the music-rocks that littered the meadow. It ended with a long, high, mournful howl that held and rang, then dwindled away into the night. The evening was still, except for the shrilling of crickets and, somewhere in the distance, the drumming of a bullfrog—or was that a music-rock?

But Spinball was nodding. He whisked something long and thin out of a sleeve.

"A magic wand?" Rod asked.

But Spinball put the wand to his lips and began to play. A lovely melody lilted out into the night, wafting toward the wolf, rising and falling in time to the beat of the music-rocks. Then Spinball took the pipe away from his lips, and began to sing:

> *"One is one, and all alone,*
> *And ever more shall be so!*
> *Yet two are two, and ever do*
> *Have other ones to seek to know!*
>
> *To reach, and nothing gain, is pain;*
> *To reach and touch is warming.*
> *To see another may be bother,*
> *But often may be charming!*
>
> *They who slay shall never stay*
> *To fulfill themselves in others.*
> *They who hate shall never sate*
> *The hollowness that shudders!*
>
> *Reach and touch, and feel and heal!*
> *Tumult soothe in sharing!*
> *Be kin and kind, and seek and find!*
> *Angst unknot in caring!"*

The wolf sat, head cocked to the side, studying the wizard, who with a flourish raised his pipe to his lips again, blew a last, lighthearted, skipping tune, then whisked the pipe away as he bowed to the wolf. He rose out of the bow to stand, head cocked to the side at the same angle as the lupine's.

The huge wolf rose, danced lightly up to the wizard, and held up a paw.

Spinball took the huge pads with a grave bow, looked into the wolf's eyes, and nodded. The wolf returned the nod, turned away, and stepped back into the woodland from which it had come.

Gwen released a long-held breath, and Rod said, "Astonishing! Did he really understand what you were trying to tell him?"

"Oh, yes, of course! What I couldn't tell him with words, I told him with melody! After all, a dancing wolf does have music in his heart, you know."

"I do now," Rod said, and Gwen added, "Art thou certain he will harm no human person?"

"Quite sure," said Spinball, "for the music brought our minds into harmony for a brief time. But I promise you, I'll seek out his thoughts every day for a few weeks, just to be absolutely certain."

"I thank thee," Gwen said slowly. "Such befriending of a wild thing doth surpass my gifts."

Spinball reddened with pleasure, but said, "Oh, no, my lady, not at all! I couldn't even come close to your abilities, no, not if you're even half as deft as rumor says. You must be a far greater magician than I!"

That brought a smile to Gwen's lips. "Say not so, good sir. Yet I must also thank your friend, who called you to us in this hour of need."

"Who, Hoot?" Spinball looked up, surprised. "But he didn't call me, you know—he made me!"

Hoot gave an angry call.

"No, it's true, Hoot, and you know it!" Spinball said stoutly, then turned to explain. "He says that it was I who made him, but of course we know that's nonsense, now don't we? Yes, of course it is, for how could such a dizzy-head as I have sense enough to imagine a wondrous bird like Hoot?"

"*Who-o-o-o-o-o!*" the great owl said, with conviction.

"Oh, that's silly!" Spinball scoffed. "And don't you ever call yourself a birdbrain again! I'll have you know you're my special friend, yes, my closest friend in all the universe, at least in the part that's alive, so there!"

*"Who!"* the owl said, mollified, and lapsed into a satisfied sulk.

"It's an old argument." Spinball sighed, turning back to Rod and Gwen. "He insists that I made him, and *I* insist that he made *me*. I don't expect we'll ever see eye to eye about it. The only thing we disagree on, too."

"A most excellent choice," Gwen said, smiling, "if friends must disagree at all."

"Oh, they must," Rod said softly. "Every now and then, they must. We can't stand being *too* close, you know."

That earned him a peculiar look from both wizard and wife, but the great owl spoke up with a long and loud *"Who-o-o-o-o-o-o!"* that sounded very satisfied with Rod's version of the affair.

Rod glanced up, caught by a sudden change in the music. "You know, I think you've had an effect on the ambience."

"What, the rocks' music?" Spinball dismissed the notion with a wave. "Hoot always does that. Every time he shows up, they change their tune. Not that we mind, you understand. Keeps things friendly all around."

"But we did seek to follow, to discover how the rocks progressed!" Gwen turned to him. "We must find where they have begun, for we seek to understand what this new force is that doth strain the land, ere it doth rend it asunder."

Again, Spinball waved the idea away. "Oh, don't be such a worrywart. After all, it's just entertainment."

"I've heard that before, someplace," Rod said, "and I'm beginning to become a little wary of it. You wouldn't happen to know where this all started, would you?"

Spinball shook his head. "I wouldn't, for I seem to have started with it, and so has Hoot. But we think it's south, yes, perhaps south, and certainly west."

Gwen glanced at Rod with doubt; he nodded and said, "Well, I suppose the best we can do is follow where the rocks came from, then. Funny how this one seems to be going north."

"I thought so, too," Spinball admitted. "They seem to grow as a tree does, branching out from a common trunk—but the roots lie in the west, yes, and the south.

Still, as each branch grows older its music seems to change—and, of course, it spreads out, so that you find two rocks with entirely different kinds of music, right next to one another."

"They ought to put labels on 'em," Rod grunted. "That's how we came to follow this branch, in fact—we found a rock near the other ones we were investigating. Well, thanks for all your help. We're off to the west, then."

"My lord," said Gwen, "we speak to no one."

Rod looked up, startled, and realized that Spinball had disappeared. "Well! Not very polite of him, to run off without saying goodbye."

"Goodbye!" said a voice from empty air, and a long, mournful hoot echoed down from the sky.

Rod and Gwen exchanged a glance, then started quickly toward the dark wood ahead. Over his shoulder, Rod called back, "Bye!"

# 10

Many miles away, the children followed the guide Puck had assigned them.

"Yet what *is* a vampire?" Cordelia asked.

"Have a care," said a reedy voice in front of them. "A root doth bulk up, to trip thee."

"Oh! I thank thee, elf." Cordelia lifted her skirts and stepped carefully over the root, following the foot-high manikin who led them. " 'Tis hard going as the woods darken."

"It will be night soon," Fess said, "and the vampire will be active. We should return home and come here again by daylight, when the monster sleeps within his cave."

Magnus frowned. "Wherefore doth he so?"

"Because he will turn to dust if sunlight strikes him." Fess lifted his head sharply. "What am I speaking of? Vampires are mythical!"

"Any myth may gain weight and substance, in Gramarye," Magnus assured him. "Yet thou hast not answered Delia, Fess. What *is* a vampire?"

Fess heaved a burst of white noise and answered. "A

vampire, children, is a person who lives by drinking other people's blood."

Cordelia froze, horrified. Geoffrey made a retching noise. " 'Tis disgusting," Gregory said, looking a little green.

"Why do other folk suffer such a one to live?" Magnus demanded.

"They do not, Magnus. When people learn of a vampire's existence, they generally attempt to slay it—but the monsters cannot truly be killed, for they are no longer completely alive."

"Immortal?" Magnus asked.

"Until they are disposed of, yes. A vampire can be immobilized indefinitely by driving a stake through its heart and burying it at a crossroad—or it can be burned."

"What of their souls?" Cordelia whispered.

"I am not programmed to conjecture about spiritual matters, Cordelia."

"Then there is no certain knowledge?"

"Surely their souls must be lost!" Geoffrey protested. "Have they not slain innocent folk?"

"Not precisely. Vampires generally do not take enough blood to kill a person at one sitting. But after several visits over a period of time, the victim becomes a vampire in his or her own turn."

"Thou dost not say so!" Cordelia gasped. "Is't to *this* that Arachne hath condemned the lass she sold to the vampire?"

"We must save her," Geoffrey said, with decision. Then he frowned, uncertain. "Or hath she already become like to him?"

"How are we to know?" Magnus asked.

"By her vitality, according to the literature. If she is listless and apathetic, the vampire is still feeding upon her; but if she is energetic and burning with greed, she has become a vampire herself."

"We shall know her when we see her, then." Magnus frowned. "If we can see aught, in this gloaming."

" 'Tis still light enough for that," the elf replied. He parted some ferns and breathed, "Behold!"

The sourceless twilight showed them a clearing in front of a cliff face. In its base, a crevice widened into a cave mouth seven feet high and four feet wide, with a semicircle of beaten earth before it and rubble to either side. The rubble must have contained some music-rocks, for a three-chord melody murmured through the clearing. The heavy thrumming of its bass notes seemed to be moving the feet of the girl who danced in front of the cave. Certainly she did not seem to be stepping by herself, for her face was drawn and pale, and her whole body limp and drooping, waving vaguely to the rhythm. She was perhaps sixteen, and should have been bursting with the vitality of youth, but her eyes were only half-open.

"Regard," Geoffrey breathed. "Her throat!"

The children stared, fascinated and repelled, at the cluster of double marks on the girl's neck.

"She is apathetic," Fess murmured.

"Why, 'tis so!" Cordelia lifted her head. "She doth care for naught! She is not yet herself a vampire!"

"We may save her, then." Magnus stood up, purpose settling about him like a cloak. "Come, my sibs." He stepped forward into the clearing.

"Beware," the elf said near his ankle. "When darkness falls, the vampire will come out."

"I await him with hunger to match his own," Geoffrey answered.

"Thou shouldst hide thee, elf," Gregory advised, hurrying after his brothers and sister.

"Why, so I shall," the elf answered. "Yet be sure, a score of Wee Folk do watch, and await thy need." Then he ducked down into the grass, and was gone.

Magnus stepped up to the girl and inclined his head. "Greetings, lass. I am called Magnus, and I would speak with thee."

The girl's glance strayed to his face, then strayed away. She gave no other sign of having heard him.

"Let me try." Cordelia moved in front of Magnus, gazing up at the bigger girl. "I am Cordelia. Wilt thou not pause to speak with me?"

The lass frowned slightly, her gaze wandering toward Cordelia; but it never quite arrived, for her face smoothed out, and she ended by gazing over the younger girl's head.

"Oh!" Cordelia said. "How rude! Wilt thou not cease dancing for a few moments' speech?"

"I doubt me an she can." Magnus beckoned to Geoffrey and Gregory. "Come, brothers! We must catch and hold her, an we wish speech with her."

"Done!" Geoffrey cried, and dove into a flying tackle.

"Not *that* way!" Magnus threw his arms around the girl, holding her up. Finally her gaze met his, looking up only a little, and her eyes widened, almost completely open.

"I have her feet," Geoffrey called out from below.

"And I have her arms." Magnus leaned back a little. "Now, lass! Tell me thy name!"

The girl just blinked at him, not understanding.

"Thy name," Magnus urged. "Thy name that folk do call thee by!"

She blinked again, and said, "What matter?"

"What matter!" Cordelia cried. "Wilt thou forget thyself also?"

The girl's eyes strayed to her. She blinked again, and yawned. "Mayhap. 'Tis naught."

"Naught!" Geoffrey exploded. "Is 'naught' thy name, then? Are we to call thee 'Naught'?—'Ho, Naught! How dost thou fare? 'Tis a fine day, Naught, is't not? Come, Naught, let us . . .'"

"Geoffrey!" Cordelia pinned him with a glare. "The poor lass hath grief enow, without thy . . ."

"Nay, I have no grief." The girl puckered her brow. "Yet thou art truly a rude fellow. An thou must needs know it, my name is Nan."

Geoffrey returned Cordelia's glare. "There are times when rudeness doth serve purpose, sister."

"Aye, it angered her enow to draw her from her apathy a moment." Gregory studied Nan, watching her face smooth into blandness again. "Yet only a moment. Dost thou care so little for thy name, lass?"

"I ha' told thee, 'tis naught," the girl murmured.

"And thy life?" Gregory whispered.

Finally, Nan sighed. "What matters life? The days do pass; one doth sleep, then doth wake to another day that swimmeth by."

"Wouldst thou liefer be dead?"

"I care not." She blinked several times and yawned again.

"Thou must needs care for summat!" Geoffrey insisted.

But Nan only shrugged once more, her eyelids fluttering, closing. Her head lolled to the side.

"She sleeps," Gregory observed with a start.

"Why, certes!" Cordelia lifted her head. "She hath so little of life within her that if she doth cease to move, she doth sleep! Brother, wake her!"

"Wake?" Magnus protested. "I do well to uphold her!"

" 'Tis thine office, sister," Gregory explained. "Thou art most skilled at moving thoughts within another's mind."

"Thou art not greatly less so," Cordelia huffed, but she turned to gaze intently at Nan, brow wrinkling with concentration. After a moment, the bigger girl sighed; her eyelids fluttered again, and she lifted her head, blinking and looking about her. She started to speak, but the words turned into a yawn, and she passed her tongue-tip over her lips as she looked about her. "What . . . ? Oh. Thou art not dreams, then?"

"Nay," Magnus assured her, "but thou shalt be little more than such, an thou dost not come away with us."

"Come away?" Finally, Nan's eyes opened almost fully. "Yet wherefore ought I?"

"For that an thou dost stay, thou wilt be turned into a thing of evil!"

Nan frowned, considering, then shrugged. "What matter what I shall become? I have a dry, warm chamber within. Its walls are hung with tapestries and the floor is covered with thick carpets. There be chairs and tables that glow with the rich gleam of grand woods, and a great couch with soft feather beds. Nor am I lonely, for a proud gentleman doth company me. In truth, he doth dote upon me, bringing me rich foods and fine wines, and doth dance and talk with me till I do sleep."

"Then doth he drink thy blood," Magnus told her, his face grim. " 'Tis therefore thou art so listless; 'tis therefore thou hast those marks upon thy throat."

Nan raised a hand, fumbling toward her neck. "These . . . they are but . . ." Her voice trailed off in confusion.

"He is a vampire," Cordelia explained, more gently. "He doth keep thee to bleed thee for his supper."

Nan frowned. "Oh. Doth he truly so?"

"I assure thee that he doth," Cordelia said, shocked. "Dost thou care naught?"

Nan's gaze strayed. "I think I do not. Upon a time, I might have—yet I do not now."

"Oh, but thou must!" Cordelia cried. "Come away with us! We may still save thee!"

"Save me?" Nan frowned, blinking. "From what?"

"From becoming thyself a vampire! An he doth continue to drain thee, thou shalt become like to him!"

"Oh." Nan pursed her lips, considering. "Is that so bad?"

"Why, 'tis horrible!" Cordelia insisted. "Wouldst thou do to another what he hath done to thee? Wouldst thou take the very life from another's veins?"

Nan concentrated, thinking it over. . . .

"Do not let it trouble thee overlong," Geoffrey said, with sarcasm. "Come, wilt thou be good or evil? 'Tis as simple as that."

Nan blinked, thoroughly confused now, and Cordelia glared at her brother.

"An she truly careth naught," Gregory mused, "we have but to pose the question in another fashion. . . . Nan, why *not* come with us?"

"Aye!" Cordelia added. "Wherefore *not?*"

Nan's brow creased in concentration. Then, finally, her face smoothed again. "Wherefore not, indeed?" She actually managed a slight smile as she lifted a hand. Magnus let her go, and stepped back—but her hand came on up to touch his. "Where wilt thou go?"

"Why, to the nearest village," he said, with immense relief. "Geoffrey, lead!"

Geoffrey didn't need persuading. He turned away, drawing his sword, and led them back along the path. Magnus followed, propping up Nan, with Cordelia and Gregory behind him and Fess bringing up the rear.

Geoffrey led them around a curve and under a huge old tree. As they neared it, Magnus pulled back. "Hold! There is summat about this oak that . . ."

A shadow stirred within shadows, detached itself, and stepped toward them, smiling. His clothes were black, and skintight; his face was white as paint, his eyes shadowed into points, and his lips very, very red. "Kiss," he said, reaching for Cordelia. "Kiss. Kiss."

She struck his hand away, stepping back, and Geoffrey leaped between them, stabbing upward at the vampire, then riposting—but the vampire only looked down at his shirt-front, nettled. "Thou hast ripped my cloth."

Geoffrey stared. There was no spreading stain, no blood on his sword.

The vampire grinned at his discomfiture, showing pointed fangs. "Nay, steel shall not harm me—and I hunger. An thou wilt not give me to drink, then return my lass to me." He reached for Nan.

"Avaunt!" Magnus struck his arm down, in spite of the crawling revulsion within him. "She is no thing of thine, but a woman sole in her own right, and no man's chattel."

"Thou knowest not of what thou speakest, boy," the vampire sneered. "Tell, Nan—whose lass art thou?"

"Why, thine." Nan tried to step toward him, but Magnus held her back. "Lay off!" she cried, struggling against his arm.

"By what right dost thou keep her, when she doth desire to go?" the vampire demanded.

"By what right dost *thou* keep her, when she would desire to go were she recovered of her senses?" Gregory demanded.

"What sprat is this?" the vampire snarled. "Be gone,

mere inconvenience!" He pounced, claws reaching for Gregory.

Geoffrey shouted and leaped at him again, but this time the vampire turned, catching him and lifting him toward his mouth. "Tender," he growled, "succulent."

Magnus let go of Nan and hurtled into the vampire, knocking Geoffrey out of his grasp. The pale man went flying—and kept flying, as his cape spread out into wings and all of him shrank into a bat. He wheeled about in the air, streaking back toward Gregory.

"Why, 'tis a birdbrain!" Geoffrey laughed. "Come, hen! What fowl prank wilt thou play next? O bird absurd!"

The bat wheeled, its eyes glowing fire, and pounced— but Geoffrey dodged behind Fess. The bat didn't even try to follow—it sailed straight at Fess's neck, needle-fangs glinting—and striking down through horsehair with a re- sounding clang as they met Fess's metal neck. It spun toward the ground, stunned, and just barely managed to pull out of its nosedive and start flapping up.

But that was long enough for Magnus to find a long stick. "One bad bat doth deserve another," he grunted, and swung.

The club cracked into the vampire. He lurched and went spiralling down to the dirt, out cold.

The children stood transfixed.

Then Nan gave a wordless cry and reached out toward the fallen creature.

Geoffrey leaped to block her. "Nay! Thou art freed of him now, and shalt remain so!"

"It will be a while before she ceases to crave his presence," Fess advised him. Geoffrey nodded, caught Nan by the wrists, and pulled her away.

"What now?" Cordelia demanded. "We dare not leave him so, or he will revive and begin his depredations anew."

"Why, we have one who doth await the occasion," Gregory answered. "Magnus, summon."

Magnus straightened, gaining a smile and calling out, "Wee Folk! We have done what we can! Now come and aid!"

"Why, that will we, and right gladly!" The elves stepped out of the long grass all around. "We had hoped for such as thee, young witchfolk, who could disable this nemesis long enough for us to . . . seek its disposition."

"Then we may leave it to thee?" Magnus asked, relieved.

"Assuredly," an elf replied. "He shall ne'er trouble the folk of this shire again, I promise thee."

"In truth," a brownie agreed. "He was not here a year agone; he shall not be here after."

"Gramercy, then." But Cordelia was still troubled. "What shall we do with Nan, though? We cannot bring her with us—and she cannot care for herself now."

"Be of ease in thy mind," an elf-woman assured her. "We shall care for her till her body hath filled itself up with blood again, then take from her mind all memory of Elfland and bring her once again unto her own village."

The circle of elves closed around the form of the vampire, and the spokesman said, "Thou shouldst be gone now, younglings. We shall do as we must, yet thou hast no need to see."

"Why, therefore shall we take our leave," Cordelia said. "Fare well, good elves! Be kind to Nan!"

"We shall," the little woman assured her, and they turned away.

They had only travelled for fifteen minutes or so when another elf stepped out onto the trail ahead of them. They looked up and stopped. "What cheer?" Geoffrey called.

"All," the elf answered. "The lass sleeps, and mends; the vampire will sleep forever—unless some fool comes upon him, not knowing how much is at stake."

"Thou hast buried him at a crossroad, then?"

"Nay, for folk might come upon him there, if they sought to rear up buildings. We have hidden him in a deep, dark cave."

Magnus frowned. "There are ever human folk who cannot resist the lure of such deep places."

"Even so," the elf agreed, "so we have taken him by dark and secret ways too small for mortal folk, or for any but an elf—or bat."

" 'Tis well." But Magnus still wasn't smiling. "Yet there are folk, good elf, who have much more of enthusiasm than of good sense."

"And ever will be," the elf rejoined. "There is no guarding 'gainst them, young wizard, whatsoe'er we may do."

Magnus lifted his head, then gazed off into space. He had never heard someone call him "young wizard" before, and the thought gave him pause.

"And Nan will be well?" Cordelia asked anxiously.

"She will," the elf assured her, "though she will never again be so filled with the joy of living as she once was."

"Ah." Gregory smiled sadly. "Yet is that not the fate that doth await all folk, soon or late?"

"Not always," the elf said.

"Nay," Cordelia said, "it need not."

That brought Magnus out of his daze. He glanced at her, worried—but all he said was, "Come. Away!" And he turned to lead them on down the trail again.

# 11

They had gone some ways, Magnus on Fess's back, when he suddenly stopped and frowned down at Geoffrey. "What didst thou say?"

Geoffrey gave him a look of exasperation and spoke again, but Magnus could still barely make out the words. "Nay, say!" he demanded, more loudly.

"Why, thou loon, canst thou not hear what's clearly spoke to thee?" Goeffrey yelled.

"Aye, *now*—and mind whom thou dost call loon! An thou dost speak so softly, how am I to hear thee?"

"I did not speak softly!" Geoffrey bellowed. "I did speak as ever I do!"

"Which is to say, in impatience," Cordelia called. "If aught, Magnus, he doth ever speak too loudly. Wherefore canst thou not hear him today?"

"Wherefore dost thou call out?" Magnus returned.

Cordelia halted, surprised, and stared up at her brothers. "Why, I *did* call, did I not?"

"Thou didst," Geoffrey assured her loudly. "Wherefore?"

"I know not . . ."

"Why, for that we'd not have understood her words an she had not," Gregory said reasonably, though at much greater volume than was his custom. "Yet wherefore must she? Doth the air swallow our words?"

They all looked at one another, confounded, trying to puzzle it out.

Then, suddenly, each of them was struck with a subtle sense of wrongness. Geoffrey looked up. "Summat hath changed."

"Aye." Cordelia glanced about her, brows knit. "What is it?"

Magnus eyed the trees around them with suspicion.

Then Geoffrey said, "The music hath stopped."

They turned to him, eyes wide. "Why, so it hath!" Cordelia exclaimed.

With a sudden, jangling chord, all the rocks around them began emitting music again.

Gregory winced and clasped his hands over his ears. *"That* is why we shouted so! The music had grown so loud, it had drowned out our voices!"

"So it would seem." Cordelia smiled, head tilted to the side as she nodded with the beat. "Yet 'tis pleasant withal."

"As thou wilt have it, sister . . ."

"As she will or will not!" Magnus called. " 'Tis all about us; we can go to no place where it is not. Yet wherefore hath it grown so much louder?"

"Belike because there are so many more rocks here," Geoffrey suggested.

"Mayhap." But Magnus seemed unconvinced.

"Yet why did I not perceive that it had grown louder, till it ceased?" Cordelia wondered.

"And why did it cease?" Geoffrey demanded.

"For that all the rocks do give off the same sound," Gregory explained, "and the tune paused for a brief time."

"Aye, then would it yield silence." Magnus nodded slowly. "And as we have come west, the number of rocks making music hath increased, thus yielding louder sound."

"Yet so slowly that we did not notice!" Geoffrey agreed. "Thou hast it!"

But Gregory still looked doubtful. "There would be some such increase, aye—yet not so much as this."

"Gregory is right," Fess declared. "The proportion of rocks to decibels is not by itself enough to account for so great an increase in emitted sound."

"Then what else?" Cordelia demanded.

"Why, the music itself hath grown louder, sister," Gregory said, spreading his hands. " 'Tis the only other source of gain."

They looked at one another, astonished.

"Assuredly," Magnus said. "What else, indeed?"

"And now I bethink me, there's some other difference in the music." Geoffrey tapped his foot impatiently. "What is it?"

"Thou dost tap thy toe in time with the music, brother," Gregory pointed out.

Geoffrey stared at his toe, astonished. "Surely not! What dost thou take me for, manikin!"

"My brother," Gregory answered, "who hath ever hearkened to the soldier's drum."

"Aye . . ." Geoffrey was absorbed in the music, actually listening to it, for once. "Thou hast it aright—there are drums, though of divers kinds."

"More than there were," Cordelia agreed.

"Aye, and a scratching, raucous note to the melody that was not there aforetime," Magnus added.

"If you must call it melody," Fess said, with mechanical dryness.

"Aye, assuredly 'tis melody!" Cordelia blazed on the instant. "The strain doth rise and fall, doth it not?"

"A strain indeed. It varies by no more than six notes, and uses only four of them. Yet I must admit, it is technically a melody."

"Oh, what matter is it, when the drums, and the deep notes, have so much life in them?" Cordelia's eyes lit, and she began to move her feet in the patterns of a dance.

"What dance is that?" Geoffrey said, perplexed.

"I'll tell thee when I've finished the crafting of it."

"The rhythmic patterns have grown more complex," Fess agree, "and some are syncopated."

"Sink and pay?" Geoffrey asked. "What meaning hath that?"

"Nay, sink thy pate!" Magnus aimed a slap at his head. "Dost not know the words speak of offbeats?"

Geoffrey stepped nimbly back from the blow, leaped, and tagged Magnus, calling, "None so off the beat as thou! What matters it, when the beat is only for marching?"

"Why, when it is for dancing!" Cordelia moved lightly on her feet, her steps becoming more certain.

Magnus eyed her askance. "Wilt thou dance, when thou wert so lately compelled to?"

"Aye, for now I'm not."

"Art thou not indeed?"

"The term syncopated refers to unexpected accents in the rhythm pattern, Geoffrey," Fess put in. "Such accents usually come on downbeats; in syncopation, they come on upbeats, or in between beats."

"What beat is this thou dost speak of?" Magnus demanded.

"The intervals of time between notes," Fess explained. "When a note sounds during what we expect to be a silence, we say it is syncopated."

"Why, that is the source of its excitement!" Cordelia cried. " 'Tis the surprise of it, that it comes when we do not expect!"

Her dance had grown considerably, in scope if not in complexity.

"Is't a jig or a reel?" Geoffrey wondered, his eyes on her feet.

" 'Tis neither, brother."

"Yet to watch it, doth make *me* to reel." Magnus turned away, with determination. "Come, my sibs! Let us seek further!"

"Why must the music change so, and so quickly?" Gregory's brow was furrowed in thought. "Was not the first form of it good enough?"

"A pertinent question," Fess argued, "but one which we lack data to resolve. Let us keep it open, Gregory."

Magnus halted, looking down. "Mayhap we have found thy data, Fess."

"Of what do you speak?" The horse halted, and the children gathered round.

A stone sat on the ground, vibrating with the loudness of the sounds it blared out.

"What manner of music *is* this?" Magnus demanded.

"Why," said the rock, " 'tis but entertainment."

"It doth glisten," Cordelia murmured.

Geoffrey frowned. "Is't wet?" He reached out to touch it.

"Geoffrey, no!" Fess cried, and the boy, from long experience with Fess, halted. "An thou sayest it, I'll stay. I've ne'e'er known thy judgment to be false. Yet what need for caution dost thou see?"

"A rock that glistens when no water is near, is suspect," Fess explained. "I mistrust the nature of its moisture."

"Oh, 'tis naught of evil!" Cordelia scoffed. "Art thou, rock?"

"Nay," the rock answered, and the children started, for the rock now spoke by modulating the strains of its music. " 'Tis but entertainment."

Gregory cocked his head, studying the sound. "This is yet a different sort of sound that it doth give."

"Perhaps a minor variation . . ." Fess allowed.

"Nay, 'tis truly new!" Cordelia tried to match both beat and bray with her feet, failed, and had to writhe her body to fit both. She gyrated, crying, " 'Tis harsh, but 'tis filled with verve!"

Magnus stared at her, shaken by her sinuous movements.

Geoffrey shook his head, dissatisfied. " 'Tis not a proper sound. Its beat is too uneven."

" 'Tis oddly structured, in truth." But Gregory was beginning to look interested. "Nay, I sense some interlocking between two sorts of counts. . . ."

"It is employing two different time signatures in the same piece," Fess said briskly. "Surely that is elementary enough."

"Why, so it is!" Gregory cried. "How ingenious!"

"Largely instinctive, I fear," Fess demurred.

"And the tune! Note how the strains approach one another, till the two notes are almost one, yet not quite! Anon they strengthen one another; anon they war!"

"Yes; the product of their phases is termed a beat frequency, Gregory. Surely you cannot acclaim a lack of skill as ingenuity. . . ."

"Can we not, if they do it a-purpose?" Cordelia countered.

"I mislike it." Geoffrey started to reach for the stone again. "Let us hurl it far from us."

"No, Geoffrey! I beg you, before you touch it, to perform a simple test!"

Reluctantly, the boy straightened. "What test is this?"

"An acid test. Reach in my saddlebag, and take out the environmental kit."

Frowning, Geoffrey reached up, rummaged, and came up with a metal box.

"Open it," Fess said, "and take out the tube filled with blue slips."

"The litmus paper?" Gregory was surprised. "What dost thou think it to be, Fess?"

Geoffrey laid the box on the ground, lifted the lid, and took out a clear plastic tube. "Shall I take a strip of it?"

"Do, and touch it to the rock."

Geoffrey pulled out the litmus and reached out to touch; the stone giggled.

The paper turned bright pink.

Then it began to smoke, darkening; a hole appeared and spread. Geoffrey dropped it with an oath, just before the whole strip of paper disappeared, leaving only a fume behind.

"What was it?" Cordelia whispered, shocked.

"The rock is coated with acid," Fess explained. "I suspect that it exudes the fluid. Put the kit away, Geoffrey."

"Aye, Fess." Geoffrey bent to stopper the tube and put it back in the box. "And I thank thee. Would my skin have burned had I touched that rock?"

"I do not doubt it. . . . Yes, back in my saddlebag, that is correct."

"Yet what are we to do with this thing?" Magnus looked at the stone. "We cannot leave it here, to eat through any living creature that doth chance to wander by."

Cordelia shuddered.

Fess looked up, nostrils catching the breeze—and feeding it to molecular analyzers. "I detect a familiar aroma. . . . Geoffrey, look beyond those trees."

Geoffrey stepped over. "I see a small pit, perhaps a yard across, filled with some white powder."

"It is alkali; I know it by the aroma. The problem is solved, at least in this instance. Geoffrey, take a fallen stick and bat the stone into the pit."

Geoffrey turned, coming back, stooped, and came up with a four-foot branch. He took his stance by the stone and swung the stick up. As it swooped down, the stone saw, and in alarm, shrilled, "Do not knock the rock!" But Geoffrey had too much momentum, and wasn't about to stop anyway; the end of the stick connected with the stone, and it flew through the air, emitting a keening drone, to land in a puff of powder.

"Well aimed, Geoffrey," Fess approved.

But the boy was staring at his accomplishment. "What doth happen to it?"

The rock was drying out and, as they watched, gained an odd, crinkled texture, with here and there a glint of reflected light. The music changed, too, gaining a new sort of piercing twang.

"Its surface has undergone a chemical change," Fess explained. "It exuded acid—but you sent it into a pit of alkali, which is a base."

"Then I have scored it with a base hit?"

"And bases and acids combine to produce salts!" Gregory said. "But why doth it glisten so, Fess?"

"Presumably this alkali was a compound of one of the heavier elements, children—or perhaps even the acid itself was. In any event, the salt is metallic."

"Aye—there is something of that in the sound." Cordelia cocked her head to the side, listening.

"But how could a soft rock turn into an acid rock?" Gregory wondered.

"An excellent question, Gregory—and one which I am sure we will find answered as we journey farther west." Fess turned his back on the alkali pit. "Come, young friends. I confess I have grown curious as to the manner of the transformation, for it is one I have never seen on Gramarye before."

"Aye!" Cordelia skipped to join him. "That is the wonder of it—that it is so new!"

Her brothers fell in behind her with varying degrees of eagerness, and marched away, following their equine guide.

Behind them, the alkali pit emitted a steady stream of sound, growing harsher and harsher as the rock hardened.

Suddenly, with a sharp report, two rocks sprang out of the pit, sailing away eastward. They flew in long flat arcs, ninety degrees apart, and when they came to earth, their music was louder.

# 12

The day was waning as they came to a riverbank. Cordelia sank down. "Let us stay the night here, Fess, I pray thee! For I'm overborne with the toils of this day, and must rest!"

Fess tested the breeze with electronic sensors. "Not here, young friends, for the trees grow too close to the edge of the water. Only a little farther, I pray you."

"Courage, sister." Magnus extended a hand. " 'Tis only a little way. Lean thou on mine arm."

"Oh, I can bear mine own weight." Cordelia caught his hand and pulled herself upright. " 'Tis only the burden of all the things we've seen that doth weigh on me."

"On me, also," Gregory said.

"Aye," said Geoffrey, "yet thou art wearied by efforts other than ours, brother." He forced himself to stand straight. Together, they turned to follow the black horse, whose outline was beginning to be obscured by the dusk.

Gregory tried to blink away the sleepiness. "How dost thou mean, effort other than thine?"

"Why," said Geoffrey, "I am wearied by marching or battle, but thou art wearied by striving to comprehend anything that confounds thee."

"Everything is comprehensible," Gregory muttered.
" 'Tis only a matter of striving, until it comes clear."

"True," said Fess. "Some problems, however, require
generations of striving."

"Well, true," the little boy admitted. "Yet such riddles as
those, I can tell apart in a few hours' time. 'Tis the ones for
which I've all the knowledge I should need that confound
me."

"I think we have not yet found all that we require."
Magnus clasped his brother round the shoulder—and helped
hold him up. "I, too, am worn not only with marching, but
also with striving to understand."

"Riddle-me-ree, riddle-me-rune!" Cordelia sighed. "And
I am wearied with seeking to riddle it out."

" 'Tis the bizarre folk we've seen, in a bazaar of sound,"
Magnus protested.

"And with a rack of bizarre behaviors." Geoffrey shook
his head. "I ken it not."

Gregory plodded ahead, fighting to keep his eyes open.
"Wherefore doth the music change so oft? Is not one form
enough?"

"Or doth it truly change?" Magnus countered. " 'Tis not
so great a transformation, when all's said and done. Is it
truly so, or is it only as we hear it?"

"Oh, be done!" Geoffrey said, exasperated. "Dost thou
say all life's but a dream?"

"Nay, then, do not wake me!" Cordelia stopped, gazing
ahead. "For yonder lies a web of gossamer that no daylight
mortal could sustain!"

The river widened into a small lake, overhung by
willows. The rest of the forest drew back, leaving a little
meadow between the bank and the forest, and the current
slowed, leaving room for a great abundance of water plants.
The evening mist blended outlines, and the gathering dusk
made the landscape indeed appear to be something out of a
dream.

"Let us rest now, I prithee." Cordelia sank into the soft
meadow grass.

"Yes—this location would be appropriate," Fess said. "Boys, gather wood."

"Aye—directly, Fess." But Gregory was near to collapse, leaning back against Big Brother's knee.

"He is done," Magnus said gently.

"Nay!" Gregory struggled back upright, forcing himself to stay awake. "I am as able as any!" He looked up at the lake. "What are these flowers, Fess?"

"Some are water lilies, Gregory, but most are lotuses."

"Lotuses?" Magnus repeated. "I have ne'er seen their like before."

"We have never been so far to the west, brother, either," Cordelia reminded.

Magnus felt a weight against his leg, and looked down to see that Gregory had succumbed to sleepiness after all. He stretched his little brother out in the soft grass, with a smile of gentle amusement. "I shall gather wood, Fess. Sister, do thou . . ." He stopped, seeing Cordelia's lifted head. "What do you see?"

"Naught," she said, "yet I do hear yet another sort of music."

Magnus cocked his head, listening. After a few minutes, he said, "I can make out some hint of it."

"And I." Geoffrey wrinkled his nose. "Wherefore must it ever transform?"

"I too hear it," Fess said, and of course that decided the issue.

Around the curve of the river, lights came into view, seeming to float on the water. One single light drifted up higher.

"What manner of thing is this?" Cordelia wondered.

As the music came closer, they could see that the lights were campfires, with young people grouped around them, talking and laughing—and growing more intimate. Cordelia gaped in surprise, then glanced anxiously at her little brother, but he was sound asleep.

"How now!" Geoffrey said in wonder. "Do they float upon the water?"

"No, Geoffrey," Fess assured him, "they have rafts."

And rafts there were, a half-dozen or more, each with a handful of young men and women. Above each raft, a single lantern hung on a pole.

"How can they have fires on rafts without burning the logs?" Cordelia wondered.

"Mayhap they brought hearthstones," Geoffrey suggested.

One of the rafts bumped the shore near them, and a soft voice called, "Wherefore dost thou stay lonely?"

"Join us!" invited a bulky young man, beckoning to them with a smile. "Pass a happy hour, and . . ."

"Join us!" called a young woman's voice. "Leave thy cares to glower, and . . ."

"Join us!" called a dark-haired young beauty. "In our river bower, and . . ."

"Join us!" they called all together.

"I misdoubt me . . ." Magnus began, but Cordelia had no hesitation. "Up, sleepyhead!" She nudged Gregory awake. "Here are they who will spare us a long day's march on the morrow!"

"Nay," Geoffrey protested, "for we know not their intentions. . . ."

But Cordelia had already set foot on the raft, and what could he do but follow?

"I beg you, young friends, do not!" Fess's voice said inside their heads. "You must not put yourself at the mercy of people who may be your enemies!"

"Pooh! An we cannot defend ourselves against the likes of these, we are poor fighters indeed," Geoffrey said scornfully. "And if all else fails, we may fly."

Magnus stepped onto the raft. "Come, brother. If there's a trap of some sort, each of us must clasp our sister by an arm and loft her high." He turned to swing Gregory aboard.

"I shall parallel your course on the riverbank," Fess assured them. "Be careful."

"We shall," Magnus subvocalized.

A wiry young man pushed with a pole, and the raft floated out into the stream.

"Come, sit by me!" A handsome young man stretched

out a hand toward Cordelia. "I am Johann, and there's room a-plenty 'gainst my pillow of fragrant boughs. Come nestle with me in idle dalliance!"

"I thank thee." Cordelia sat primly, tucking her skirt about her shoes. "I've need of rest."

Johann smiled, accepting the implied refusal with equanimity. "You do seem wearied."

"Aye," Cordelia admitted, "for we have come far, and have seen much."

"And heard much," Geoffrey added. "A cacophony of sound, and seen strange ways a-plenty."

" 'Tis horribly confusing," Gregory sighed, "and most dreadfully ravelled."

"Then let it be." The dark-haired girl smiled up at Magnus. "I am Wenna. Unknit thy brow, and rest with me." She leaned back, hands behind her head, stretching.

Magnus's breath hissed in, his gaze fast upon her, and Geoffrey stared, spellbound.

Cordelia looked up, frowning at the sound, but Johann asked, "Is't so great a coil, then, that doth confound thee?"

"Aye." She turned back, relieved at being able to speak of it to a stranger. "We have found stones that make music, and in following them we have found strange creatures and seen folk who behave in senseless fashions. 'Tis a web proof 'gainst all unravelling."

"Ravelled indeed," said the girl behind Johann. "What confusion it is, seeking to discover why mothers and fathers do as they do, not to us alone, but to one another also."

Johann nodded. " 'Tis even as Yhrene saith."

"Aye," the wiry young man agreed. "Wherefore do they kneel to the priest, and bow to the knight? There is no sense in it."

"None, Alno," Yhrene agreed.

But Gregory objected. "They kneel to Our Lord, not to the priest! And the knight's of a higher station than they."

"Even so," a lumpish young man growled, nodding. "It all seemed so simple, when I was ten. But when I came to the brink of manhood, and did begin to act as I thought a man should, I was rebuked. When I protested that I did but as they had bade me, they told me that they had not meant it that way."

"Aye, Orin, I know the way of it," Johann said, with sympathy. "Long and long did I seek, till at last I riddled it out."

"Thou hast?" Gregory roused up, suddenly no longer at all sleepy. "How didst thou make sense of it?"

"Why, by seeing that there was no need to," Johann returned, with a beatific smile. "This was my great insight."

Alno nodded. "And mine."

"And mine," Yhrene said, "and all of ours. What great peace it brought us!"

"What?" Gregory asked, incredulously. "Did all of you see the same answer at the same moment?"

"And all the same idea," Geoffrey murmured.

"We did, in truth." Johann smiled, quite pleased with himself. "Of a sudden, we saw there was no need to puzzle it out—only to embark upon the flood, and be happy."

"We needed but to build rafts," said Orin, "and take ourselves aboard—ourselves, and the stones that made our music."

"Oh, it is *thy* music, is it?" Geoffrey breathed.

"Naught but music?" Gregory was still wide-eyed. "What had you to eat?"

"The river provides." Alno reached out and pulled in a lotus as he passed. Looking up, Gregory saw that the others were nibbling the plants, too. He squeezed his eyes shut, then looked up again. "Thou dost say there was no need to puzzle out the sense of the world, and its people?"

"Aye, and what a deal of peace did it bring us!" sighed a redheaded lass.

"Peace indeed, Adele. How blessed an end to all confusion," Wenna agreed.

Orin nodded with slow conviction. "Therein lay our error—in wrestling with the world, in seeking to strive."

"Nay, surely," the dark-haired beauty agreed, "for when we cease to strive, there's an ending to strife."

"But thou dost speak of ceasing to think!"

"Aye," said Johann, "and therein lies tranquility. We ceased to ponder the matter."

"And gained a ponderous peace," Geoffrey murmured.

"But how couldst thou still the workings of thy mind?" Gregory asked.

"By hearkening to the music," Johann explained. "When thou dost think of nothing but its sweet strains, all else doth ebb from thy mind."

"I cannot believe it," Gregory protested. "Attending to music cannot obliterate thought!"

*But it can*, Fess's voice said inside his head, *as concentration on any one notion can dull any other mental activity. And the lotus aids them in this, for it dulls the mind and induces a sense of euphoria. It is, after all, a narcotic.*

"Narcotic," Gregory mused. "Doth not the word mean 'deathlike'?"

*'Pertaining to death' might be a more accurate definition. It usually refers to a sleeplike state.*

"And Sleep is the brother of Death," Gregory murmured.

Johann turned to Cordelia, holding out a lotus. "Come, join our bliss."

"By ceasing to think?" she exclaimed, shocked.

"Aye! Turn off thy mind."

"Relax." Adele gave them all an inviting smile.

"Float downstream with me." Wenna gave Magnus a roguish glance. She leaned back and stretched languorously again, holding out a hand toward Magnus. He gazed at her, fascinated, and Geoffrey stared, too.

"Whether thou canst or no, thou must not!" Gregory seemed near tears. "Thou must needs strive to understand, for all else is false!"

"But what if there's no sense to be found?" Alno said, with a skeptical smile.

"Nay there is, there must be! For why else have we minds?"

*There is some sense to that notion*, Fess's voice said, *for your species evolved intelligence to comprehend its environment. By doing so, it became better able to survive and prosper. If the world were truly random and without sense, the more intelligent person would not be any better fit, and so would not survive.*

"Nay, in truth!" Gregory averred. "The sharper mind would be *less* fit for life—for the world would drive it mad!"

" 'Tis not so bad as that, little one." Yhrene smiled with sympathy and reached out to him. "The world is as it is; we cannot change it. We can but enjoy it whiles we may."

"But what of the morrow?"

"Tomorrow, we shall yet drift upon the river."

"But all the rivers flow home to the sea!" Gregory insisted. "What wilt thou do when thou art come to the ocean?"

Adele frowned. "Be still, mite!"

"Speak not so to my brother," Cordelia snapped, since it was the kind of thing she might have said herself.

Adele fixed her with a glare and was about to speak, but Johann forestalled her. "When we come to the ocean? Belike we shall float!"

Gregory rolled his eyes up, exasperated. "Nay, but think! What of the barons through whose lands thy river doth flow? Will they leave thee to thy pleasures?"

"Wherefore should we care? We leave them alone."

"Thou mayest leave Life alone, but it shall not always leave *thee* alone. What shall thou do when it doth once again touch thee?"

"Must we have aught to do with it?" Alno fixed him with a stony stare. "We have that choice. Is there a law that says we must live?"

"There is," Johann said softly, "but how shall they enforce it?"

"Aye! How shall they reach us? We float on the river!"

"Dam the river," Gregory shouted, "and they may!"

Johann waved the notion away with the first signs of exasperation. "Peace, peace! An thou wilt have it, then, there will come a day when we must strive again for an answer! Will that appease thee?"

"Nay," Gregory answered. "Dost thou not see thou must seek the means to deal with that day ere it doth come?"

"Dost *thou* not see that even the most earnest seeker doth need rest?" Yhrene countered, striving to keep her tone gentle.

Gregory paused, then finally admitted, "Aye. Even our minds need some ease. Yet tell—how long is this rest to be?"

"Oh—a day, a week!" Adele said crossly. "What matter?"

"Why," said Gregory, "so long a rest is a sleep."

"What matters it?" said Yhrene, amused now. "This is the little sleep, not the great one."

Geoffrey shrugged impatiently. "A great sleep, a little death—what difference?"

"Try the Little Death with me, and learn." Wenna stretched her arms up.

"Come dally with me!" Johann reached out for Cordelia. "Golden slumbers kiss thine eyes! Smiles shall wake thee when thou dost rise!"

"Nay," Cordelia said, as though it were dragged out of her. "I must remain vigilant."

Adele exhaled a sigh of frustration, and Johann said, smiling, "But even the watchman must rest, soon or late. Come, repose thy brain awhile, as we do. Hearken to the words of the music and let them fill thy mind."

"Words?" Geoffrey looked up, alert. "What words are these?"

"Why, in the music," said Orin. "Has thou not heard them?"

"Pay heed," Yhrene suggested.

The Gallowglasses frowned, listening.

"I hear it," said Cordelia, "but 'tis not a voice. 'Tis the music itself doth speak."

"Yet I ken not the sense of it," Geoffrey said dubiously.

"Thou hast but to attend," Yhrene assured them. "It will begin again. It ever does."

And it did, repeating itself. It only lasted a few minutes, but it started again immediately—and again and again, cycling on and on. Gradually, the words became clearer:

*Why do they do the things they do?*
*Why is the world as it is?*
*Why are there customs, and why are there laws?*
*Why must we labor, with never a pause?*
*Why are we living, and where is our cause?*
*And why must we never stray? Why not just turn away?*

*Why do our parents do as they do?*
*Who bade them leach out their time?*
*Why must they labor all day on the soil?*
*Why must so many grieve, and so many toil?*
*Why to those who command them must they ever be loyal?*
*Why so many questions to cause us turmoil?*
*And why must we obey? Why not just turn away?*

*Why are there rulers, and why must we bow?*
*What is their worth to the world?*
*Why are there kings, and why are there lords?*
*Why must they all bear armor and swords?*
*Why are they misers who lock away hoards?*
*And why should we obey? When we could just turn away?*

*Why so many frowns on so many faces?*
*Why are there so few who smile?*
*Why must the lasses refuse our embraces?*
*Why must we try not to give them caresses?*
*Why so many "noes" and so very few "yes'es?*
*And why should we obey? Why not just drift away?*

*Why must we do the things that they do?*
*Why must we never seek joy?*
*Why so much sorrow and why so much pain?*
*Why so much striving without any gain?*
*Why do these questions belabor my brain?*
*And why not just drift away? Why not just drift away?*

*Why should we do as our parents have done?*
*Why wear their shackles and chains?*

*Why not eat lotus, and let the world be?*
*Find lotus, on rivers that flow to the sea!*
*Taste lotus, recline, and seek pleasure with me!*
*Let us taste of each other and drift away free!*
*And let us go drift away, let us go drift away* . . .

Gregory's eyes were huge. "Why, what manner of song is this?"

"Aye," Magnus agreed. "There's a scant meter, and little enough of rhyme in it."

"And less of reason," Geoffrey declared, "to say to do naught, for no better reason than that the why of it doth not leap up to strike one in the eye! Do they not see that a man must strive?"

"Wherefore?" Johann said simply.

"Wherefore?" Gregory asked in consternation. "Why—because without it, he has no worth!"

"But there is no virtue in labor by itself," Orin protested. "What purpose doth it serve?"

"But there *is* virtue in it! Men need labor as a plant needs sun!"

"Why, what a poxy lie is this?" Alno stirred impatiently. "Hast thou not heard but now? There is no worth in toil!"

Gregory persisted. "And who hath told this to thee, with what proof?"

"None need tell me! 'Tis plainly seen!"

"And thou dost believe it?"

"Aye! Wherefore not?"

"Yet wherefore *shouldst* thou?" Geoffrey said, low.

*Because*, said Fess's voice, *he has heard the song say it. He has heard it time after time without noting the words, though they did register in the back of his mind. Then, once he understood them, he paid attention to them for only a few recitals; after that, each time he hears the song, he does not truly pay attention to it.*

"The backs of your minds do heed these words you scarce understand," Geoffrey explained to Alno.

Orin frowned, unsure whether or not to take offense.

*Yes, because they do not expect to be targets of persuasion; they only expect to be entertained. Simple repetition by itself would persuade them, when it is perceived at so fundamental a level.*

"Yet why should you listen to a song when you cannot understand the words?" Geoffrey wondered.

"Why, for the pleasure of the music," Wenna said, with a sinuous wriggle.

*Do not grind your teeth, Geoffrey. The young woman speaks truly—the music has a beat and lilt that elicits the sensations that people of this age wish to feel.*

"Sensations," Magnus mused, his gaze on Wenna. "The songs speak of pleasures you wish to enjoy, but have been told you must not—until you are wed."

Wenna flushed, and Alno sat up, annoyed. "Is there nothing to life for thee, save rules and orders?"

"I but spoke of marriage," Magnus said easily, and Alno started to retort, but noticed the women looking at him, and closed his mouth with a snap.

*The point is taken*, Fess's voice said. *Yes—if the words of the song justify the behavior they wish to practice but have been taught not to, they will wish to believe those words. From there, it is only a very small step to persuade oneself that they are true.*

"Yet surely," Cordelia protested, "these songs are but entertainment."

Fess was silent.

"The song bade them eat lotus, sister," Geoffrey pointed out.

"Aye." Orin smiled. "I told thee it spake truly."

*Yes, Geoffrey*, came Fess's voice again, *that is the final stage in the persuasive process—the call to action. The song ends with an imperative—and it is heeded.*

"Thy lotus," Cordelia said, seized by a sudden notion. "Doth it enhance the music?"

Johann sat up, leaning close to her. "Why, how couldst thou have known?"

*Yes, Cordelia—once they have begun to eat lotus, it dulls*

*their thinking processes, and makes them much more suggestible.*

"For that it bids thee do what thou dost wish to be told to do," Geoffrey answered. " 'Tis simply a matter of telling thee what thou dost want to hear, and mixing into it what someone else doth wish thee to do."

Alno sat bolt upright. "Why, how is this?"

"It is the source of thine 'insight,'" Magnus inferred. " 'Tis given thee in the music, and thou dost make it thine own."

He was met with a full chorus of denials. "Nay, not so!" "What we believe, we have seen of ourselves!" "None have taught us—we have learned of our own!"

"Learned, forsooth!" Gregory cried, exasperated. "Thou dost but repeat what the stones tell thee!"

"And is there not truth in the rocks that endures?" Alno challenged.

"Truth in words that have been fed thee like bran in a manger?" Cordelia retorted.

"What need for an army?" Geoffrey said, with a laugh. "I could take a city with but a handful of men, had I music like this to precede me!"

"Conquest! Battle! Rule!" Johann's face darkened. "Canst thou think of naught but strife?"

"Why, if I do not think of it, another will," Geoffrey gibed. " 'Tis sad, but 'tis the way of men, is't not? There will ever be one who will not let others bide in peace, when he could bring them under his sway!"

"Thou shalt not do so to us!" Johann rushed him, hands out to grasp his neck.

Geoffrey twitched aside, and Johann sailed into the river with a huge splash.

"A rescue, a rescue!" Yhrene cried. "He cannot swim!"

Then Orin fell on Geoffrey like a wall.

Magnus leaped to pull him off, but a chance elbow caught him under the jaw. Then the big youth's body heaved as Geoffrey slipped out from beneath, scrambling to his feet; but the wiry Alno seized him, kicking and biting. Frowning, Geoffrey twisted around, catching Alno's collar and wrist in a lock that should have given him unbearable pain; but the lanky lad only whined, his eyes bulging, and tried to swivel the bound thumb into Geoffrey's eye as his knee slammed into Geoffrey's groin. Geoffrey emitted a loud groan, folding but pulling Alno down with him, the two of them holding one another up.

Then Magnus caught the wiry one and threw him aside into the water, and swung back to prop up his brother. "Art thou well?"

"Hurting, but not hurt," Geoffrey groaned again and forced himself to bend and stretch, biting down to stifle the pain. "I must . . . before I am set . . ." He rested a moment, panting, leaning on Magnus's shoulder. "What of . . . Orin?"

"He sleeps, though not entirely willingly."

"Oh, help Alno!" Adele cried. "He too cannot swim!"

"An I must, I must." Gregory sighed, and stared at Alno's thrashing form. Slowly, it rose out of the water and drifted back to the raft.

"Thou art witchfolk," Adele whispered.

"She saith it with fear," Geoffrey muttered, "she, who hugs things of magic to her bosom for their sweet sounds!"

Magnus turned, frowning. "What of the first man overboard?"

"He is here, brother." Cordelia stood, arms akimbo, glaring at Johann, who floated thrashing and squalling in midair. "Nay, thou'lt not come down till thou art done seeking to strike out!"

"Why, who art thou to give commands!" Yhrene demanded in indignation.

Cordelia stood stiff with surprise for a moment, then turned slowly to Yhrene, her eyes narrowing. "Why, I am she who hath hauled thy lad from the river! Shall I let him go?"

"How like the old folk they be," Adele said contemptuously, "to think that mere might doth give them right to command."

"Aye," Cordelia spat, "even as Johann sought to sway

my brother by sweet reasoned discourse! Nay, wherefore should I uphold a hypocrite?"

Johann hit the water with a champion splash again. But he managed to catch the edge of the raft this time and hauled himself up, spluttering and blowing.

"Oh, poor darling!" Yhrene cried, dropping to her knees and helping him pull himself onto the raft.

"I . . . I wish them gone," Johann gasped, and managed to push himself upright. He stood before the Gallowglasses, soused but commanding, "We need no witchfolk here. Get thee hence!"

"Aye." Alno came dripping up behind him. "Go! If thou canst not be tranquil and enjoy sweet sensation with us, go!"

"Even so," Johann agreed. "This raft is for none but they who love peace!"

"Love the lotus, thou dost mean," Geoffrey grated, still bent and clasping Magnus's shoulder. "And the music. Nay, my sibs, let us go. They shall have the life they have earned."

"Earned, earned!" Wenna exploded. "Dost thou never think of aught but earning?"

"Nay, we never do," said Magnus, "just as thou dost never think of gravity."

"Why, wherefore should I wish to be grave?"

"Thou hast no need—yet wilt thy feet stay on the ground."

"If they are there at all," Cordelia added.

Wenna glared at her, not wanting to admit her own lack of comprehension. "Thou dost not think an air of gravity would help thee fly!"

"Nay, certes," Cordelia retorted, "though the sort of flying thou dost seek will make thee gravid."

Wenna flushed with anger, finally understanding. She was about to start clawing, when the raft jarred against the shore.

Johann stared. "How came we here?"

Gregory looked up from his station by the edge of the raft, all innocence. "A trick of the current, belike."

"Or a current trick." Johann's eyes narrowed. "Nay, assuredly we have no need of thy kind! Get thee hence!"

Magnus bowed with a flourish. "Ever are we glad to please those whom we respect."

"Aye," Geoffrey agreed, looking about, puzzled, "but where shall we find any?"

Johann reddened. "Begone!"

"Thou art of acute perception," Geoffrey growled. "We have." He glared at the raft, and it slid off into the current so suddenly that Wenna and Johann fell, and the others rocked on their feet, crying out.

Cordelia rounded on Geoffrey. "That was ill-done! Couldst thou not have let them depart with dignity?"

"I am somewhat preoccupied with mine aches," Geoffrey rasped, still bent. "Why, dost thou think they would mind?"

"Certes thou dost not think so poorly of them!"

Geoffrey shrugged, and nodded toward the raft. "Behold, sister."

Cordelia looked. Johann had fallen close enough to Wenna so that he was able to reach out to touch her—and he was doing so, as their lips met.

"Why, the scoundrel!" Cordelia gasped, scandalized. "Was he not Yhrene's lad?"

"At that moment," Magnus allowed. "Yet what cares he which lips he doth kiss?"

"He is a lad for all lasses," Geoffrey muttered.

Cordelia turned away, her face flaming.

Magnus glanced at her, concerned.

"I must walk, or I'll be lamed awhile," Geoffrey groaned. "Brother, give aid."

"Gregory!" Cordelia scolded. "Do not stare! Nay, do not even look at what they do! Turn thine eyes away!"

Gregory looked up, surprised, then turned away with a shrug.

Magnus relaxed. "We'll have naught more to do with the floating world, I warrant."

"Aye, forsooth," Cordelia agreed. "It seemed pleasant enough whiles I did tarry there, but its folk care so little for what they do that they cannot be trusted."

"For what they do," Geoffrey grated, "or for one another, or their duties. Nay, I am schooled."

"Aye," Magnus agreed. "To them, honor's a mere scutcheon—and thus ends their catechism."

# 13

Meanwhile, the elder Gallowglasses continued their part of the quest.

The sun set, turning the sky into rose and pink, reaching long streamers out toward Rod and Gwen as they hiked toward it.

"I had felt tired," Gwen said, "and a-hungered—but now, by some happenstance, I do feel invigorated, and mine hunger has abated."

"A bait that I would have taken," Rod said, "and dealt with the trap if I'd had to. But I know what you mean—I'm ready to greet the day. Only it's dusk."

"Could it be the music that hath done it?" Gwen asked.

"Can you call it music?" Rod returned.

"Whatever 'tis, 'tis wondrous," Gwen answered.

And it was—a magical blending of sound that almost seemed to lift them and lend wings to their heels. They walked on into the sunset with a spring in their steps. Almost without realizing it, they joined hands.

But the pinks went on much longer than they should have; surely the sun must have set long ago! Nonetheless, all the sky was rosy still, and Rod suddenly realized that everything around them was pink-hued too. "Gwen—we're looking at the world through rose-colored glasses!"

Gwen looked about, eyes widening. "So it would seem—yet we wear no spectacles. How comes this, my lord?"

"Don't ask me—you're the magic expert." Rod grinned. "Why worry, anyway? Let's just enjoy it."

For a second, he could have sworn the breeze whispered in his ear, " 'Tis but entertainment." But he knew it must have been his imagination.

"Rose-colored glasses, indeed," Gwen said after a while. "The pinks have deepened."

"Yes, they have," Rod mused. "In fact, some of them have turned a definite red."

Then suddenly, the music that had been all about them was in front of them, and scarlet light glimmered through a screen of leaves ahead.

"What have we here?" Gwen murmured.

"Go gently," Rod whispered.

Together, they stole up to the screen of leaves, and peered in.

It was a throne room—it had to be. There was a huge chair on a high dais, which could only have been a throne, and a mass of courtiers treading the measure before it. They were all different shades of red—ruby, scarlet, deep rose—and the man who sat on the throne was crimson, with a crown of red gold adorned with rubies. He nodded and beat time with his sceptre, for it was rock music they danced to—and even the tallest of them could scarcely have reached Rod's knee.

"I thought that I knew all of the Wee Folk, or at least knew of all their kingdoms," Gwen whispered, "yet ne'er have I heard of these."

"They may not have been here before," Rod whispered back. "After all, that music they're dancing to wasn't here before, either. Maybe they came with it."

The courtiers bowed and curtsied, rose and swirled, and the crimson king nodded and smiled over all, delighting in his subjects' bliss.

" 'Twould be shame to trouble them," Gwen whispered. "Come, my lord, let us go."

They stole away, leaving the king and all his court to their endless ball.

But as they went farther and farther into the wood, the tones of color deepened and changed—maroon, then purple, and finally indigo—and the music became slower, even rather sad, but with a strident beat that lifted the spirits before they could sink too low.

"I am saddened." Gwen leaned her head on Rod's shoulder. "I have no reason to be, I know—yet I am."

"Must be the music that's doing it." Rod held her close, trying to cradle her as they walked. "I feel it too. Lean on me, love—it makes it better."

"I shall," she murmured. "Thou must needs support me now."

"I promised to once, in front of a congregation of elves, didn't I?" Rod smiled. "We really must get around to a church wedding one of these days."

"Would not our children be scandalized, though?" she murmured.

"Are you kidding? You'll have all you can do to keep Cordelia from making the arrangements."

She lifted her head, smiling up into his eyes. "Thou canst ever buoy me up when I sink, Rod Gallowglass. Mayhap 'tis that for which I love thee."

"Well, you manage to put up with some awfully rough changes in my temperament," he reminded her. "You're not the only one who's moody now and then."

"Now most of all," she said. "Come, speed my steps. We must move out from this place of blue hues, or it will sadden us to death."

"Only a little farther now," he murmured. "It's getting darker."

"Can that be good?"

"Of course. It has to get darker before it can start getting lighter, doesn't it?"

She gave him a thin smile in answer, but her face was growing pale. With a stab of anxiety, Rod noticed that she had become heavier, as though some weight were dragging her down. Looking up, he saw that all the leaves had fallen, and bare branches glimmered in starlight. Off to his right, a dark lake lay like the gathering place of lost hopes, a well of despair, and Rod shuddered and pushed on, half-carrying his wife now. Her feet still moved, but her eyes had closed, and she was murmuring as though in a fever. All around them, the music still strummed with a steady beat, but a slow one now, sad and lonely. High above it, like an arpeggio, came a long, eerie howling that sank and died into a gloating laugh. It was distant, but it made Rod shiver. He pushed on, walking a little faster.

Finally, the haunted woodland sank behind them—but they were in a place that was bleaker still, a barren land broken by harsh upthrusts of rock, sharp-edged and unworn, like flints new-broken in a new-made world. Light glimmered on their points and edges, but starlight only. It didn't bother Rod, really—he had grown up on an asteroid, and to him, it seemed almost like home. Yes, quite like Maxima, or perhaps even Luna, between sunset and earthrise—the dark side of the moon.

Rod took a deep breath and actually relaxed a little—it might be stark, but at least it was clean. That other place had felt of sickening and decay.

Gwen lifted her head, eyelids fluttering open. "My lord . . . what did I . . ."

"The blues got to you, darling," he said softly. He felt good about having helped her out for once. "We're into a new land, now. In fact, it looks very new."

Gwen looked about her, and shuddered. She nestled closer to Rod. "Cold . . . I feel so chilled. . . ."

"Well, you just woke up, sort of. But keep walking, dear. If nothing else, the dawn must come sometime. Just keep moving your feet, and we'll be out of it."

"I will," she murmured. "'Tis not so hard, now. The music doth aid."

And it did, rising and soaring, still with that pronounced beat, but you had to listen for it sometimes now, and Rod could even recognize the sounds of strings.

Softly, almost in silence, they came to a place where the land dipped down, and a river ran. It should have been silver, or at least reflected the glitter of the stars, but it was black, totally black, dark as velvet. Their path followed the incline down to a landing, where a boat waited, with a ferryman leaning on his pole, head bowed.

"I mislike that river," Gwen murmured.

"I know what you mean," Rod said, "but I like what's behind us even less. Come on, darling—the boat looks safe."

As they came up to the pier, though, the old man lifted his head, then raised his pole to bar their path. "Wilt thou not carry us?" Gwen pleaded, but the ferryman shook his head.

"Here, maybe he wants money." Rod opened his belt pouch and drew out a silver coin. The old man released his pole with one hand, which came out cupped. Rod dropped the coin into his palm and reached down to his pouch again. "Maybe I have another . . ."

But the old man shook his head again and turned away, slipping his pole into the dark water, waving a hand toward the seats in his boat.

Rod held the gunwale while Gwen got in, a bit awkwardly—she hadn't been in boats very often. Then Rod climbed in himself and sat beside her, holding her close. The old man's expression was kindly enough, but there was something forbidding about him all the same. He pushed on his pole, and the boat glided out into the current.

That was a very eerie trip indeed, totally in silence, except for the music coming from the shore, which waned as they moved out into the middle of the river. There it was silent indeed. Curls of mist rose from the water, more and more of them, thickening and twining together, swelling into roughly anthropoid shapes with darknesses for eyes and mouths, gesticulating and beckoning. Gwen gasped and crowded closer to Rod, which he was very glad of, since he wasn't feeling any too cocky himself. They slid through the silent shapes, mists of ghosts wreathing up all about them, until finally they began to hear music, faint but unmistakable, coming from the approaching shore.

Then they could see the land, and they knew dawn was near.

The ferryman pushed the boat up against a pier, and they stepped out into the false dawn. Rod reached into his pouch again, but the ferryman was already turning away, shaking his head and poling out into the middle of the stream.

"Strange old duck," Rod murmured, but the jaunty words had the false ring of bravado.

Together, they clambered up the bank into a meadow.

Rod yelped with pain and surprise. The missile that had hit him glanced away, spinning up and around, swooping back at him. It was a discus, looking like two dinner plates glued together rim to rim, only it was made of metal.

"Duck!" Rod shouted. "That edge is sharp!"

They dove for the ground, but the strange missile skimmed past a bare foot above them—and it was being joined by others like it, a dozen, two dozen. As they came, they made a humming, thumping, syncopated music that drowned out the magical sounds Gwen and Rod had followed through the long night.

Gwen glared at them. With a surge of relief, Rod remembered that she was telekinetic. Then he remembered that he was, too, and glared at a saucer that was skipping through the air toward him, thinking *down* and *away*.

It went right on skipping.

Rod felt a surge of indignation—how dare it ignore him? But Gwen said, "My lord, they will not answer!"

"So don't ask," Rod snapped. Then he realized what she had said, and whirled to her. "They *what?*"

"They will not answer," she said again. "I think at them, I seek to turn them with my mind, but they do not respond."

"You mean these flying discos have nothing to do with mind power?" Rod frowned. "Well, we'll have to cope with them, anyway."

"What can we do?" Gwen asked.

"Rise above it!" Rod answered. "Ready, dear? Up and away!"

She shot off the ground on her broomstick, and Rod rose up right behind her. The discos oriented on them and came singing after, but they were out of their league, and the High Warlock and his wife left them far behind.

# 14

Back on the shore of the river, the children trudged on.

"We still have not found the magic that maketh the soft rocks exude acid," Gregory reminded.

"I doubt not we'll discover it," Magnus said grimly, "at least, if that one we came upon was not alone among its kind."

"Well, we have found *summat*." Geoffrey stopped, looking down.

There on a patch of bare earth, a knot of grass was walking.

"What is't?" Cordelia breathed.

" 'Twould seem to be a bunch of dill weed that hath been cut off from its roots," Gregory observed.

"A bob of dill? How came it to walk?"

"How came thy toes to tap?" Geoffrey returned. "This music about us would set the dead to prancing, sister! How much more likely, then, is't for a living thing?"

But Gregory, more practical, observed, " 'Tis a thing of witch-moss."

"I doubt it not," Magnus agreed. "Must not all these music rocks be so?"

"Behold! 'Tis our beetles again!" Geoffrey exclaimed, pointing.

The others turned to look. The four insects crouched around the circle, almost exactly alike, watching the dill with sharp attention.

"Scarabs," Fess pronounced. "They would seem to be identical with the ones you saw earlier."

"Can they be the same?" Cordelia wondered.

Magnus knit his brows. "How could they have come so far, so fast?"

" 'Tis a wonder if they have." Geoffrey gazed thoughtfully down at the little panorama. "What doth the dill?"

The animated grass was dusting its way to a soft rock that sat at the edge of the bare patch. It reached out with its stem tops to touch the pebble, and froze.

"Doth it have so great a liking for the sound, that it must touch?" Gregory wondered.

A thin curl of lavender spiralled up from the stone.

"What smoke is that?" Gregory asked.

"Mayhap a thing of hurt!" Cordelia caught his arm and yanked him back. "Away, little brother! It might sear thee!"

"Hist! The tone doth harden!" Geoffrey said.

Gregory watched, wide-eyed—for the timbre of the music had indeed changed, to a more brazen sound.

"It doth glisten!" Cordelia breathed.

Sure enough, where the dill touched the surface of the stone, moisture grew and spread, expanding to cover the pebble.

The dill broke contact and turned around toward the scarabs with a flourish, seeming almost boastful.

The scarabs waved their antennae, then scurried away into the grass.

The children sat for a second, taken by surprise. "What do they?" Cordelia breathed.

"Follow!" Geoffrey cried.

The children scattered, each seeking out a scarab.

"Yours has turned northward, Geoffrey," Fess directed, tracking the silver with his radar. "Magnus, yours has turned right. . . . South by southeast, Cordelia . . . Gregory, you have overshot the mark; yours has already stopped."

Gregory slid to a halt, whirled about, and stepped back, eyes on the ground. Then he called out softly, "It hath found a soft rock, Fess."

"So hath mine," Cordelia answered.

"What do they do, children?"

"Mine doth reach out to the rock with its antennae," Gregory called back. "It doth touch the surface."

"Fess!" Cordelia cried. "Moisture doth spread from the beetle to the stone!"

"As doth mine," Magnus called.

"And mine!" Geoffrey echoed.

Four curls of lavender mist rose up from the grass, deepening in color as they spiralled higher.

"Surely it cannot, children!" Fess stepped over to look. "How can silver and silica create acid?"

"Mayhap the silver is only the scarab's shell," Gregory suggested. "Within, their ichor could be acidic."

"Whatever the means," Geoffrey responded, "it doth occur! Dost thou doubt, Fess? Shall I take it up to hurl?"

"No, do not!" the robot said quickly. "We can tell it by its music, children—the rock has indeed turned to acid."

"But what substance can the bobbed dill have spread to the scarabs, that they may use to transform rock itself?" Gregory marvelled.

Geoffrey looked up, brows knit. "Doth the day darken already?"

They looked about.

"It would seem that it doth," Magnus said.

Fess was quiet, analyzing their surroundings with spectrometer and chemical assayers. After a minute, he said, "It is not the sunlight, children, but some localized substance which seems to fill the air."

"The purple mist!" Gregory cried. "It hath risen and spread into a haze!"

Five more curls of lavender rose about the clearing, deepening and adding their mist to the ambience.

"What manner of mist is this?" Gregory wondered.

"Whatever it may be, I do not trust it!" Fess paced forward into the mélange of droning, pulsing music. "This springs from no natural chemical reaction, children! Such things cannot happen—and the inference is obvious!"

"Magic," Cordelia breathed.

"Illusion, sent by an enemy," Geoffrey snapped.

"A projected illusion, carried by the rock and strengthened by the beetles," Gregory deduced. "What genius of magic hath concocted *this* spell?"

"A genius indeed," breathed a husky voice, "if he hath led me to you!"

It was a nymph, coalescing out of the haze, wrapped in a mauve gown of gauzy mist, with long, purple hair that twined about her to hide her secret. She undulated through the air, curling about Magnus.

"A succubus!" Cordelia leaped to her feet in indignation. "Avaunt thee, witch!"

But Magnus was staring, spellbound.

"Be not so hard," a warm masculine voice cajoled. "Let them be, and come to me."

He was a strikingly handsome young man, glad in jerkin and hose of purple, drifting through the air to bow low before Cordelia, to catch and kiss her hand.

"However bad the nymph may be, thou art worse!" Geoffrey's sword whispered out of its scabbard. "Stand away from my sister!"

But the purple man only laughed.

Geoffrey reddened and thrust out his sword to prick the stranger's throat.

The point passed through the skin.

Cordelia cried out in alarm.

Once again the stranger only laughed, and slid on down the blade toward Geoffrey. "Thy sword avails thee naught, foolish lad—for it is but a dream, and I am real."

"Thou liest, foul image!" Geoffrey fairly screamed. "The sword is real—the truest steel!"

"Nay," said the image, " 'tis *I* am real—for look upon my riches." He turned with a flourish and gestured towards a castle towering above them. The drawbridge was down, the

portcullis up, and through the gatehouse, they could see
chairs of gold and cups of amethyst, with chests of rubies
and sapphires around them.

"All this is real," the young man breathed. "Come in
with me."

"And me," the nymph cooed.

"Why, how is this?" Gregory stepped forward, confounded. "How canst thou be real, who art but a dream of
purple haze?"

"I?" the stranger laughed. "I am true, I am a man of
substance! Thou art *my* dream, child, and all thy life is but
an idle invention of my slumbering brain!"

"This cannot be true!" Gregory argued. "I must exist, for
I do think!"

"Thou dost but *think* that thou dost think," the nymph
murmured. " 'Tis all a part of my brother's dream—that
thou dost walk, remember, talk, and think."

"But . . . but . . ." Gregory sputtered, at a loss to
prove his own existence.

"Behold!" The young man turned with another flourish.
"Yonder lie what all children wish! I know thy desires, for
I did make them!"

On the golden table inside the castle, a huge sugarplum
appeared, two feet across if it was an inch.

Gregory's eyes grew big, and he took a mechanical,
dragging step forward.

Fess saw the white all around his eyes and knew the
agony of soul for what it was. "Do not be deceived,
Gregory. You are real, and these riders of the purple haze
are only dreams."

"Why, thou firm illusion!" the young man mocked.
"How canst thou say that thou art real?"

"Because I am not organic, and cannot be influenced any
more by specious arguments than by glamours of mist. I
was not born, but made in a factory, and recall every second
of five hundred years and more. You have existed for
exactly seven minutes, thirty-four seconds . . . thirty-
five, now. And no longer!"

The young man stared, incredulous, then laughed with a harsh and mocking sound.

Fess turned his back on the illusion. "Let us go, children! You are real, and proof against delusions—for you are of the line of d'Armand! Come! Reality awaits!"

He stepped away toward the surrounding forest, not even looking back to see if they were following.

Gregory shivered and whirled about, staring after Fess, then ran to catch up. Geoffrey marched after him, face burning with anger, but obedient to command.

"Away, hussy!" Cordelia caught Magnus's hand. "What, brother! Wilt thou be enslaved by thine own waking dream?"

Magnus shook himself, and turned away from the purple nymph, moving slowly and mechanically, but moving.

"'Tis *I* shall be *thy* slave," the purple youth purred. "Only stay with me!"

Cordelia wavered, leaning toward his ready embrace.

Magnus's head snapped up as though he'd been slapped. Then his eyes narrowed, and he strode forward to catch Cordelia's wrist. "Why, what a poxy lie is this, that would seek to entrance a maiden with her own longings! Begone, foul seducer! My sister's not for thee!" And to Cordelia, "What—wilt thou not wait for a true love who's truly real? Is not a real man, however flawed, of greater worth to thee than barren dreams?"

"Mayhap not," she murmured, but fell into step with him. "I cannot tell. . . ."

"I can!" Magnus proffered his arm, somehow managing to catch her hand around his biceps without releasing his hold on her wrist. "Come away, fair sister! Come, walk with me . . . so! Forever, we shall walk together . . . and thus shall we save one another!"

And so they did, each following the other's movements, step by step, up out of the haze of illusion, back into the light of day.

Before them, their brothers marched, following the robot, whose horse sense could pierce through dreams.

As they caught up, Gregory was saying plaintively, "Yet

how can I *prove* it, Fess? How can I *know* that I am real?"

"Aye." Geoffrey was scowling. "This Bishop Berkeley that thou dost speak of—was he not right? Does nothing exist if it is not perceived?"

"That is a matter decided some years ago," Fess answered, "if ever it can be." He lashed out with a hoof, and a rock spun through the air, bounced off a tree, and fell to the forest floor—all without missing a beat. "Thus did Dr. Johnson refute Berkeley," Fess replied. "And I submit that, like Dr. Johnson, you, Geoffrey, gave as much evidence as we can have, when you batted the acid rock into the pit."

Gregory perked up. "Why, how is that proof? If 'tis our eyes that are fooled as well as our ears, did we truly see the rock fly through the air, or did we but dream it?"

"'Twas true enough for me," Geoffrey assured him. "The stone did sail through the air; I saw it do so, I felt the shock as the stick hit the rock!"

"That was Doctor Johnson's point when he kicked a cobblestone, Geoffrey."

"Yet his eyes might be deceived as easily as thine ears," Gregory objected.

"And what of his foot?" Geoffrey jeered.

"Yet that too could have been illusion! The sight of the rock flying through the air was only what mine eyes did tell me! It might be as much illusion as that purple castle—for did not mine eyes also tell me of that?"

"Yes," said Fess, "but your senses were distorted when they received that impression, distorted by the purple haze."

"Were they?" Gregory challenged. "How are we to know that?"

"Because I did not see them directly," Fess answered. "I perceived them only at second hand, through your thoughts."

Gregory stopped, eyes losing focus. "Nay, then . . . Assuredly, they were not there . . ."

"Yet, Fess, we will not always have you with us," Magnus said.

"I fear not. Remember, then, that Bishop Berkeley's

main point holds—we cannot totally prove what is real and what is not; some iota of faith is necessary, even if it is only faith that what we perceive, when our senses are clear, is real."

"Yet how are we to know if it is truly real, or is not!"

"By whether or not it is there when you come out into the light again," Fess said severely, "by whether or not what you see by night is still there in the morning: by your interaction with other objects, and their interaction with you. The cobblestone might have been illusion, but if so, it created a very convincing illusion of flying away from Dr. Johnson's foot. Dr. Johnson may have been an illusion, but I suspect he had a very convincing sense of pain when his toe hit the cobble."

"But we cannot prove . . ." Gregory let the sentence trail off, not sounding terribly worried anymore.

"Thou dost say that whether it is real or not, it will hurt as though it was," Geoffrey amplified. "My sword may be an illusion, but it will nonetheless spill another illusion's blood."

"You approach the solution. What if you had touched the gleaming rock, even though I bade you not to?"

"Then my illusory hand would have felt illusory agony, and my illusory skin would have rotted as the illusory acid seemed to eat it away," Geoffrey answered, "and my illusory self would liefer not, thank you! Thou mayest burn thine *own* illusion, an thou dost wish!"

"But then . . . our whole frame of reference may be illusion . . ." Gregory ventured, his expression troubled.

"That is the point." Fess nodded. "It is real within our frame. Whether it is ultimately real or not is beside the point; it is pragmatically real. It is the reality you must live with, like it or not."

"I see." Gregory's face cleared. "It may not be ultimate, but it is the only reality we have."

"Even so."

Magnus frowned. "Then the purple lad and lavender lass, they were not real at all?"

"Certes, they were not real!" Cordelia said with a

shudder, "and I thank thee for saving me from them, brother."

"As I thank thee, for saving me," Magnus returned. "Yet how can we have needed saving from them, if they were not real?"

"Because they *were* real illusions," Fess explained. "Be sure, children—illusions can do as much harm as anything else in this world. By clouding your perception of reality, illusions can kill."

# 15

Many miles away, Rod and Gwen finally began to hear the roar of surf. Coming out of the forest, they found themselves on a rocky beach with a thin strip of sand near the foaming breakers.

"How beautiful!" Gwen exclaimed.

"It is," Rod agreed, gazing at the dark green mass of water, smelling the salt air. "I keep forgetting."

They strolled toward the tide line, watching the gulls wheel about the sky. But they couldn't hear them— whenever there was a lull in the sound of the surf, all they could hear was the snarling and beating of the music of the metallic rocks.

"Here?" Gwen cried. "Even *here?*"

"I suppose," Rod said with resignation. "They fanned out from wherever they originated—and there's no reason why this edge of the fan should end, just because it's come to the ocean."

Something exploded, just barely heard above the roar of the surf, and they saw a rock go flying off into the waves. The other rock went . . .

"Duck!" Rod dove for the sand, pulling Gwen with him. The rock sailed by right where her head had been.

"Look!" Gwen pointed.

"Do I have to?" Rod was noticing how wonderfully the fragrance of her hair went with the scent of the surf.

"Oh, canst thou never pay heed to aught else when I am by?" she said, with exasperation (but not much). "See! The waves do hurl the rock back at us!"

Rod followed the pointing of her finger and saw the new rock come sailing back, shooting by over their heads. They heard its whining thumping as it hurtled past.

"The sea will not have it!" Gwen exclaimed.

"Sure won't." Rod pointed to a yard-wide swath of thumping, twanging stones at the edge of the water, shifting like sand with each surge and ebb of the waves. "Thank Heaven." He had a sudden vision of the sea filling up with layer upon layer of stones, each vibrating with its own rasping beat. Then he realized that the same phenomenon was happening on land. "Gwen—is there any end to how many music-rocks can be produced?"

She shrugged. "As much as there is a limit to the witch-moss of which they are made, my lord."

"And there's no shortage of that—new patches crop up after every rain. It spreads like a fungus—which it is." Rod struggled to his feet. "Come on. We've got to find out where those rocks come from and put a stop to their making, or they'll bury the whole land."

"Husband, beware!" Gwen cried. "The waves . . ."

Rod leaped back as a new wave towered above him. "My Lord! Where did *that* one come from?"

The new wave hammered down on the heavy metal rocks and, for a moment, their music was drowned in its roar. Then, as the wave receded, the music made itself heard again.

Gwen came up behind Rod, touching his arm. "Husband mine . . . the music . . ."

"Yes," Rod said. "It *has* changed again."

"But can we call that a change?" Gwen murmured.

It was a good question. The music had the repetitive

melodic line and metrical beat they had first heard, near Runnymede.

"Well, it's a change," Rod said, "but it seems as though that wave has washed everything new out of them. It's the same music as it was at first."

"No, wait." Gwen frowned. "I think . . ."

Rod waited, watching her closely.

Finally, Gwen shook her head. "What e'er it was, 'twas so slight that I could not distinguish it. For all that I can tell, 'tis as it first was."

"And so we end where we began." Rod caught her hand and turned away. "Come on—if the music can go back to its beginning, so can we."

"To the place where the music began?"

"Yes. Every time a rock split, we followed the northern pebble—and this is where it ends. Time to swing south. If this is the end, the beginning must be down there."

"There is sense to that." Gwen fell in beside him, but found a huge swell of peace and joy in her heart. To be walking with him, by the sea, was enough; she found she didn't really care whether or not they found what they were looking for.

"This rock music has a strange effect on me," Rod muttered.

"I am glad," Gwen murmured.

"How's that again?"

"Naught."

"Oh. Right." Rod's stride became more purposeful. "Yes. We do have to find the source of this rock music, you know."

"Oh, aye."

"That's right. The stones already around are all well enough, but we've got to choke off the source, before Gramarye is totally buried under rock."

"Yes," Gwen agreed, "we must."

And they went off south, hand in hand, with the sea and the sunset on their right, and a land of music on their left.

* * *

Far to the south, Magnus came wide awake. He frowned, looking about the clearing where they had camped for the night. The embers of the fire showed him the blanket-wrapped forms of his brothers and sister, and the bare outline of Fess, black against night, brooding over the scene.

What had wakened him?

"I heard him, too, Magnus," the great black horse assured him. "It is no dream."

But Magnus didn't even remember a dream of someone talking. Before he could ask, "What?" it came again, inside his head. *Magnus.* His father's voice.

*Aye, Papa,* he answered, watching his siblings.

*We're on the way back now,* Rod said. *Where are you?*

*Some ways south and west of Runnymede, Papa,* Magnus replied, and looked up at Fess with a question.

*Ninety-eight miles southwest of Runnymede, Rod,* Fess advised.

*Right. We're about fifty miles northwest of you,* Rod said. *Should meet you in two days, but it could be tomorrow about noon. Should we rush?*

Magnus looked at Fess again, then said, *There is no need.*

*Good. See you tomorrow, then.*

*Papa, wait!*

*Yes, my son?*

*What hast thou found?*

*Some things that are very interesting, but nothing that seems to provide much information,* Rod reported. *Tell you all about it over dinner two nights from now.*

*Aye, Papa. Safe journey to you.*

*Godspeed.* And he was gone.

Magnus lay down again, feeling rather disconcerted. But after all, at seventeen, he couldn't very well admit that he had felt reassured by even the mental presence of his father—now, could he? No, of course not. Not even to himself. Instead, he rolled up in his blankets and recited a koan. He fell asleep listening for the sound of one hand clapping.

# 16

The next evening, Gregory piped up, "I am hungry."

"Let it not trouble thee," Geoffrey advised. "It is but illusion."

"Illusion or not, you had best answer it with real food." Fess came to a halt, turning back to face them. "Or would you rather have an illusory dinner?"

"True substance, by choice." Geoffrey pressed a hand over his stomach. "Now that I bethink me of it, my little brother speaketh aright."

"'Tis only past sunset, Geoffrey."

The boy shrugged. "I care not. I can be a-hungered at any hour."

"Yet thou didst dine but four hours agone."

"Aye, 'tis gone indeed." Geoffrey frowned around him. "There is sign of game hereabouts. Mayhap we should hunt down our dinner now."

"What," Magnus scoffed, "lose time for naught but an empty belly? Nay, where is thy soldier's fortitude?"

"It hath fled with the last of my dried beef," Geoffrey answered. "Naetheless, thou hast the right of it, brother—I must endure."

But Gregory pointed to a column of smoke that stood against the sky. "Yon are folk. Mayhap they will have some victuals to sell."

They followed the path through the trees, till it opened out into a meadow. "Go warily, children," Fess cautioned. "Let us be sure they are friendly."

"As thou wilt." Cordelia sighed, and stepped through the last screen of leaves.

"It is certainly no village," Geoffrey said.

All over the meadow, young men and women were sitting up and shaking their heads, as though waking. They yawned, stretched, and put something in their mouths. A few were straggling down to a stream to drink and splash water on their faces; others were returning, far more sprightly than when they had left. Two others added sticks to a small tongue of flame, their movements quick, but so energetic that they sometimes nearly buried it.

"They are so gaunt!" Magnus said, unbelieving.

And they were—not emaciated, but devoid of any ounce of fat, pared down to stringy muscle. Their cheeks were hollow, their eyes too bright.

"The poor folk!" Geoffrey turned away, drawing a sling from a pouch at his waist. "Come, brothers! Let us find them meat!"

Fifteen minutes later, they approached the fire shoulder to shoulder, laden with squirrels, rabbits, and partridge.

The couple around the fire were chatting with each other, scarcely pausing for breath. They looked up, surprised; then the girl recoiled, face twisting in disugust. "Faugh! The poor beasts!"

"Aye." The young man frowned. "Wherefore didst thou slay them!"

They spoke so rapidly that the Gallowglasses could scarcely understand them.

"Why . . . why . . ." Geoffrey, his gift spurned, was at a loss.

"We have brought thee food," Magnus explained. "All thy folk do seem a-hungered."

The lad and lass stared at them in amazement. Then, abruptly, they burst into laughter—too loud, too hard.

"Why . . . wherefore . . ." Gregory looked around, perplexed.

"How ill-bred art thou!" Cordelia stormed at the couple. She threw her bundle of game down by the fire and set her hands on her hips. "To so laugh at those who seek to aid thee!"

But other young folk were gathering around now, and joining in the laughter.

"Be not offended, I prithee." A young man, perhaps a little less hard-faced than the others, choked back his laughter and smiled at them. "And your gift is welcome, for we must eat now and again, whether we wish to or no."

"Not wish to?" Geoffrey asked. "How is this? Wherefore wouldst thou not wish to eat?"

"Why, for that we have these." A girl who had once had a shapely figure held out a double handful of white pebbles. "Eat of one, and thou'lt be no more a-hungered."

Geoffrey shied away, and Cordelia eyed the pebbles askance. "How now! Is not mistletoe a poison?"

"They are not mistletoe," another lad assured her, "but magic stones. What Greta offers thee are near to being the apples of Idun!"

"What, they that conferred eternal youth?" Magnus took up a pebble and inspected it narrowly. It had an unhealthy look somehow, a translucence that hinted at corruption just under the surface.

"Well, mayhap Tarmin doth overspeak his case," the first youth allowed, "though when thou hast swallowed these stones, they fill thee with so great a sense of well-being that thou dost indeed feel as though thou wouldst ever be young."

"And end thine hunger," Greta asserted. "Thou wilt not wish to eat, and will be bursting with vigor."

"Here! Try!" Tarmin's hand shot out toward Magnus's mouth, a white pebble pinched between thumb and forefinger.

He almost punched Magnus in the nose, but Magnus

recoiled just in time. "How now! I've no wish to eat of it!"

"Nor I," Geoffrey said, scowling about, "if it will waste me as much as it hath thyselves."

"Waste!" the first young man cried, offended. "Why, I am the picture of health!"

"He is!" another girl asserted. "Alonzo is the very portrait of robust young manhood!"

"Busted, mayhap," Geoffrey allowed. "I thank thee, but I'll not eat."

"Nay, thou wilt," Alonzo insisted. "What! Wilt thou thrust *our* gifts back in our faces?"

"We do not wish to offend," Magnus soothed, "but we will not eat."

"Why, how rude art thou!" Greta said, offended. "When we do but wish to share with thee. We would not be alone."

"Dost thou say that we do wrong to eat of them?" Tarmin demanded, glowering.

"Now that thou hast said it," Geoffrey replied, "aye."

"Then thou must needs partake of them," Alonzo stated. "We will not be wrong! Everybody must get stoned! Kindred! Catch and hold!"

And the circle closed in with a shout.

But a spirit screamed behind them, a huge black form towering out of the night above them, steel teeth flashing in the firelight, steel hooves flailing down.

The young folk screamed, terrified, and cowered before the night-demon—and the Gallowglasses ran through the gap toward Fess.

"Around me, and run!" the horse told them, and they shot past him, off into the night.

Alonzo shouted, seeing his prey escape, and leaped after them. Fess slammed his hooves down—he didn't have enough cause to really attack, but he could bar the way. Alonzo jarred into his steel side and reeled back, arms flailing, into Greta's embrace. The other young people raised a huge shout and, seeing that the demon was only a horse, leaped past it after the fleeing Gallowglasses.

"Where . . . to?" Gregory panted. Night had fallen, and he could not see.

"Over here, brother!" Geoffrey called. "There is a path!" He pounded away, taking the lead, his night-sight better than the others'.

"Fly," Cordelia called to her little brother, "or thou'lt be caught for weariness!"

"*They* will not." Magnus looked back over his shoulder. "Whence gained they such a store of strength, with so little meat upon them?"

"Do not ask, brother! Run!"

The leaders had yanked sticks out of the fire, pursuing them by torchlight. Magnus glanced back at the bobbing lights. "They come . . . closer," he panted. "Nay, find some way . . . to lose them! Or they'll . . . outrun us yet!"

"Into the wood!" Geoffrey called, and swerved in among the trees.

Behind them, a joyful shout split the air.

"They cheer with reason," Magnus cried. "We must go slowly here!"

"So must they," Geoffrey called back, "for I've spied a bog!"

The trees became more widely spaced, and between them some sort of sticky, mudlike substance roiled. Here and there, it puffed up into a bubble, sometimes of amazing dimensions, which finally popped and subsided into a sticky mess that closed off its own crater.

"The trees are all of one kind." Cordelia looked up about her. "What sort are they?"

"Gum, by the look of them," Magnus answered, "though 'tis too dark to see clearly."

Cordelia turned back to the business at hand. "How shall *we* cross?"

"There are stepping stones!" Geoffrey called. "Step where I step!"

They hopped across the bog, the boys levitating, ready to dash to catch their sister on the instant. But she sprang from rock to rock, more sure-footed than any of them.

Behind them, the mob came up against the sticky substance and jarred to a halt, one step from the mire.

"They stop," Cordelia cried. "They'll have none of this bog!"

"Small wonder." Magnus wrinkled his nose at the sickly sweet smell that rose from the bursting bubbles. "What manner of mud is this, that is pink?"

"Mayhap 'tis not its true color," Geoffrey called back. "We see by starlight, look you."

"I look," Magnus answered, "and I hear, and wish I did not."

The air about them was filled with soft rock music, perhaps softer than ever. Certainly the melodic line was simpler, varying only by a few notes, repeating over and over.

"I find it pleasant," Gregory said, smiling.

"Aye," Cordelia puffed, "but I'll warrant thou dost find the scent of this bog to thy liking, also."

"Why, so I do. How couldst thou know?"

"Because thou alone among us art still young enough to be truly a child, brother, and children do ever like sweetness."

"What, will I one day dislike it?" Gregory asked in surprise.

"Belike," Magnus admitted. "I find I have come to have a liking for sharper flavors."

"Then why dost thou not like the music we have heard?"

"I do find some of it suiting my taste," Magnus admitted.

"Safe ground!" Geoffrey cried, with one last bound. He climbed up the bank several paces and sank down to rest. "That was trying. Rest, my sibs, but not o'erlong."

"Aye." Cordelia joined him. "Those lean ones may yet find their way around this bog."

"But what of Fess?"

Geoffrey looked up at a slight sound. "He comes—or trouble doth."

"I am not trouble, Geoffrey." The great black horse shouldered out of the night. "As you guessed, however, your pursuers are coming around the bog; there is a trail, and they know their way."

" 'Tis their country." Magnus pushed himself to his feet with a groan. "Come, my sibs! The chase is on!"

They dodged around tree trunks and did their best to avoid thorns. "Is there truly a trail, Geoffrey?" Magnus called.

"Not truly, no. There is a game track that I follow."

"It should lead us to a larger." Cordelia looked back with apprehension; jarring music echoed in the distance behind them, with faint but enthusiastic shouting. "Find it quickly, I prithee! They gain!"

"We must fly, then," Magnus said, tight-lipped, "and 'tis dangerous enough in a daytime forest, let alone one benighted."

"Not so," Geoffrey called as he broke through some underbrush. "Here is a pathway!"

"Then we can run," Cordelia panted. She followed Geoffrey through the gap and began to sprint down the pathway. Magnus and Gregory followed, the younger boy gliding an inch off the ground, keeping pace with Cordelia.

Behind them, a huge crash announced their pursuers' breaking in upon the path. A whoop filled the air behind them, then the thunder of pounding feet.

"They follow," Magnus panted. "Run!"

And they did—but the mob stayed hard on their heels, whooping with glee.

"Where does . . . this path . . . lead?" Magnus puffed.

"I have . . . no notion . . . brother!" Geoffrey replied.

"So long as 'tis . . . away from them," Cordelia called.

Gregory piped up, "Is not that . . . tree ahead . . . the one near which . . . we came onto . . . the path?"

As they shot by it, they saw the broken screen of brush where the mob had tumbled through onto the trail.

"It is!" Geoffrey cried. "We are on a circle!"

"Then our pursuers are, also," Cordelia called back.

But Magnus frowned. "I hear them—but not . . . behind us."

"Aye," Gregory called. "By the sound, they are beneath!" And he stopped, peering down at the path.

"Nay, brother!" Magnus caught him up and started him running again. "An they still follow, we must not let them gain!"

But it was the Gallowglasses who gained; the sound of the mob began to fall behind them again.

"How is this?" Gregory wheezed. "I could swear we have passed them!"

Cordelia looked up, frowning. "Their voices come from the side, now."

They all looked—and the spectacle made them jar to a halt. The mob was in sight, but across from them, on the other side of a curve—and the young peasants were running upside down, seeming to hang from the path.

"What manner of magic is *this?*" Geoffrey demanded.

"Whatsoe'er it may be, they still follow, and we must flee!" Magnus stated. "Yet they will run us to ground if we keep to our feet. Up, sibs, and fly!"

He and Geoffrey grasped wrists in a fireman's carry, swooped Cordelia off her feet, and rose up a foot above the path, sailing away down its length. Gregory wafted alongside them, demanding, "How can they run inverted?"

"I know not," Geoffrey grated, "but we must run faster if we wish to lose them. See! They are still across from us!"

Gregory stared. "How can that be? We have flown a quarter-mile, at least!"

" 'Ware!" Geoffrey called. "We come to where we came in again!"

"Aye!" Magnus swerved toward the break in the underbrush. "And whence we came in, we can leave!"

But as they shot toward the break, it seemed to start moving itself, staying just a few feet ahead of them.

"Why, how is this?" Geoffrey demanded. "Doth the circle turn?"

They were all silent as insight hit a hammer blow.

"Many circles turn, brother," Cordelia said. "They are wheels."

"And so is this, upon which we run! Nay, then, we must

go faster than the wheel, to catch its entrance! Fly, my sibs! At thy fastest speed!"

And fly they did, flat out, exerting every ounce of psi energy they possessed—but the gap stayed just ahead.

"Wherefore . . . did it not flee . . . before?" Cordelia panted.

"Belike because we did not seek to catch it! Save thy breath, sister, and fly!"

It was Geoffrey who realized their danger. "Slacken, sibs! Or we will overtake our pursuers!"

Sure enough, the mob's torches were just barely visible in front of them—right side up again.

"What unholy manner of loop is this?" Geoffrey moaned.

"Who asks?" called a clear alto, and two figures stepped through from the brush screen. The Gallowglasses cried out, and did their best to stop—but couldn't arrest their motion fast enough; they sailed into the strangers . . .

Who caught Cordelia and Gregory in one-armed hugs, and reached out to catch the older boys by the arm. Magnus jolted back, trying to break free, saw the stranger's face, and froze. "Papa!"

"Mama!" Cordelia cried, throwing her arms around her mother. "Oh, praise Heaven thou art come!"

Geoffrey squeezed his father in a quick bear hug before he remembered how old he was and drifted back, saying, "Alas! Now thou, too, art caught here with us!"

"Caught?" Gwen asked in alarm. "Have we come into a trap, then?"

"Aye! For this path is a circle, and we must run faster and faster to escape it!"

"But speed is not enough!" Cordelia explained. "The entrance stays ever ahead of us!"

"And there are those who chase us." Magnus looked back over his shoulder nervously. "By your leave, my parents, let us fly."

"Well, an thou wilt." Gwen levelled her broomstick; Cordelia hopped aboard. They drifted up above the path, and the boys rose to parallel them.

"If I fly, I can't really do much thinking." Rod started trotting alongside.

"You must ride, then, Rod." The great black horse shouldered through the brush and onto the trail.

"Fess! Praise the saints!" Cordelia called. "I feared they might ha' given thee a seizure!"

"No, Cordelia, though I thank you for thinking of me." Fess nodded to Rod, who mounted. "The gaunt young people ran past me; I had but to follow, since they pursued you."

"Why didn't you join them sooner?" Rod asked.

"I had to wait for them to come around again, Rod."

"Around? So it *is* a circle, then."

"But a most strange one, Papa," Cordelia burbled. "Anon our pursuers are across from us—but upside down!"

"Aye," Gregory agreed, "but after some time, they are before us again—yet right side up!"

Gwen frowned. "Husband, what manner of spell is this?"

"Probably a projective illusion," Rod said thoughtfully.

"Oh, I ken the manner of its casting!" his wife said impatiently. "Yet what hath been cast?"

"From the sound of it, I'd guess a Möbius loop."

"A Möbius loop?" Gregory questioned. "What is that, Papa?"

"A loop with a half-twist in it—it only has one side. Stay on it, and you eventually come back to where you started—but on the other side of its single surface."

" 'Tis nonsense," Geoffrey said flatly.

"Nay, 'tis wondrous!" Gregory's eyes were huge. "Wherefore have I not heard of it aforetime?" He gave Fess an accusing look.

"Because you are not yet ready for topology, Gregory," the horse answered. "I must insist on your learning calculus first."

"Teach it quickly, then!"

"Not now." Magnus looked back over his shoulder with apprehension. "We have either lagged, or gone too fast—they approach from behind again."

"Faster," Geoffrey urged, and they all picked up the pace.

"How shall we break out of this circle, husband?" Gwen asked.

"We must run faster!" Geoffrey declared. "Soon or late, we will catch the break in the brush through which we came!"

"Not so, brother," Magnus reminded him, "for the faster we go, the faster it doth go."

"Synchronizing its rotation rate to yours, huh?" Rod pursed his lips. "So you have to run faster and faster to get out of the trap—but there's a catch."

"Yes," Fess corroborated. "The faster you run, the faster the loop's rotation—and the faster its rotation, the greater its attraction."

"The more speed, the more you're stuck in the rut." Rod nodded. "That makes a weird sort of sense."

"Weird it is," Gwen agreed. "A trap."

Magnus stared. "Dost thou say that as we run harder, we hold ourselves better to it?"

"Of course!" Geoffrey cried, "even as a sling-stone sticks to the pouch of the sling!"

"Then loose, and throw," Magnus urged.

"Good idea." Rod skidded to a halt just short of the break in the underbrush, caught Gregory, and threw him through the gap. He squalled, then remembered to fly as he sailed up and over. He sank out of sight, then bobbed up again, calling, "I am free!"

"I thought so." Rod nodded. "Just a matter of making the effort to break the vicious cycle. Hold still, everybody— then jump!"

They all came to a halt—and the gap slowed with them, then halted, seeming ready to take off again.

"Now!" Gwen called, and the whole family arced up and over. They landed in a crackling of underbrush and bounded to their feet. "You too, Fess!" Rod called.

The great horse followed, landing in their midst.

Howling approached, and torches flared near. The young folk sailed by in a storm of thundering feet.

"They do not even know we're gone," Cordelia said, staring after them.

"I think they do not care," Magnus said, with a cynical smile. "They take joy in the running; they care not if they never come to their destination."

"What destination?" Geoffrey wondered.

"Well asked," Magnus agreed.

"Leave them be," Rod said firmly, and turned his boys' heads away from the Möbius trail. "Some people you just can't help."

"But we must try, Papa!" Cordelia protested.

"It is to no purpose, daughter," Gwen said gently. "You cannot succor those who do not wish a rescue. Come, leave them to their trap, and let us seek our beds."

Everything considered, Fess forbore to wake them and, by the time Rod rose, the sun was high in the sky. The family had a late breakfast of journey rations, with the parents asking the youngsters what they'd seen. They were only too glad to oblige, and by the time they got around to asking what their parents had seen, it was noon. Gwen filled them in, with a few details from Rod. The youngsters shivered with delight at their descriptions and, when they'd finished, Gregory asked:

"Have we now enough facts to make some guess as to who hath wrought this coil? Or is't but happenstance?"

"Surely not happenstance!" Geoffrey said. " 'Tis too much of a pattern."

"Ah," said Gwen. "What pattern dost thou see?"

"Chaos!" Cordelia answered, and Rod nodded. "I'd say that's pretty good. It's almost as though the younger people become addicted to the music, and disregard any social rules they've been taught."

"I would not say that," Geoffrey demurred. "There is some faint ranking that I've seen, some one who doth assert himself as leader, each and every time."

"Thou couldst say that, too, of birds and beasts," Gregory objected.

"An excellent point," Fess said. "What little social order is left, is of the most primitive."

Rod sat there and glowed as he watched his offspring putting their heads together to work out a problem.

Magnus lifted his head. "No order but the most primitive? That hath the ring of anarchy!"

"Not quite," Rod disagreed. "The ideal anarchy has everybody cooperating with everybody else, and nobody giving orders."

Gregory stared. "Is't possible?"

"Oh, surely," Cordelia scoffed, "and 'tis possible that a fairy came to take thy tooth away and leave thee a penny for it!"

Gregory stared at her, in shocked disbelief. "Dost thou mean the fairy comes not?"

Cordelia bit her lip, irked with herself. "Nay, certes not. We but spoke of what is possible, brother, not of what doth truly exist."

Neat try at covering, but the cat was out of the bag now, and Gregory had that much less left of childhood's wonder. Rod had to remind himself that intelligence can only make a child *seem* to be more mature.

But Magnus was nodding. "Such an ideal anarchy may be as possible as the Wee Folk, but is far less likely; it doth require that all folk agree without saying so, and that none seek to violate that common trust for his own gain. Can people truly believe that such a thing may hap?"

"People can believe anything, if they want to badly enough," Rod murmured, "and the anarchists who are trying to subvert Gramarye want very badly to believe that no one is better than they are. Not the other way around, of course—but they're not really worried about proving that *they* can't be superior."

"So," Magnus said, "it would seem that these music-rocks are made and spread by thine ancient enemies, the anarchists."

"Not *ancient*—but, let's say, well established, anyway. And, yes, I'd stake my job on the future anarchists' being behind this phenomenon."

"How have they wrought it, then?" Magnus asked. "Have they won a convert among Gramarye espers?"

"That's their standard operating procedure, and I don't see any reason to think they're *not* doing that now. Might be more than one—it would take a dozen espers to spread these music-rocks all over Gramarye."

Gwen shook her head. "I cannot believe there could be more than one. 'Tis a wondrous accomplishment, husband, to make rocks such as these that will make their music, and make more of themselves, when they are far from their crafter—and 'twould take an amazing mind to think of it, too. He or she would be a very genius of a witch."

"But intelligence and shrewdness don't always go together, dear. We're talking about someone who's not only an amazingly gifted crafter, but who also has a very thorough grasp of organization and leadership."

Magnus frowned. "That hath the sound of two separate people."

Husband and wife looked up, amazed. Then Gwen said slowly, "Why, so it hath. Gramercy, my son."

Magnus shook off the compliment with irritation—he was getting a little old to be *showing* pleasure at praise. "I thank thee, Mama, yet 'tis of greater import to discern who is which, and where they are."

"As to where," said Cordelia, "I've seen naught to make us think 'tis not come from the West."

"All the evidence does seem to point in that direction," Fess agreed.

"Why, then, there's an end to it." Magnus rose, dusting off his hands. "Westward ho!"

"Aye." Gwen looked up at him, her eyes bright. "Yet where shall we go to in the West, my son?"

Magnus shrugged. "There is not enough to tell us that yet. We must be alert for clues and signs that may direct us as we go. Must we not, sprout?" He slapped Gregory's shoulder affectionately.

Little Brother looked up, his eyes alight. "Aye, Magnus! Assuredly, we know not yet all the answer—but I've no doubt we shall learn it. Let us go!"

"Bury the fire." Gwen rose, and began packing up the journey bread and pemmican. The boys kicked dirt over the flames, made sure they were dead out, then turned to follow her toward the sun's destination.

Rod followed, subvocalizing, "The kid amazes me, Fess. He's showing a talent for leadership that I hadn't expected."

"Yes, Rod. His seeking of confirmation of his conclusions was deftly done."

Rod nodded. "After all, Big Brother couldn't admit that Little Brother might be better at thinking things through—at least, not if he wanted to keep leading."

"It is not Gregory who would question his leadership."

"No, but Cordelia and Geoffrey both would, if they thought Magnus had to refer his decisions to the youngest—and he has to keep them on his side if he wants to get anything done." Rod nodded. "Oh, yes. If anybody can keep them working together, Magnus can."

"Or Gwen, Rod. Or yourself."

"Well, yes," Rod agreed, "but we won't always be here, will we?"

"Prudent, Rod, but rather morbid. Shall we think of more pleasant things?"

"Such as finding out who's behind these music-rocks? An excellent idea, Fess. Let's go."

# 17

A day's journey was uneventful, and a night's sleep the same. The next morning they were dousing the fire as the sun cleared the horizon. The day was fresh and clear, and might have been filled with birdsong, but the strains of rock music drowned them out.

" 'Tis odd how we did sleep through the night, without the music's slackening," Geoffrey opined.

"Not for thee," Cordelia taunted. "Thou wouldst sleep through the Trump of Doom!"

Geoffrey considered the notion, and nodded. "True. Gabriel will not summon us to battle."

"Hist!" Magnus put out a hand to silence him. "Look up!"

They all did—and saw it float by, glinting in the dawn light, gray against the early blue of the sky.

" 'Tis a giant egg!"

"Nay—'tis far too elongated," Gregory disagreed. "What manner of object is't, Papa?"

"A blimp." Rod was taut as a guitar string, eyes narrowed. "Like a balloon, only made of metal."

"So much iron as that?" Gwen sounded doubtful.

"Not iron, dear—aluminum. It's a lot lighter."

"But it doth not glister," Gregory objected.

"A point." Rod thought a moment. "Maybe some other metal."

"Yet it is not of Gramarye," Gwen inferred.

The children looked up in alarm.

"No," Rod said. "It takes a much higher technology than we have here."

"So it is of our enemies," Geoffrey said flatly.

"Why, yes, son." Rod felt a small glow that his offspring so readily assumed Rod's enemies were his. "It definitely is."

"Might it have aught to do with the dancing dead, and the stones that bring music?" Cordelia guessed.

Rod shrugged. "It *does* seem likely."

"Not really, Rod," Fess protested. "The phenomena merely coincide chronologically; there is no indication of causality."

"Not by thine own teaching," Geoffrey said stoutly. "Thou hast taught me that once may be chance, and twice may be coincidence, but thrice is the work of intelligence."

"I do remember saying something of the sort," the horse sighed.

"Then we follow it!" Geoffrey set off after the blimp, not waiting for anyone else.

"Why call him back?" Rod asked rhetorically. *"En avant*, troops!"

They set off, following a bubble.

Fortunately, the sun was behind them, so they were able to see the broad reach of the sky as they came out of the woodlands; and equally fortunately, they were following the blimp, so they were looking up.

Magnus frowned. "Why are there so many hawks ahead?"

"Belike due to a plenitude of game, brother," Geoffrey guessed.

"Mayhap," Gregory conceded, "but wherefore doth the blimp course toward them?"

"Why, it doth steer toward the west," Gwen answered, "and here, at least, I think we may say 'tis coincidence."

Gregory shrugged. "As thou wilt."

But as they hiked westward, one of the hawks broke loose from its mates and sailed toward them.

"What?" said Magnus. "Doth it seek us out?"

The small blot grew bigger in the sky.

"Either it's mighty close," Rod said, "or . . ."

" 'Tis a giant!" Geoffrey snapped.

It had to be, with a wingspan of at least thirty feet. As they watched, those wings folded, and the bird suddenly dropped toward them, swelling hugely.

"It doth stoop—upon *us!*" Geoffrey cried. "Back, all back!"

"In a semicircle!" Rod shouted. "And get ready to hit it with everything you've got!"

The bird plunged with a cry that filled the air—straight toward Gregory. The boy tried to dodge, but huge talons caught him up.

"Hit him!" Rod yelled, and his dagger shot through the air, with Magnus's and Geoffrey's right behind it, to bury themselves in the bird's breast. A storm of rocks and sticks shot up from Cordelia and Gwen, and Rod hurtled into the midst of them, sword first. The giant hawk screamed and tried to rise, but Rod slammed into it before it could lift more than a yard. The hawk slashed with its beak, and blood welled in a long gash on Rod's left arm, shoving him slightly off target. He howled with the pain but drove the sword in, then wrestled it out and stabbed again—and the bird's face was peppered with stones and sticks. It reeled, keeled over, and fell to earth with a thud. Gregory sprang free, and Gwen swept him up in her arms.

Rod sprang for the bird's head, but saw the eyes glaze. He stood, trembling, watching its last spasmodic shudder, muttering obscenities.

"Vile raptor, to prey upon children," Magnus spat, and slashed its throat.

"Well done, my son," Gwen said. "Thus may it be to all

who seek to harm little ones! There, now, Gregory, thou art not hurted."

The boy's trembling slackened.

Rod stood looking down at the dead hawk.

*Come away, Rod,* Fess's voice said inside his head. *It is dead.*

"Yes." Rod's eyes were hidden under his brows. "I've just taken the life of a living being. Why don't I feel guilty?"

"Because it deserved to die!" Cordelia spat. "Be exalted, Father! It was evil!"

"Yes. It was, wasn't it?" Rod turned away. "Fess, what kind of bird was that, anyway?"

"A chicken hawk, Rod, though immensely gross."

"And evil." Gwen set Gregory free, and Magnus clapped him on the shoulder and took him aside. Gwen turned to Rod. "Now, husband, we must see to that wound. There is no telling what manner of foulness may have been in such a monster. We must use strong spells, to banish its corruption."

"We can try, anyway," Rod grunted.

Half an hour later, they were back on the trail. The blimp was only a smudge on the western sky, but it was still in sight.

"Look out!"

Rod reached out to catch Gregory around the middle and yanked him back just in time. A foot-thick boulder came crashing and banging down the hillside in front of the family, narrowly missing them. Rod let out a shaky breath. "Son, I keep telling you—when you're mulling over a problem, sit down! Don't go wandering around half-aware!"

Gregory swallowed. "Aye, Papa."

" 'Ware!" Gwen cried, and Rod looked up the hillside to see another small cannonball bowling toward them. He leaped back, hoisting Gregory high.

"Fly, Papa!" Magnus called.

Rod spat an impolite word; when would using his psi

powers start becoming automatic for him? He concentrated on pushing the earth away, and the world grew dim; the rattling and bouncing of the boulders seeming distant. Then Gregory wriggled out of his arms, and Rod's concentration disappeared as he made a frantic grab for his son. But he saw that Gregory was floating ten feet off the ground, realized he himself was falling, and just barely managed to push the ground away in time to loft him above the trajectory of the next cannonball. Not quite high enough—it smacked him a wicked one on the great toe—but he managed to stifle a yelp, keep his concentration, and still observe the hillside, in a remote sort of way.

The first thing he noticed was that his wife and daughter were circling over it on their broomsticks. The next was that his sons were floating in the updrafts.

The third was that there were an awful lot of those spinning, jouncing stones.

"Why are they so round?" Cordelia called.

"Because they have rolled so far down the hillside, sister," Gregory answered. " 'Tis a very long hillside, and hard."

So it was—only a ten-degree slope, but it had to be a quarter of a mile long. That was a plateau up there, not a crest—and the hillside itself was rough and rocky, with glints of flint. "That's a long way to slide, once you start to slip," Rod said.

And totally barren, of course. Anything that had tried to grow there, the tumbling boulders had mashed flat.

Fess posed a question. "How long have they been rolling?"

Geoffrey retorted, "What made them start?"

Gregory's eyes lost focus again. "The hill slopes up toward the east. Belike there are soft rocks down here that split, and shoot their offspring up—and those that cannot fly past the ridge above come tumbling back down here."

A loud crack sounded. They looked up in surprise, and saw two rocks flying toward the top of the hill.

"Why," said Cordelia, "that was a rock that lodged in a cranny, until it was time for it to split!"

Rod nodded. "And thus they do eventually get up to the top; it's just that some of them probably go up that hill and come back down several times, before they're finally lucky enough to lodge against an outcrop that will hold them."

"But every time they start again," Gwen called, "they do so by splitting. Nay, of course there are so many here!"

"An excellent resolution," Fess carolled. "Really, Rod, your whole family fills me with pride! Though of course I cannot take any credit for Lady . . ."

"Wait a minute." Rod frowned. "That rock that mashed my toe wasn't so soft."

They all studied the rocks, struck by the notion.

Then Fess said, "Could it be that the long tumble back down the hill hardens them?"

"Of course!" Gregory cried. "As they roll, they compress!"

"And as they compress, they harden." Magnus nodded. "Yet how large they are!"

"They have been long here," Cordelia said. "Mayhap they swell as they wait."

"Or mayhap," said Gregory, " 'tis simply that we near the stones' source."

Rod had another question. "But why does becoming hard make their music so much more strident?"

Everybody was silent, trying to puzzle it out.

Finally, Fess said, "We have noticed constant mutation in the music, as though some force were ever striving to create some new form. But such evolution must surely be cultural, not physical."

"I take it you mean 'cultural' in the broadest sense." Rod scowled. "Look, can we move on, please? I'm getting a headache."

"Poor Papa!" Cordelia sympathized. "And surely we will lose the skycraft if we tarry longer."

"Aye. Away!" Gwen called. She banked toward the west, the boys swooping to follow her.

Or at least two of them did. "Magnus!" Rod called. "Snap out of it!"

Magnus looked up, startled. "What, Papa?" He looked

around and saw his mother and younger brothers drifting away. "Oh, aye! Forgive my distraction!" Then he drove off after them—but his feet were still tapping the air, in time to the music of the hard rocks.

Someone else was still hovering about.

"Daughter," Rod intoned.

Cordelia looked up from the intricate routine she was trying to work out, involving the front end of the broomstick moving in circles while the bristles went up and down—and all, Rod could have sworn, in time to two different sets of beats coming from the same music. His daughter finally focused on his face, looked startled, glanced quickly around, then gave a little cry and peeled off after her mother.

Rod heaved a sigh and sailed off after her. "You coming, Fess?" he called out. "Fess!"

"Here, Rod. I had my audio amplification turned down. Yes, I am following along on the ground."

"That's reassuring, anyway." Rod glanced back at the hillside with trepidation. "So by the time any rock gets over that ridge, all those trips down the hillside have turned it hard."

"That is true, Rod."

"And that means that after a while, all the rocks east of here will be hard, too."

Fess was silent for a moment, then said, "I think not, Rod. There are already many soft rocks in the lands we have passed through, and they are multiplying. There is room for both types of rock in the East."

"I hope you're right." Rod lofted higher, hoping the music would become fainter. It did, but not much. He sailed on west, with only one glance back at the hillside where the rolling stones developed into hard rock.

# 18

The children were beginning to stumble with weariness as the sun set, and Rod was about to call a halt if Gwen didn't; the metal blimp would just have to get away. But as the dusk gathered, the blimp slowed and stopped.

Gwen halted, eyes still fixed on its swollen form. "Doth it sleep?"

"It would seem so," Rod said slowly. "If it throws out a mooring line . . ."

An anchor swung down from the blimp and snagged in the top of a tree. Rod relaxed, nodding. "It's set for the night. Collapse, kids. I'll find the raw materials." As the youngsters sank down, he touched Gwen's hand. "You could rest a little, too."

"I thank thee." She smiled up at him. "Yet I'm not so tired as I might be."

"You're a wonder—it's been a long hike."

"I, too, could last some while longer, Papa."

Rod looked up at Magnus and decided they could both benefit from the lad's proving how tireless he was. "Okay— *you* go bag a couple of rabbits."

Magnus smiled, turning away and taking out his sling. "Will squirrels do?"

"Oh, no!" An unfamiliar voice called out. "Get back, get back!" They looked up, startled. A young man in glittering garments was coming out of the wood, manic energy in every step. "No, no!" he cried. "Be nice, be nice!"

Cordelia reached up to catch Gwen's hand. "Mama—his face!"

Gwen looked, then gasped. "Even so, daughter! Doth he mock?"

"He must," Cordelia said.

Geoffrey frowned. "What ails thee?"

"Why," said Cordelia, "that young man doth—for thus will Prince Alain look when he is grown."

Geoffrey swung back to stare, amazed. " 'Tis even so!" He leaped to his feet, sword flickering out. "Avaunt thee, pretender!"

"Avaunt!" the mimic mocked. "Get back, get back! Who gives orders? What a fool!"

Rod's eyes narrowed. "Watch your tongue!"

"Oh, great man!" The mimic held up his hands in mock horror. "Oh, shall I bow? No—*thou* shalt bow, to thy prince!"

"The true prince is only half thine age," Gwen snapped, "and thy mockery hath little of amusement in it."

"A joke, a joke! The lady doth smoke!"

"Nay, but thou shalt, if thou wardest not thy tongue." Magnus stepped forward. "Shall I slay rabbits as thou slayest humor?"

"A slayer, a butcher!" the man screamed. "Murdering thief! Get back! Get back!" He leaped at Magnus, foot lashing out in a kick.

Magnus ducked easily, but the mock prince slapped him as he went by, catching Magnus a sharp blow on the cheek. The young warlock's face reddened; he lashed out with his empty sling.

"A weapon!" the mock prince cried. "I have one, too!" He yanked off his doublet and hurled it at Magnus, who slapped it away and stepped in to swing at the man—but he caught a boot square in the eye. He howled in anger, ducked the next boot, and came up swinging—to catch the youth's hose right in his face. The mock prince hooted with delight and slashed another kick—but Magnus caught the foot, twisted, and shoved. The mock prince hopped backward with a howl and fell, but did a backward somersault and rose, hurling his singlet at Magnus and catching at his loincloth.

Cordelia stared, not believing what she was seeing—only for a split second, though, before her mother clapped a hand over her eyes.

But the mock prince had only pulled a knife out of his loincloth, and that was his undoing. He slashed at Magnus, who caught the wrist, whirled, and cracked the young man's arm backward across his knee, locking the mock prince's elbow in the crook of his own arm. The imposter howled, eyes bulging, and the knife dropped from his fingers.

"Wait, hold it right there!" Rod called. "He's in the ideal bargaining position!"

Magnus looked up. The bellowing imposter twisted, and Magnus reacted barely in time to tighten the elbow lock. "What can he know?"

"Only the item we're wanting most." Rod went over and caught the young man by the hair. As the mock prince jerked his head up to yell at Magnus, he howled. "*Yeowtch!*"

"Yes, that gives you a reason to hold your head still," Rod said. "Now, pay attention for a second."

"What for, big man?"

Magnus applied a little more leverage. The imposter groaned, eyes bulging.

"Now that we have a basis for discussion," Rod said, "maybe you can tell us where these music-rocks came from."

"Oh no, big man." The youth tried to shake his head, winced, and gave it up as a bad job. "Oh no, I can't. I only know they came one day—and never has my living life been dull a moment since."

"I wonder an he doth tell the truth." Magnus bore down,

and the young man yelped. "The dead! Only the dead know, only the dead! I mean it . . . *YEOWTCH!*"

"Magnus!" Gwen scolded. "What honor's in this? Thou hast reason to hold him still, naught more!"

Magnus looked up, realization dawning. "I cannot stay here all year, Mama."

"Mama, Mama," the young man mocked. "Oh, pretty honor, little b—OWWWW!"

"You shouldn't have made him angry," Rod explained. "Either control your mouth, or don't use it. As to your dilemma, son—we *could* put him to sleep."

Magnus shook his head. "He would but follow us when he waked, Papa."

"What dost thou intend!" Gwen said with indignation.

"I know not," Magnus confessed.

"Give him more of what he doth wish," Gregory suggested.

"No can do, little man! I want everything!"

"Aye, but what dost thou want most?"

The imposter's eyes roved toward Cordelia, but his arm creaked, and he groaned. "Music. Most of all, music!"

"He shall have music, wherever he goes." Geoffrey shrugged.

"An excellent idea, brother!" Gregory caught up two rocks.

"What?" Geoffrey stared blankly. "What have I said?"

"That he should have music, wheresoe'er he doth go!" Gregory placed the two rocks over the youth's ears. Instantly, his eyes dulled and lost focus.

"Maybe, just maybe," Rod said thoughtfully.

"Bind them in place," Gregory suggested.

Geoffrey caught up the youth's singlet, tore off a strip, and tied it around his head, crown to chin. Then he tore another and bound it from nape to forehead. "They shall stay, unless he doth take them off."

"He won't, or I miss my guess," Rod said. "Let him go, son."

Magnus let go, and the young man fell like a stone.

Magnus looked down at him with disgust. "What, hast thou no pride? Rise and walk, man!"

The prince-mocker picked himself up, looking dazed, and ambled away. He walked right between Gwen and Cordelia, unseeing, and wandered into the wood.

Rod nodded with satisfaction. "Wonderful idea, boys! He's out of trouble for the rest of his life!"

"Or until someone doth take the rocks off from him," Geoffrey pointed out.

"By then, we shall be long gone," Magnus said with satisfaction, "and our trail grown very cold." Then he frowned. "What did he mean by saying, 'only the dead know'?"

"A metaphor," Gregory suggested, "to show that none living can have any idea of the rocks' origin."

"No." Rod was quite certain. "What started this whole exploration, son?"

Gregory looked up, startled. "Why . . . the dancing dead."

Rod nodded. "So if he says that only the dead know, those zombies might just be the dead he speaks of."

"But where," asked Cordelia, "shall we find the walking dead?"

"Somewhere between sunrise and dawn." Rod turned to pick up sticks. "But I, for one, am not minded to go searching just now. Fire and food, kids. We'll go hunting tomorrow. Maybe the blimp will show us."

"Aye," Gwen agreed. "For now, dinner and bed."

They managed to sleep well in spite of all the music—or perhaps because of it. Rod's last thought, as he drifted into sleep, was that maybe his ears were beginning to grow numb.

# 19

The next day was a hard one. They followed the blimp from sunrise to sunset and beyond. Past dark, they came to a village.

"We truly ought to have stopped some while ago, husband, whiles there was still light."

"I know, dear, but you'd been talking about wanting to sleep in a real bed, and frankly, I just couldn't resist the notion. Besides, I thought you might appreciate not having to cook." Rod frowned down at the village below them in the gloaming. "But I'm beginning to wonder if this hamlet is big enough to have an inn."

"It hath a graveyard," Magnus noted.

They stood atop a ridge, with the village nestled in a bowl of trees below them, centered around a small church with a broad yard dotted with grave markers. Lights warmed the darkness here and there, but none bright enough to indicate an inn.

"Well, if there is an hostel, it'll be near the church," Rod noted. "We can always go on through and camp on the outskirts, if we come up dry."

"Papa . . ."

"Patience, Geoffrey," said Gwen. "If there is an inn, thou'lt have thy dinner straightaway."

The boy sighed and followed his father down the hill.

But as they passed the churchyard, Gregory winced at the volume of sound. "Is this reverent, Papa? How can there be so much more noise here?"

"It *is* suspicious," Rod admitted with a glance toward the church, "almost as though someone were attacking the chapel. . . ."

"We have seen a meadow where folk did throw music-rocks, to be rid of them," Magnus contributed.

Gwen frowned. "But wherefore would they throw stones at the church?"

Gregory jolted to a halt, staring.

Rod stopped. "What's the matter, son?"

"The graves," Gregory gasped, affrighted. "Papa . . . so many . . ."

In front of a score of tombstones there were gaping, ragged holes. Rod was aghast. "What is it?" he asked. "The plague?"

"No, Rod," Fess answered. "I am enhancing my night-vision, and can see that the holes are those of old graves. It is not the work of a sexton, though it might be the detritus of grave robbers."

"Or ghouls," Cordelia said, with a delicious shiver.

"I think not, Cordelia. From the pattern in which the dirt has fallen, I would say that the graves have been opened from within."

The whole family was very quiet for a minute or so.

Then Magnus said, "Fess—dost thou say these graves were . . ."

The ground in front of one of the tombstones began to tremble.

Gregory cried out, and Gwen caught him up in her arms. "Peace, my little one, peace . . . Husband, away!"

"Good idea." Rod crouched down to hide behind the wall. "You folks get going."

Gwen hopped onto her broomstick, then turned back, startled. "Assuredly thou dost not mean to stay!"

"What danger could there be?" Rod asked. "Don't worry, I'm only going to watch."

"Wherefore take the chance!"

"Because," Rod whispered, "I think we just may have found out where our zombies came from."

Gwen made a little noise of exasperation, then commanded. "Cordelia! Geoffrey! Aloft!"

The younger children circled up reluctantly—until Geoffrey noticed that his mother had that withdrawn look that she had whenever she was readying magic. He had a notion he might just see a flying tombstone.

For the moment, though, he saw his father and his big brother crouched behind a wall and, in a patch of moonlight, ground bulging in front of a headstone. It bulged, it heaved—and clods of earth spewed up as a hole appeared and widened. Then the dirt stopped flying, and two hands of bone rose out of the hole. They groped about, found purchase on the ground at the sides, and heaved. A skull catapulted out of the hole with the rest of the skeleton behind it. It knelt on the edge of the grave, scrabbled for purchase, then rose up tall in the moonlight, gleaming white, wrapped in the rotting remnants of a shroud.

Gregory moaned and hid his head in Gwen's shoulder. She made soothing noises as she glared at the tombstone; the skeleton didn't see it tremble.

No, it was the skeleton who was trembling—or rather, nodding. It made a happy noise, then moved away from its grave, stepping in time to the music, its whole body bobbing and weaving as its skull rotated, seeking. Suddenly it stiffened, facing west, then leaped in the air, landing with the sound of a xylophone run. It gave a joyous yelp and set off in a stiff and awkward dance, moving away down the main street of the village. Shutters slammed in its wake, but it didn't notice.

Rod and Magnus rose from behind the wall. "If I hadn't seen it, I wouldn't have believed it!" Rod breathed.

"It doth not seem ill-intentioned," Magnus pointed out in a shaky voice.

Fess stepped up behind him out of the night. "It does seem harmless."

*"Ya-a-a-h!"* Magnus leaped five feet straight up. "Must thou move so silently!"

"My apologies, Magnus. Rod, may I recommend seeking a campsite?"

"Uh, not just yet." Rod set off down the road.

"Where dost thou go?" Gwen cried down in anguish.

"Why, after that skeleton, of course. You can't think it would mean any harm! Why, it's fairly whistling!"

"To whistle," Fess pointed out, "one must have lips."

"And it needs vocal folds to sing, but it's doing a pretty good job of that. Gwen, you didn't tell me witch-moss could grow in graves."

"I had not thought it," she admitted, swooping low. "Now that thou dost speak of it, I wonder an it doth occur by nature's way."

"Nay! Someone did seed each grave with witch-moss!" Geoffrey cried, alighting next to Rod.

Rod looked at him askance. "And where do you think *you're* going?"

"Why, with my father! If 'tis as safe as thou sayest, then I am at no hazard!"

Rod opened his mouth to answer, then closed it with a sigh. "One of these days, I'll start saying no."

"Tomorrow," Cordelia suggested, "or mayhap next year."

"A possibility. Okay, family, let's go see where the skull is headed. Just be ready to hit the treetops on a moment's notice, okay?"

The skeleton led them out of town, past three fields, and into a pasture that was bordered with a circle of piled stones—musical ones. The night was filled with hard, jangling sound, and the cows had fled to the nearby wood-lot. Rod had a notion there wouldn't be much milk in the morning.

Not that the field was empty, of course. In fact, it was rather full—of bones. Not heaped, but articulated. It was a night of the walking dead, in various stages of mummification.

There were only twenty of them, though—Rod counted. The rest of the crowd . . .

"Papa," Cordelia gasped, "they are living folk!"

"Yes, dear—their descendants, no doubt. A little on the young side, too."

In fact, they were still trickling in—young folk in their teens and early twenties, heads nodding, feet weaving in intricate patterns, bodies moving in time to the music.

"Are they blind to the presence of the dead?" Magnus demanded.

Rod was about to say "yes" when he saw a zombie rise up in the center of a circle of young folk, who shouted and clapped their hands as their ancestor cavorted. After a few minutes, they left off clapping and began to dance with one another in the stiff, awkward movements of the skeleton, while he beat time over their heads, signalling them in their progress through the dance.

"Nay," Gwen said, coming down to earth. "They see, but do not see."

Rod frowned. "How can that be?"

"Like the drifters we met," Magnus explained. "They used lotus to rid their minds of thought—but for these young folk, the music alone doth suffice to achieve that end."

Rod turned to him, appalled. "You don't mean they're trying *not* to think!"

"Aye," Cordelia said. "They told us they had wearied of the sad and endless task of seeking to make sense of the world."

Rod remembered his own adolescence, and held his peace. He turned back to watch the dancers for a while, then whispered, "Of course. They seek to be like the zombies."

"Rod."

He shook off the mood. "Yes, Fess?"

"You must establish the mechanism and, if possible, determine who has created this situation."

"A good point." Rod frowned. "Any advice on methodology?"

"Gather data."

"How are we to do that?" Magnus asked. "Will watching tell us aught more?"

"Maybe," Rod said, "but I'd like to try a more direct approach." And, before anybody could stop him, he dove into the center of the circle of dancers. Gwen gave a scream, then clamped her lips shut, pale with anger.

"He will be well, Mama," Cordelia said faintly.

"An he is not, we shall drag him out! Children! Be ready!"

Rod surfaced inside the circle, coming up right next to the dancing bones. Now he could see why the skeleton stood head and shoulders above the youths—it danced on a broad stump.

Rod waved. "Hi, there!"

The skeleton turned about, bobbing and beating time, not seeing him.

Rod steeled himself and reached up to tap a scapula. "Hey! Got a minute?"

"Eternity." Now the skull swivelled toward him, the sightless eyes seeking his own. "What wouldst thou of me?"

Rod swallowed. "Just some information. Mind telling me the reason for the party?"

"What is a 'party'?"

No, the culture wasn't ready for democracy yet. "This festival, then. Any particular reason you climbed up out of your grave? Or did you just feel like taking a walk?"

The skeleton made a dry, rattling sound that Rod hoped was a laugh. "I only know that I swam up from darkness to feel a steady rhythm round me, like to a heartbeat. I wished to hear more of it; I swam up through the earth, and the closer I came, the more clearly I heard—till I broke through to air, and climbed again upon the surface."

Rod stared. "You mean the music was loud enough to wake the dead?"

"Aye. I was the first; anon I gathered all the pretty rocks that made such wondrous sound, and brought them here, to set in a circle by which I might dance. Ere the night had ended, others had waked from their long sleep to join me."

Rod swallowed. "Well—at least it doesn't seem to be doing you any harm."

"Oh, nay!" the skeleton carolled, and pirouetted for joy, stamping a foot down to stop so that it faced Rod again, and all its bones rattled like castanets. "Nay, this music doth make me stir as though with life again; it doth fill my bones with the need to dance! Oh, happy are we all for this second chance at life, and ten times thankful to be waked!"

Just what Gramarye needed—a band of grateful dead. "You're setting a bad example, you know."

"What—by dancing?" The skeleton stared with sightless eyes, incredulous. "How can that be so bad?"

"Because your descendants are imitating you. They were raised to respect their elders, after all."

" 'Twas we who were raised, not they." But the skeleton looked about at the young people. "How is our example harmful to them?"

"Because they're trying to become just like you—mindless zombies. You don't want them to grow up to be deadheads, do you?"

"Wherefore not?" The skeleton turned a toothy grin on him.

Rod was still trying to phrase an answer, when the skeleton looked past his dancing circle and saw the family. "Oh, I see! Thou hast children of thine own, and dost fear to lose them!"

"Well, there is that, yes."

"Let me see!" The skeleton hopped down off its stump and pushed through the dancers, over to the ring of stones. The children saw it coming, and drew back—but the skeleton halted a dozen paces away. "These are not of my village."

Rod brightened. "Does that mean they're immune to your music?"

"Aye—but they have ancestors of their own."

Rod relaxed, reflecting that most of the children's local ancestors were not only still alive, but likely to remain so. Their more frail progenitors were thirty light-years away. "You know, I can't help wondering . . ."

"Poor fellow. Only listen to the music awhile, and it will cure thee of that malady."

"Yes, I don't doubt it. But, um, I was going to say—you *are* beginning to look a little weary."

The skeleton was silent for a minute, then admitted, "Aye. I feel the first faint edge of tiring. I am not so young as once I was, a hundred years agone."

"I kind of thought so. You're going to want to rest before too long."

"I doubt it not." The sigh was a gust of breeze. "Yet I have rested so long that I am loath to lie down again."

"Don't push it too hard." Rod glanced at the dancers with apprehension. "You may need a vacation from your holiday."

"And if thou dost not, thy young folk will." Gwen gazed past the skeleton to the dancers, with concern. "Wilt thou never release them from this spell?"

"Only if they wish it—and I think that they will not. Be not troubled in thy heart, kind lady—there have ever been deadheads, and ever will be. In truth . . ." Its empty gaze lingered speculatively on Magnus and Cordelia.

"Don't even think it," Rod snapped.

"Fear not. I can see that these have too much joy in thought; they would be loath to be deadheads."

Gregory tugged at Rod's sleeve. "Papa—dost thou recall? That pretentious prince did say that only the dead did know."

Rod looked up at the zombie, startled. "That's right, he did, didn't he? And here are the dead!"

"Of what dost thou speak?" asked the zombie.

"The music-rocks." Rod demanded. "Can you tell us where they came from?"

"Nay, only that I am right glad they did. Yet mayhap Destina would know." He turned his hollow eyes back toward the crowd, crying, "Destina, come!"

Cordelia frowned. "What is Destina?"

Another zombie came dancing out of the crowd toward them. From the tatters of a skirt and bodice adorning its bones, they could tell it must have been a woman once.

"Destina," said the leader. "Tell: Whence come the music-rocks?"

"Ah," said she, "the first did fall from the Sky Egg. But find and follow it"—she turned toward the Gallowglasses— "and belike thou shalt find . . . Why, so!"

"What?" They all gave her a blank look.

"A right comely lad!" Her bony hand reached out to chuck Magnus under the chin. "Art thou wed, sweet chuck?"

Magnus recoiled. "Nay!"

"He is too young," Gwen said, with steel in her voice.

"Wherefore? My first was a father by the time he had come to this height! Nay, I've need of another husband, handsome youth. Wilt thou come with me to wed?"

"Oh, no!" Magnus took another step backward. "Thou canst not mean it!"

"I doubt not she doth," the leader said. "Nay, come along with us, and taste life eternal!"

"I'm afraid she's not quite what I had in mind for a daughter-in-law . . ." Rod began.

"Thou shalt be of another mind when thou hast kissed me." The skull-face thrust closer to Magnus.

"Thou dost lie!" Magnus stumbled back. "Pray Heaven thou dost lie!"

"Come, essay it!" The leader reached out for Magnus, and Destina giggled and stepped forward. "We shall insist thou stay with us a while!"

"He most assuredly shall not!" Gwen stepped between her son and the zombie, arm raised—then hesitated.

"Do not, Mama." Magnus's voice trembled, but he persisted. "They are but poor and empty things!"

Gwen's mouth twitched. "I am loath to give hurt to ones

who have, at long last, gained so pitiful a measure of pleasure."

"Measure of pleasure!" The leader lifted his skull, eyes lighting. "A measure of pleasure! Aye, a measure indeed!" And he began to beat a rhythm on his pelvis and a tune on his rib cage, chanting,

> *"He shall have a measure,*
> *A quantity of pleasure!*
> *Let him with us tarry,*
> *Dally and be merry!"*

Magnus swallowed. "Said he, 'be merry,' or 'be-marry'?"

"Now, *come!*" The leader sprang at Magnus.

The lad leaped back as his father leaned in; the skeleton slammed into Rod's chest and fell in a jumble of bones.

"What hast thou done!" Destina keened.

"More to the point, what should we be doing?" Rod corrected.

The leader began to pull himself together.

"I am loath to fight them." Coming from Geoffrey, that was saying a great deal.

"What else can we do?" Cordelia asked.

The leader rose up, singing,

> *"We do not measure please,*
> *But give pleasure in full measure!*
> *So if thou wouldst thy pleasure measure . . ."*

"We can *run!*" Rod shooed them away from him.

They ran.

The zombies yelped with joy and bounded into a bone-shaking chase.

"Where can we go?" Gregory panted.

"Where but straight ahead!" Magnus outdistanced them all.

"Fly!" Gwen commanded. "Lest thou dost break thy leg in a fall!"

They all rose up a foot off the ground, skimming along as fast as they dared in unknown country. Behind them, the young people added their enthusiastic shouting to the chase. The music-rocks picked up the excitement, and began to boom and howl all about them.

Then, suddenly, they crested a rise—and found themselves in a cul-de-sac, a box canyon, surrounded by stone on all sides.

"Back!" Magnus whirled about. "Out from this place, ere our pursuers . . ."

The mouth of the canyon filled with walking bones and bonny youths.

"Too late." Rod spread his arms, trying to shield his whole family. Before them, the crowd advanced with glee and stones, holding out rocks that were racketing with an unholy din.

Then the noise began to beat at them from the back.

"It doth echo off the cliff walls!" Cordelia called.

"Nay," Magnus shouted, "they do take it up!"

It was true. The canyon walls had begun to vibrate in sympathy, resonating and re-emitting the music of the stones.

"What can we do now!" Gregory wailed. "We are caught between their rocks and a hard place!"

"We can fly!" Gwen snapped.

On the word, Cordelia's broomstick took off like a rocket. All three boys shot up after her, with Rod and Gwen right behind them.

Below, a disappointed moan filled all the canyon.

The music dwindled behind and below them.

"Praise Heaven!" Magnus shuddered. "I feared I would have to dismember them!"

"Where shall we go now?" Geoffrey asked.

Rod looked up with a sudden smile. "Hey! We're in the right place to look for it. . . ."

"For what?" Gwen asked.

"That female zombie said something about following a Sky Egg!"

"But how can there be an egg in the sky?" Gregory said reasonably.

"Mayhap she meant the moon," Cordelia suggested.

"An that be so," Gwen pointed out, "we must wait—for the moon hath set."

"All right, I suppose we should"—Rod sighed—"especially since I'm afraid she didn't mean the moon but just that blimp we've been following."

"Why—'tis so!" Cordelia said, surprised.

"Even so," Geoffrey agreed. "Dost recall that when first I saw it I said 'twas a giant egg?"

"It seems to run all through this terrain," Rod growled.

"Have we come in a circle, then?" Gwen asked.

" 'Fraid so, dear—and we'll have to break out of it, tomorrow. But for tonight, let's get some sleep. Pick a good camping place. Sorry about that bed you wanted."

She sailed up alongside him to squeeze his hand. " 'Twas more a door I had a-mind—but let it rest."

"Not much choice, now," Rod said, resigned. "Come on, my love. Let's see if we can get a little sleep, at least."

"And food," Geoffrey reminded them.

# 20

They had journeyed an hour or two the next day when Cordelia tilted her head back and sniffed the wind. "I smell brine."

"We do come near to the sea, then," her mother said. "Magnus, go aloft and tell if thou dost see water."

Magnus bobbed up as though he'd hit a thermal, sky-rocketing to a thousand feet. His mental voice said, *Aye, Mama! Ah, 'tis ever a noble sight! Such a vast expanse of water, so wide and flat, clear to the edge of the world!*

"Stop being so poetic," Rod said, grinning. "It's just the horizon."

*Ah, but who doth know what may lie beyond this horizon?*

"More water, and you know it darn well." Rod felt a stab of anxiety, though; Magnus was almost of an age to begin wandering. How soon would his son leave him?

"How far is it?" Gwen asked.

*Twenty miles or more, Mother. Two days' journey afoot, at least.*

"Anything worth looking at in between?" Rod asked.

*Dost thou wish to look at fens and marshland?*

"Let us leave no stone unturned." Rod sighed. "Come down, son, and let's see what the fen has in store for us."

But they found out on the way. They happened across a road and, as they neared the scrub growth that marked the fen, they saw a group of people ahead—and another even farther ahead. Rod frowned. "What is this, a procession?"

"Aye," said Gregory. "Behind us, Papa."

Rod looked back and saw another handful of people following a hundred yards to the rear. "We seem to be popular."

"Or the fen is," Gwen pointed out.

"Wherefore are there only small children among them?" Cordelia asked.

"Interesting point, that." Rod lengthened his stride. "Let's ask someone."

They caught up with the group ahead—two men and two women in their forties, a woman in her sixties, and three small children.

"Where are you going?" Rod asked, but the people plodded on as though they hadn't heard. Rod throttled his irritation and was about to ask again, when Fess noted, "They wear bandages about their heads, Rod. Between that and the clamor of the rock music, they may not have heard you."

"Good point." Rod reached out and tapped the shoulder of the peasant in front. The man shied away like a critic hearing a countdown, then took in the sight of Gwen and the children. He relaxed a little, but eyed Magnus and Cordelia with caution, almost hostility.

Their voices echoed in Rod's head. *Who hath hurt him, Papa? Of what is he so wary?*

*Of us, sister,* Magnus answered. *But why should he fear a youth and a maiden?*

*Let's ask.* Rod pointed to his ear and said, "Can you hear us?" loudly and slowly. The peasant frowned, shaking his head. He pulled the bandage off his head, popped a wax cover off his ear, and promptly winced. "Aiee! The noise! I trust Your Worship hath good reason to rob me of my ward."

"I just want to know why so many of you are going to the fen," Rod called, trying to project over the sound of the music.

"Why, to escape this coil of howling," the peasant called back. "Come, but ask no more until we've gained shelter, I beg of thee." Still, he didn't turn away; Rob was obviously gentry.

Impatiently, Rob called, "Right. Go ahead."

The peasant smiled in gratitude and replaced his earcover, pulling the bandage back to hold it in place. He relaxed visibly, then gave the Gallowglasses a smile and turned away to trudge toward the fen.

"Can they truly seek refuge from the music?" Cordelia asked, wide-eyed.

"They can," Gwen assured her. "For myself, I do not wonder at it; 'tis a veritable cacophony."

"Nay, Mama! 'Tis pretty! Well . . . not 'pretty,' surely. But 'tis most appealing!"

"If that's appeal, I'll steal the bell," Rod growled. "Come on, family. If there's silence ahead, I crave it."

"If thou wilt." Magnus sighed, and followed after.

"Magnus," said Fess, behind him, "must you put in extra steps for each stride?"

"It doth no harm, Fess," Magnus answered, "and this music doth make me feel so filled with movement that I must needs find some way to let it out."

"Well, if you must, you must." The horse sighed, and followed the family, remembering how Will Kemp had danced his way from London to the seacoast, never taking a normal step for nine days.

The ground became marshy to either side of the road. Soon small pools appeared. Then they were in among the low scrub growth, and the peasant family stopped to take off their bandages and earcovers, warily at first, then quickly, with sighs of relief.

"Was it truly needful, Mama?" a ten-year-old asked.

"Mayhap not for thee, sweet chuck," his mother answered, "but it was for me."

"We would liefer not have thee heed the clamor about us, as thy brother and sister have done," his father explained.

"What clamor?" the boy said. " 'Tis most sweet strains, here."

And they were. The music was soft, very melodic—and so peaceful that Rod almost didn't realize it was there, until he stopped to listen. The tunes had a much greater range of notes, and the bass line and rhythm were no longer dominant.

"Aye, there be sweet sounds *here*," said the other man. "Thou art within the fen, and its music doth bar that howling that we have waded through these two days."

"The music doth emanate from some place ahead," Magnus pointed out.

"Let us go to it," one of the men said, "for I crave its shelter."

Everyone started down the road again, but it wasn't wide enough for more than four abreast, so the Gallowglasses followed after.

"Husband," said Gwen, "go up among these folk, and learn why they have come."

"If you say so—but I would have said it was pretty obvious." Rod lengthened his stride and caught up with the peasants. "If you don't mind, goodman—I need a bit of information."

"Assuredly, my lord! What wouldst thou?"

"Well, for starters—how did you find out about this place?"

"Word of it hath run through every farm and village," the wife answered, "wherever folk do groan under the burden of this clamor that hath begun these few months past."

More than two months, then, Rod noted. "You've had to try to keep up with your daily work all that time?"

"Aye, and it hath become a trial greater and more sore as the days have rolled," her husband said. "A neighbor told us there was sanctuary in the fen, yet we had crops in the field, and sought to keep our daily round."

"Yet our heads began to ache, and sorely," the wife added. "We stopped our hearing with waxen covers for our ears, we tied bandages to hold them—yet still the strident thumping came through, to make us falter."

"I began to stumble as I went out to the pasture," the other peasant man explained. "I found that I did trip as I sought to follow the plow."

"Anon the burden became too great to bear," his wife said, "and so we came here, for sanctuary."

"Ere any others of our children were reived from us," the first wife said darkly.

"Children reived!" Cordelia stiffened. "Who would do so craven a deed?"

"The music, maiden," the first man answered. "The music, that doth capture the affections of our older children."

"Why, how is this?" But there was foreboding in Cordelia's voice; she remembered the groups of young people she had seen.

"Our son was aged twelve, when he began to twitch with the music's rhythm," the second wife answered. "Our daughter was fourteen. Her head began to nod, and she commenced singing wordless songs as she went about her chores. . . ."

"Not wordless," the ten-year-old protested.

"Well, if there were words to them, I could not make them out. She did move more slowly about her tasks, and more slowly still, till finally she threw them over, and went off to join the other maidens in the forest."

"Pray Heaven they are maidens still!" the second father said with a shudder, "for the older boys and young men have gone to the forest, too. Mine eldest was twenty, mine other son sixteen. Where are they now?"

Magnus saw the real worry that lined his face. "Peace, goodman. He's well, I doubt not."

"Then thou hast not seen what we have seen," the first father grunted. "The twitching and spasms they call dancing, the strange foods they gather, the bands of them that wind about the countryside with strange kicking steps, knowing not whither they go— Pray Heaven they have not come to their undoing!"

Magnus started to say that he hadn't seen the youths doing anything dangerous, but remembering the sense of peril he had felt with the lotus-eaters, the cadaverous pebble-eaters, and the vampire, he held his peace.

"So many families!" Gwen saved him with a change of subject. "And look, they do come from all points of the compass!"

They could see for a mile or two in each direction, for the fens were flat and level, and covered only with bushes and tussocks, with here and there a small stand of trees. Against the waning sun came the silhouettes of families and groups of older peasants, trooping in from all directions.

"Where are they going?" Rod asked.

"We shall know soon enough," Gwen assured him.

"The music has grown louder," Gregory noted.

It had, though not unpleasantly so. Rod glanced at his children, and saw that even Geoffrey was beginning to relax—and he was relieved that Magnus and Cordelia had stopped twitching.

Then they came into a grove of small, stunted, twisted trees, and saw a large pool in front of them. It lay still, molten gold in the late-afternoon sun, its surface rippled only by a passing breeze—and the whole pond seemed to resonate with the gentle melody. All around its edge, people were sitting or reclining, doing simple chores such as whittling or mending. Campfires blossomed.

"Water at last!" Magnus knelt by the pool. "I thirst!"

"I would not," the older peasant said, but Magnus had already dipped up a handful. He sipped, then shook the water off, making a face. " 'Tis brackish."

"Aye," the peasant said. "This is fen-land, look you, young master. We are near the sea; the water is salt."

"Even as our blood is," Rod murmured.

"How sayest thou, gentleman?"

"Nothing major." Rod sat down with a sigh. "We'll have to get a campfire going, of course."

"Certes." Gwen sat beside him. "Yet we may rest awhile."

"I shall search for water," Magnus said.

"Don't bother, son." Rod held up a hand. "Any water you find will taste of the sea. Anything in that waterskin, Gwen?"

His wife held up a leather bottle that was almost flat. Suddenly, it bulged. "Aye," she said. "Here, my son."

Magnus took the skin thankfully and squirted a long stream into his mouth.

"Cordelia," Gwen called, "what dost thou?"

The girl was ten yards away, by the brink of the pool. "Only looking to see what lies under the water, Mama," she called, all innocence—but she was making faces, giving exaggerated looks behind her, where Gregory was prowling along the shoreline on hands and knees, studying the water with a pensive expression.

Gwen smiled. "Oh, aye. Thou hast not seen such a pool aforetime, hast thou?"

"Nay, Mama," Cordelia said, with a smile of relief. She turned back to making sure that Little Brother didn't fall in—when he was so consumed by curiosity, he tended to ignore little things like safety. But of course it would have hurt his feelings if Cordelia had come right out and said she had to take care of him—or thought it, for that matter.

"Are there other places like this?" Rod asked one of the peasants.

The man looked up from setting kindling. "We have heard of some. A minstrel came by with clay o'er his ears; he had come from a grove to the north, where some chandlers had moved their shops, and did sing of the sea. He did say he was bound for the south, to an island on which some troubadors had gathered, where the music of the sea did keep the clamor at bay."

"A few little oases of calm, all up and down the coast, I'll bet." Rod nodded and turned to Gwen. "We'll have to encourage their growth inland."

"Aye, my lord. There is need for refuges from the wild life."

"Mama! Papa!" Cordelia called. "Come see! 'Tis most amazing!"

"Not truly, sister," Gregory disagreed. "They are but clams, after all. Wouldst thou not expect to find such near to the tidewater?"

"Not such as these, addlepate! 'Tis they who do make the music!"

Gregory looked up, incredulous.

Rod pulled himself to his feet. "I think we'd better have a look at this."

"Aye," Gwen agreed. "What manner of creatures are these?"

They moved around the curve of the pool, followed by Geoffrey and Magnus. Fess stayed where he was, but kept an eye on them.

Cordelia had followed Gregory out onto a sand-spit that ran twenty feet into the pool—and, sure enough, there they were, on a ledge two feet under the water: five clams, standing on end in the sand, almost in the middle of the pond, and they were moving, though slightly, in time to the music.

"But how can clams make music?" Gregory wondered.

"Why," said a voice from the water, "how can I keep from singing?"

The children did a double take, and Gregory asked, "Was it thou who didst speak, little clam?"

"Aye," she answered, "if 'twas thou didst ask."

"These," Rod whispered to Gwen, "are not your average clams."

"I had guessed it," she returned.

"It was a little obvious," Rod admitted. "Is there no end to the wonders of this island?"

"Only in people's hearts and minds, my lord."

"Dost thou sing only because thou must?" Cordelia asked.

The clam gave a melodious chuckle. "Is that so little?"

Cordelia blushed, and Gregory said, "Then why *must* thou needs sing?"

"Why," said a deeper voice, "we seek to keep alive the music that otherwise might die for want of singing."

"Do you unearth new tunes, then?"

"Some new, but many old. We seek to keep alive simple music, and ornate music, and songs with words worth hearing—but, more than aught else, we seek to foster melody, that the Land of Song may not die."

" 'Tis poetry, look thou," said another clam, "the lyric poetry that had its birth in song."

" 'Tis beauty," said a fourth, "beauty of poetry and melody alike."

"But if you keep it alive," said Geoffrey, "then it must have begun before thee."

"Thou speakest aright," said two clams at once, and a third said, "The fen was once filled with the sounds of natural music until the hard rocks drowned them out, and we clams do keep the music of the fen alive."

"Also the music of the folk," said the fourth clam.

Gregory sidled over to Rod and said, low-voiced, "I have discerned the manner of five small beings making music enough to fill this grove."

"I don't think they're doing it deliberately," Rod pointed out.

"That they may not realize how much they do? Aye. Yet their sounds are carried by the water, making the whole pond to vibrate—and thus their music spreads."

*You are correct, Gregory*, said Fess's voice. *They have set up a ripple effect.*

"Yet if what thou dost say is true," Cordelia said to the clams, "thou must needs treasure all music."

"All good music, aye."

"Is there no good rock music then?" she protested.

"Music that the rocks have brought? Aye! There do be some!" the first clam said, but even as she spoke, a bass voice near her had begun to thrum in a steady rhythm. Then three other voices began to vocalize in a higher register, repeating a wordless refrain.

The Gallowglasses looked at one another, astonished.
" 'Tis like the music of the first soft rocks we did hear," Magnus said.

"It is the same," Cordelia said.

Then the tenor clam broke in, singing,

*"Live with me, and be my love,*
*And we shall all the pleasures prove*
*That hills and valleys, dales and fields,*
*And all the craggy mountains yields.*

*There will we sit upon the rocks,*
*And see the shepherds and their flocks,*
*By shallow rivers, by whose falls*
*Melodious birds sing madrigals.*

*There will I make thee a bed of roses,*
*With a thousand fragrant posies,*
*A cap of flowers and a kirtle*
*Emblazoned all with leaves of myrtle.*

*A belt of straw and ivy buds,*
*With coral clasps and amber studs,*
*And if these pleasures may thee move,*
*Then live with me and be my love."*

The soprano clam sang the answer:

*"If that the world and love were young,*
*And truth in every shepherd's tongue,*
*These pretty pleasures might me move*
*To live with thee and be thy love."*

"Why, 'tis beauteous!" Gwen said, enthralled. "At the least, it is when *thou* dost sing it."

But Cordelia frowned. "The tune, I know—yet the words are new."

"Thou speakest aright," said a baritone clam. "It was but melody when first we heard it. Later, there were words, but we liked them not, so we gave the tune to other verses that we'd heard anon."

Rod frowned. "I don't know if I quite like the drift of that song's sentiments."

"Oh, thou art but one who would kill joy!" Cordelia scoffed. "Is not the lass's reply enough for thee?"

"It is," Rod said, "if you remember it."

"It was indeed the music of the soft rock," Gregory said. "Yet assuredly thou canst find no delight in the hard rocks' music!"

"Wherefore not, brother?" Geoffrey asked. "That, at least, I can begin to comprehend, for it hath the sound of an army on the march."

The clams began to vibrate with a strong, quick rhythm, and chanted:

> *"Crabbed age and youth*
> *Cannot live together,*
> *For youth is full of pleasure,*
> *Age is full of care!*
>
> *Youth, like summer morn,*
> *Age, like winter weather;*
> *Youth, like summer brave,*
> *Age like winter bare.*
>
> *Youth is full of sport,*
> *Age's breath is short,*
> *Youth is nimble, age is lame,*
> *Age, I do abhor thee!"*

"Now, wait a minute," Rod said; but the music rode right on over his words:

> *"Youth, I do adore thee!*
> *Oh, my love, my love is young!*
> *Age, I do defy thee!*
> *Oh, sweet shepherd, hie thee,*
> *For methinks thou stay'st too long!"*

"Definitely," Rod said, "I find that offensive."

"Wherefore?" asked a baritone clam. "Thou art not aged."

Rod froze, agape, then managed to close his mouth. Cordelia giggled. Rod gave her a black look, then said to Gwen, "Of course, I do kind of agree with the sentiments of that last verse."

But her eyes were already glowing at him.

"Twas fair, I will allow," Geoffrey said. "Yet surely thou canst do naught with this plague of noise that doth come from the heavy metal stones!"

"Oh, but we have heard good sounds from them!" another baritone clam cried. "Aye, mayhap nine in ten are worthless—but is not that true of all things? The tenth is well worth keeping."

But the tenor clam was already vibrating, and Rod was awestruck at the sound.

It was like surf breaking on a shingled shore, like wind howling over a frozen tundra. It was an ancient locomotive, throbbing across that barren plain; it was a driving rhythm that beat and battered at him, then broke into a cascade of jangling notes as the tenor voice cried out:

> "I, who am not shaped for lover's tricks,
> And made to shun my looking glass,
> I, that am rudely shaped,
> Cheated of feature by all-lying nature,
> Deformed, unfinished, sent before my time
> Into this breathing world scarce half made up,
> And that so lamely and unfashionable
> That dogs bark at me as I limp by them—
> Why, I, in this weak piping time of peace,
> Have no delight to pass away the time,
> Unless to spy my shadow in the sun,
> And descant on mine own deformity,
> And therefore—since I cannot prove a lover,
> I am determined to prove a villain,
> And hate the idle pleasures of these days!"

The final chord rang, and died. The Gallowglasses sat, stunned.

Finally, Rod cleared his throat and said, "Yes. I guess that's good."

" 'Tis wondrous!" Cordelia breathed.

"No music is good or bad in itself," the bass voice said. "It is what people make of it."

"Each music hath its purpose," one of the clams admonished. "Each form of music hath its verse."

"The words, though," Rod protested. "Some of the songs I've been hearing have words that are downright poisonous!"

But Fess's quiet voice said, *There have always been those who have turned music to evil purposes. Shall I speak of ancient hymns to bloodthirsty gods? Or of the twisted paeans sung by medieval witches?*

"Or of the sirens' songs." Rod nodded. "Yes, I take your point."

Magnus asked the clams, "Whose words are these that thou didst sing? For surely I have not heard them from the stones."

"Nay," said the tenor clam. "They are an older poet's, I think—but we sing them of the witch who doth sow these music-rocks broadcast."

"A witch behind the music-rocks?" Rod tensed. "Who is she? Where?"

"Here on the West Coast, though to the north. She doth name herself Ubu Mare."

"Ubu Mare, eh?" Rod locked glances with Gwen. "Now we have a name, at least."

Gwen shook her head. "I have not heard it before, my lord."

"We'll hear it again," Rod promised. "Come on, kids—time to go hunting."

"Oh, not yet, Papa!" Cordelia protested, and Magnus agreed, "Aye. Let us hear one more song, at least."

"It will not be so long, husband." Gwen touched his hand. "And our poor minds do need rest, surely."

"Well . . . okay." Rod wasn't very hard to convince; he wasn't exactly looking forward to another trip into pandemonium.

But the clams were already singing again, a ballad about a lighthouse keeper, lively and quick. The children began to nod their heads—and Gregory, belly-down with his chin in his hands, watching the clams, began to tap his toes against air.

"Music hath charms," Gwen murmured, "and they are the most charmed of all."

A scream tore the fabric of the song, and men began to shout.

The Gallowglasses looked up, startled.

Out of the trees came two of the strangest animals they had ever seen—four feet tall and four feet thick, like fur-covered globes, with thick, stumpy legs and shaggy dappled coats. Tiny eyes glittered toward the top of each ball, just above a long, tapering nose. They waddled toward the water, and the clams gave a burbling scream of fear.

"Have no care—we shall ward thee," Geoffrey said quickly. "What doth affright thee so?"

"Those beasts!" cried a clam. "Hast thou never seen them?"

"Never. What's there to fear in such foolish animals?"

"Their noses!" cried a clam. "They will suck us up, they will tear us from our bed!"

"Not whiles we are here to guard thee," Cordelia assured them. "What manner of beast are these?"

"They are clamdiggers!"

The peasant men caught up clubs and attacked the things with blows and shouts, but the globular animals scarcely seemed to notice. They reached the water and splashed in.

"Zap 'em, kids!" Rod cried.

Magnus and Geoffrey launched into the air and swooped toward the beasts, drawing their swords. They stabbed at the clamdiggers, trying to turn them, but the beasts scarcely seemed to notice, the moreso because Cordelia was pelting them with sticks and pebbles from the bank. But Geoffrey lost his temper and dive-bombed, stabbing hard, and a long thin nose swept around in a blur, to swat him out of the air. He splashed down, and the beast lumbered toward him. Gwen screamed, shooting over the water like a rocket, whirling about to swat the reaching nose with her broom. The nose recoiled.

Rod leaped onto Fess's back. "Charge!"

But on the bank by the clams, Gregory glared, narrowing his eyes.

Soft implosions sucked air inward toward the center of the pond, and where the clamdiggers had splashed, two rectangular objects floated, bobbing in the ripples. They had no eyes or noses, only straps and buckles.

Rod stared. "Do my eyes deceive me, or did my son change those clamdiggers into . . ."

"A pair of trunks," Fess finished. "That is exactly what he has done, Rod. You have seen it clearly."

Geoffrey shot back over the water to clap his brother on the shoulder with a dripping hand. "Most marvelously done, little brother! How chanced thou to hit 'pon so excellent a scheme!"

Gregory blushed with pleasure. "Why, such ungainly beasts as they could only be things of witch-moss, look you—so I thought at them, to change their shape to something harmless."

"A thousand thanks," said a shaky clam-voice.

"Aye," said three more, and a fourth, "If there is aught that we may ever do for thee, thou hast but to ask it."

"Why," said Gregory, at a loss, "I can only ask that thou dost keep this fen free for all that is best in music, as a sanctuary for all of good heart."

"And tender ear," Rod muttered.

"Why, that shall we do!" the clams assured him. "And we shall ever sing thy praises!"

Gregory reddened again. "Spare my blushes, I pray thee! Sing only hearty songs of excellence, as thou wast wont to do!"

"As thou shalt have," a baritone clam said. "Yet I doubt not we'll sing of they who defend the weak, also."

"Why," said Gregory, "I can only therefore praise thee."

"Then let's go look for someone who's picking on the weak." Rod took his son firmly by the hand and turned him away. "What do you say, Gwen?"

"Aye, my husband." Gwen glanced at the sky. "We must make five more miles ere nightfall. Magnus, Cordelia! Geoffrey! Come!" They turned away, walking back along the sand-spit.

"I had liefer stay, Papa," Geoffrey volunteered.

"Stay! Are you kidding? When there might be a battle on our trail?"

"Art thou sure? There hath been naught but skirmishes thus far."

"All right, so you're on a diet." Rod halted and looked around. "I think we're a little shorthanded here."

"Magnus! Cordelia!" Gwen cried. "Come—and now!"

"Eh? Oh! Certes, Mama!" Cordelia shot toward her like a broomstick juggernaut. "Their music is so entrancing."

"Thy pardon, Mama." Magnus sighed as he came up. "They are wondrous minstrels."

"Farewell, good clams," Cordelia called back, and the song broke off for a burbling chorus of goodbyes. Then the Gallowglasses strode away, while behind them a voice cried, "Come, another roundelay!" and the singing began again.

# 21

They left the fen refreshed, but they were instantly immersed in pandemonium again. They followed the blimp from a distance, and by late afternoon they were dazed and reeling as they topped a ridge and saw a village below them, tranquil under the evening sun, with peasants coming in from the fields, hoes over their shoulders. Wreaths of smoke rose from the central holes in the thatches of the cottages. Wives came out to chat with one another for a few minutes, then returned to their homes. Adolescent girls shooed children and chickens. On the village green, young men kicked an inflated bladder around.

Magnus looked, then looked again. "Why, their young folk abide with them!"

"Yes, and they're doing something besides listening to the music." Rod smiled. "There's a certain amount of promise in this. Let's go find out how they're doing it."

They went down into the town, finding the large hut with the bunch of greenery hanging from a pole.

"Pretty dried-out bush," Rod said, with critical appraisal. "Old ale, then."

"Thou hast told me old ale is better, betimes," Magnus reminded him. "Come, Papa—at the least, 'twill be another's cooking tonight."

"Hast thou aught to complain of?" Gwen demanded as they walked in.

"Naught, yet thou hast," Cordelia reminded her. "Wilt thou truly regret not preparing a meal o'er a campfire?"

"Well, I shall suffer it," Gwen allowed.

They sat at a table. The landlord looked up, then looked again in surprise. "Good e'en, gentlemen and ladies!"

"Just travelling through," Rod assured him. "I could stand a flagon of ale, landlord. Is there a supper?"

"Aye, milord—Timon, ho!"

A lanky teen-ager came in from the back room, saw the Gallowglasses, and smiled in welcome. Then he saw Cordelia, and the welcome deepened. She smiled back, coming a little more alive somehow, and Magnus cleared his throat. "Good e'en, goodman!"

"And to thee." Timon wrenched his eyes away from Cordelia, amused, and turned to the landlord. "What need, Dad?"

"Ale, my lad, and quickly, for these good folks!"

"Only the two," Gwen qualified. "As to the rest, hast thou clear water?"

"Aye, most surely. That too, lad."

"As thou wilt, Dad." Timon turned away and ducked back through the doorway.

"Ho! 'Dad,' is it?" Magnus grinned. "What meaning hath that?"

"Oh, it's just another intimate form of 'Father'—the one I expected my own children to use, in fact. But you four preferred 'Papa.'"

"I shall no longer, then! Oh, nay, I would not disappoint thee so! Aye, 'Dad' it shall be henceforth! Oh, ho!" And Magnus couldn't quite hold his laughter in.

Rod frowned, turning to Gwen. "What's the joke?"

"I ken not," she replied, "save that 'tis a term they've not heard before."

The other three had picked up Magnus's mood, and were grinning now.

Timon came back in with a tray. He set a tankard in front of each of them, saying, "I regret there's naught but stew this night, milord, milady. We had no notion of thy coming."

"I have no doubt thy stew will suit," Gwen assured him. "Bread, too, an thou wilt."

"Oh, of a certainty!"

Magnus grimaced, overdoing it a little, and said, "How dost thou withstand the noise all about?"

"Noise?" Timon looked up, frowning, head cocked to the side, listening. "Oh, the music of the rocks, dost thou mean? Aye, 'tis still there, is't not?"

Cordelia stared. "How canst thou have missed it?"

Timon shrugged. "A month agone we were ever in the meadows, dancing to fair strains; yet somehow, of late, we have taken less and less notice of it."

"Timon!"

"Aye, Dad!" He flashed a grin back at the Gallowglasses. "I've a notion thy stew is ready." He strode off toward the inner doorway.

"So that is the fashion of it," Magnus said thoughtfully.

"How can they cease to notice the music?" Cordelia wondered.

Geoffrey shrugged. "Mayhap through over-familiarity. We treasure least what we have known too long. Yet I find that hard to credit, when 'tis so loud."

*At any level,* Fess's voice said inside their head, *it can be ignored, when people are saturated with it. Some scholars claim that the mind protects itself by becoming numb when it is overloaded, and blocks out the irritation.*

Magnus scowled. "How now! 'Tis pleasant sound, not irritation!"

*Too much of anything can be an irritant.*

"Each of us," Gwen said diplomatically, "hath gorged too much on sweetmeats."

Magnus flushed, not liking the reminder of his child-hood, and Gregory looked guilty.

*An excellent example,* Fess agreed, *and when you have eaten too much of any food, no matter how tasty, the mere aroma of it sickens you. In the same fashion, these people's minds have erected blockades of numbness.*

Geoffrey gained a sudden wary look. "Yet blockades can be breached, Fess."

"Oh, be not so silly," Cordelia scoffed. "We speak of music, not of castles. How can one breach a wall of surfeit?"

*Why,* said Fess, *by a change in the music, one that catches attention.*

Gregory asked, "What manner of change is that?"

A howl sounded from outside.

They stared at one another, startled. Then they jumped up, turning away to the door.

They went out, looking toward the sound—for the howl had died, but was replaced by a rough, rhythmic scraping, and chanting in time to it:

> *"Whips and chains!*
> *Blows that rain!*
> *Bloody stains!*
> *Lash insane!"*

The children stood stock-still, and Gregory asked, "Can this be music?"

*You may need to redefine your terms,* Fess suggested.

"Assuredly," said Gwen, "it cannot be verse."

"I don't know," Rod said, "though I did think it was as bad as it could get."

*It has meter and rhyme,* Fess pointed out. *It must be so classified.*

"But its source!" Magnus protested. "Are there rocks now that chant?"

With a prickle of uneasiness, Rod noticed that the young folk of the village were looking out of windows and doorways.

Down the street they came, clad in roughly tanned leather garments that left their backs bare—young men and young women in their teens, moving in time to the beat, stepping three times and, on the fourth beat, slashing at each other's backs with whips.

"Flagellants," Rod whispered, horrified. "But why? There's no plague here."

" 'Tis not repentance," Gwen said, her tone hardening. "Hearken to their words, husband."

Rod heard, but could scarcely tell whether the sounds came from the young people, or from the rocks they wore tied around their necks:

> *"Hunger, lust!*
> *All that must*
> *Be rendered keen*
> *By the sheen*
> *Of whiplash law!*
> *Backs made raw*
> *Feel more deep!*
> *Naught can keep*
> *Music's strain*
> *As stings of pain!*
> *Ecstasy,*
> *Abide with me*
> *In agony!"*

"Nay!" Cordelia's voice trembled. "Assuredly the voice doth not tell them that pain is pleasure!"

"It doth," Gwen said, mouth a thin, grim line, "and I assure thee, daughter, 'tis the foulest lie that e'er I heard!"

"But how can the music say it, an it is false?" Magnus asked, bewildered.

"Because," Rod said, "these rocks were made by somebody, and that somebody can put lies in them if he wants to."

*Quite probable,* Fess agreed. *At the very least, I question their programming.*

Somebody jostled them; Rod staggered back, with a cry of anger, then stepped forward, hand going to his sword— but slammed back against the inn again, as the innkeeper bumped past him, calling, "Nay, lad! Timon, no! Come back!"

But tall Timon, eyes unfocused, had torn off his tunic and caught up a broom. He tailed onto the end of the line, shuffling along and slashing with the broom straws at the back in front of him. A young girl jumped in behind him, instantly adopting the three-step shuffle, untying her sash and striking at Timon's back with it. Another lad stepped in behind her, tearing away the back of her dress and lashing at her with a rope's end.

Cordelia turned away, stumbling back into the inn, eyes squeezed shut.

"Magnus, no!" Gwen screamed, for her eldest, glassy-eyed, was moving forward toward the line of flagellants, stepping into place, fumbling at the buckle of his sword-belt . . .

Rod reached out and clamped pincer-fingers into his son's shoulder.

Magnus winced and twisted from his grasp with a yell of pain. His hands left the buckle and leaped to the sword.

Rod yanked him out of the line. Still angry, the youth drew out his blade. . . .

Rod caught his son's wrist and forced it down. It surged back up—Rod was amazed at how strong his son had grown—but Geoffrey reached up, catching his brother's elbow, thumb probing. Magnus sagged, eyes bulging, with a high, thin whine of agony. His face came down to a level with Geoffrey's, and his younger brother snapped, "Shall I admire thee now? Art thou the toy of women, then, that thou mayest be enslaved by song?"

Magnus's face reddened with anger again. "Be still, sprout!"

Rod sagged with relief—it was brother talking to brother, not a teen entranced.

Then Magnus looked up, his glance darting around. "What . . . wherefore . . ."

"The music had entrapped thee, son," Gwen said gently.

"Aye." Geoffrey's lip curled with contempt. "And wilt thou let it hold these others enslaved?"

"Nay!" Magnus roared, covering his embarrassment. He whirled, sheathing his sword but drawing his dagger, and leaped after the line of youths, running up to the first who had a stone hung round his neck, slipping the dagger in, cutting the thong, and hurling the stone away. The youth snapped upright and turned on him with an angry roar, lashing out with his whip.

But Magnus was already on down the line to the next, slashing and snatching, working his way quickly toward the front, hurling the glinting stones far away.

Geoffrey leaped to join him, but Rod caught his shoulder. "You don't have the height for this one."

"Daughter!" Gwen called, and Cordelia hurried out from the inn. "Hurl," Gwen commanded, and turned to glare at Magnus.

Cordelia looked, startled, saw what Magnus was doing, and narrowed her gaze to the rock flying from his hand. It lurched and flew farther, much farther, out over the village and into the nearby stream.

In a few minutes, the rocks were all gone, and the young people converged on Magnus with angry shouting.

Gwen gave Rod a stony look. Rod nodded and stepped forward. "Fess, fifteen thousand Hertz."

"Certainly, Rod."

A sharp, piercing tone slid over the village. Gwen and the children clapped their hands over their ears, for the sound seemed to stab right through their heads. It only lasted five seconds, then cut off—but the flagellants were down, rolling on the ground in agony, hands over their ears, howling. Magnus alone still stood, staggering, bringing his hands away. He looked up at his father, dazed.

Rod stepped up beside him, and turned to look at the peasant youths all about him. Gradually, the youths began to realize that someone out of their league was looking down on them. They quieted; faces settled into truculent expressions.

"How are your backs?" Rod said quietly.

They stared at him, taken aback by the question. Then

they looked at one another, saw the stripes and blood, and the wailing began.

Half an hour later, Magnus was just finishing gulping down a tankard of ale. Timon set another in front of him. "Drink, I pray. 'Tis the least thanks I can make, sin that thou hast saved my back and brain."

Magnus lowered the tankard with a gasp and reached for the new one, but Gwen laid a hand over his. "Give it time to work," she said gently. "Too much, and thou wilt be the toy of this music that doth surround thee."

Magnus shuddered and pulled his hand back.

"Stew," Rod said to Timon.

"I could not eat!" Magnus protested.

"Let him smell it," Rod assured Timon. "He'll find his appetite."

"Thou hast saved them, Magnus," Gregory said, his eyes huge.

"Aye," said Magnus, "but only by Dad and Geoffrey saving me!"

"At least," said Rod, "you had your question answered."

Gregory looked up. "What question was that?"

"Why," said Rod, "you wanted to know what kind of music it would take to break through the mind's defense of numbness."

Magnus lifted his head. "Aye, even so! Yet what was the manner of it?"

"Sheer ugliness, I guess," Rod said. "Every time people become used to one sort of music, the crafter breaks through to them by coming up with something that's even more distorted. It shocks them into paying attention again." He shrugged. "Just a guess, though."

But Gregory's eyes had filled with tears. "I did not mean . . ."

"Peace, brother." Cordelia wrapped an arm around him. "These poor folk were entrapped days before thou didst think to ask."

"Aye," said Gwen. " 'Twas not thy doing."

But Geoffrey's eyes narrowed. "Papa, where a wall is

breached, there is a captain who commanded a siege engine."

"Yes," Rod agreed. "A musical change like that does seem rather deliberate, doesn't it?"

"Good Timon!" Magnus rose and turned to the tall youth by the inner door. "Whence could that train of youths have come?"

The lad looked surprised, then nodded. "I will ask." He stepped through the door and was gone.

"Shall we spend the night here, Papa?" Gregory asked.

Rod turned to Gwen; she nodded. He turned back. "Yes, son—but I think we'll camp by that stream out there. I'd like to make sure no one goes fishing tonight."

# 22

The next afternoon, they finally found out where the blimp was leading them—they, and the half-mile or so of dancers who were following behind them. They found out, because they came into a zone where heavy metal rocks glistened all about them, drowning out the sounds of the blimp. They looked about with astonishment, and Rod put his mouth near Gwen's ear. "Is this its home country or something?"

The dancers thought it was great. They leaped and whirled out into the meadow on both sides of the roadway, gamboling and dancing to their hearts' delight. Considering how thickly the ground was strewn with music-rocks, it was amazing they didn't break their legs.

"Look!" Geoffrey's voice was just barely audible above the racket. Rod turned, and saw him pointing skyward. He looked up, to see that the blimp had become translucent; the sunlight was shining through it. As he watched, it became even more faint, until it shimmered, and was gone.

The family were dumbfounded.

Then Gregory's voice said, in wonder, *Was it illusion, then?*

They seized on his idea, using telepathy because the music was too loud.

*I had thought it was made of witch-moss, at least,* Magnus answered.

*Seems it was just a mental construct, purely illusory.* Rod frowned. *Bait to lead youth here—but what for?*

*Whither journey we now?* Cordelia wondered.

*Aye,* Gwen asserted. *The music is so widespread that we can no longer use the rocks' direction as a guide.*

*No vector,* Rod added.

But Fess's voice interposed smoothly: *If the blimp was a projection, surely it had a projector.*

*Certes!* Geoffrey agreed with enthusiasm. *Let us find the blimp's maker! He should know whence came these rocks!*

*But how shall we find him?* Magnus demanded.

Gregory pointed. *See! The young folk do tend toward the west!*

Sure enough, though they weren't single-file anymore, the groups of dancers were more or less all moving toward the west.

*Then whoever wanted to bring them here, may still be leading them.* Rod nodded. *But the blimp was no longer of use, because once its music was drowned out by the rocks, nobody paid any attention to it anymore.*

*Then let us pay heed to its maker,* Gwen suggested. *Follow, family!*

They trailed off after the dancers.

The witch wasn't hard to find, once they caught up with the head of the mob. She wasn't hard to find, because she was the only person in sight who was clearly middle-aged. She was also one of the very few who was fat.

She must have caught some mental trace of the Gallow-glasses, because she looked up at their approach, and her mouth opened in an unheard scream. She pointed at them, and a searing flower of heat bloomed in their minds. But it withered just as quickly under Gwen's projection of a wintry blast. Instead, a huge barbarian suddenly confronted them, clad in leather and metal armbands, long hair tied in knots, earrings flashing, spear stabbing.

*Illusion!* Gwen's label was quick, and she and Cordelia fixed their eyes on the image, which thinned and faded even as it strode toward them. But another leaped up in its place, a woman with long, straight black hair, clad in short, tight-fitting leathers, unfurling a bullwhip. The boys stared, fascinated by the combination of pulchritude and punishment, but Rod knew the compound from experience. The flame of his anger lashed out and blasted the image to instant ashes—but rain drizzled onto them, and a manic vampire sprouted up like a plant, blood-red lips gaping wide to show his fangs, mop of hair flapping like a set of banners. His garments fit so tightly they seemed to be painted on.

Geoffrey's surge of disgust rippled through everyone. He was revolted by the notion that such a thing should wear a male form. Under the mental stress produced by him and his brothers the illusion shredded, and blew away in tatters.

The witch gave up and grabbed for her broomstick.

Cordelia was faster, swooping around to cut in front of the woman. She hesitated, just long enough for the boys to catch her robe. They yanked down hard, and the woman fell; then they yanked up, and her robe tore, but she landed gently. A boiling cauldron of anger and fear bubbled out of her, directed at them—but it subsided, stilled, and was gone as Gwen's calming, slowing tide of thoughts rocked her into sleep. The others paid avid attention to her thoughts, and Rod inserted the formless question, only a mental current, that asked (but not in words) where the music-rocks came from. All they gained from her, though, as she slipped into unconsciousness, was the phrase, ". . . the man who is nowhere . . ."

Cordelia looked down in exasperation at the sleeping form. *How is this? What can she mean?*

*How can there be a man who is nowhere?* Geoffrey demanded.

*A man, at least.* Gwen's thought was cool water on their

inflamed emotions. *Seek among this throng, for only the moiety of them came when we did.*

The Gallowglasses looked out on a vast, churning mob of young folk.

*How many are there here, Mama?* Gregory's thought was dazed.

*Some thousands, at least,* she answered, and Fess thought-corrected, *Five thousand three hundred seventy-one, Gregory.*

*Somebody must know where this witch-moss-crafting man is!* Rod insisted. *Eavesdrop on their minds, folks—but stay together.*

Bravely, they tried. For half an hour, they probed and listened. Finally, Gregory dropped cross-legged on the grass, and Gwen called off the session with a curt finishing thought.

*No one knows,* Magnus mused, benumbed.

*I did at least catch some shady picture of a man bearing stones,* Gregory thought wearily.

*I, too,* Cordelia answered, *but none had the least notion as to where he dwelled.*

*Only that he doth exist,* Gwen agreed. *How can this be, husband?*

*It's really your field,* Rod said slowly, *but to me, it smacks of post-hypnotic suggestion.*

Gwen looked up at him, amazed. *Why, thou hast it! Such few as these as have known of him, have had the memory stolen from their minds!*

Magnus frowned. *Aye . . . 'twould not be so hard to do—only to strengthen the resistance of a handful of synapses. . . .*

*Simplicity itself.* Anger tinged Gwen's thought. *They seek to keep this man's existence a secret, then.*

*But why?* Cordelia wondered.

*Angry peasants.* Rod's thoughts weren't exactly halcyon, either. *All right, family—how do you find someone whom no one remembers?*

They were silent, puzzling it out. Fess waited, and when no one spoke, he explained, *Memory is holistic. The conscious recollection would be relatively easy to erase, yes, but it would be duplicated throughout the cerebrum.*

Gregory looked up sharply. *Fascinating—yet how shall we apply it?*

*'Tis not so hard as all that.* Gwen stood, resolution in every line of her body. *Fetch me one who hath some hazy memory of this man who is nowhere, lads.*

Half an hour later, they left the peasant youth sleeping with his head on a tussock, and walked off toward a distant hill and the stream at its foot.

*We have not hurt him, have we, Mama?* Cordelia thought anxiously.

*Not a whit,* Gwen assured her. *When he doth wake, he will find that he hath slept better than ever he hath aforetime. Come, children. We hunt.*

There was a desert there, on the other side of the stream. Animal skulls and low scrub decorated barren sand, and clouds of alkali blew over them.

Cordelia shuddered. *How could aught live there, Mama?*

*How canst thou believe thine eyes, after all the illusions we have seen?* Geoffrey retorted. *Fear not, sister—never have I seen a wasteland bordering a stream before.*

Cordelia's head snapped up at his remark, but Gwen didn't give her time to start feeling chagrined. She threw her broomstick out, staring at it. In midair, its form changed, stretched—and it landed as a six-foot-wide set of planks, held together by cross-boards.

*Cross over the bridge,* Gwen bade her family, *and see what we may discover.*

Two by two, they followed their mother and father into the forbidding waste.

# 23

They ran into the first signs as soon as they crossed the bridge that arched over the stream. It was almost as though they had entered a picture-book land, with graceful willow trees bordering the stream and silver birches spaced widely apart to let in the sun. Finches sang in cherry trees, and the broad expanse of grass was cropped into a lawn.

"Why, how charming!" Cordelia exclaimed.

"Sure is." Rod looked around. "Somebody's putting an awful lot of work into it, too."

"This music is not so loud," Gregory pointed out.

It wasn't, now that Rod thought about it. He hadn't noticed it immediately, because the rock music was still there—but it was muted. He frowned. "Odd—there look to be more rocks than ever."

"One every yard, it doth seem," Gwen agreed. "Yet their music's less painful."

Magnus picked up a rock, staring at it in surprise. "'Tis only stone, not metal!"

"Aye," said Geoffrey, "and its strains stir my blood, but do not overwhelm it."

"Stir *your* blood? Here, let me see!" Rod came over and took the rock. "Just as I suspected—it's a march."

"A rock march?" Gregory asked, wide-eyed.

It was a march—but with the characteristic heavy beat underneath it.

"Here is one whose strains are slowed, and pretty!" Cordelia called.

Gwen came over to her and nodded. " 'Tis quite melodious."

"This one doth make sounds, but no music," Magnus called. He had picked up another rock. Rod followed him, and heard birdsong, then a wind swelling under it, the birdsong fading as the wind-song merged into a rolling gong, then faded into the sound of rushing water with high, clear tones above it. Yet, underneath it all thrummed a strong, unyielding beat.

Rod took a deep breath. "No, son. That's music— Nature's music, maybe, but it's organized into something more."

Gregory regarded a large pebble in his hand. "This lacks a beat."

Sure enough, it did—and its melody dipped and soared, but the tones were pure and reverberating. Somehow, nonetheless, it was like the music of all the other rocks they'd heard, even without a bass or drum line.

Fess said, "Rod—someone is experimenting."

Rod stilled, feeling apprehension boost his awareness. "You know something, Old Iron? That makes too much sense."

"Papa," Geoffrey called, "yon lies a cottage."

"Let me see," Cordelia commanded, dashing over to him. "Oh! 'Tis enchanting!"

"That's what I'm afraid of." Rod hurried over to look.

Gwen reached the children just ahead of him. "It is, husband—most wondrously made."

It was a small house with a thatched roof, such as any peasant might live in—but where the peasant's cottage would have been plastered with mud, this one was sided with clapboard, painted cherry-red. The windows were curtained, and flowers grew all around.

"Husband," said Gwen, "yon lives a crafter of amazing talent."

"Yes," Rod said, "and one who delights in making things. But it can't be the one we're looking for, Gwen— this one has a sense of beauty."

"If we would know, we must ask," she said with determination, and set out toward the door.

"Hey! Wait up!" Rod leaped after her, and they went up the neat, flagstoned path between borders of hedge-roses. Rod didn't realize it, but the children trailed after them.

They came to the door. "Now what do we do?" Rod demanded. "Knock?"

"An thou sayest?" Gwen rapped on the door.

"Hey! I didn't mean . . ." Rod subsided, mulling it over. "Why not, come to think of it?"

"We do not *know* he is an enemy," Geoffrey pointed out.

Rod turned. "What're *you* four doing here? I thought I told you . . ."

But Magnus was shaking his head, and Rod realized, belatedly, that he hadn't said anything.

Then the door opened, and he whirled about.

His first impression was of supreme, unvarnished happiness. Then he took a closer look, and decided it was only benign good humor. Whatever it was, it was contained in a plump peasant of medium height who was dressed in completely ordinary tunic and hose—completely ordinary, except that his tunic was turquoise and his hose were yellow with red cross-garters. His belt was red, too, and his face was circular and smiling, with a fringe of black hair around a bald top.

"Company!" he cried. "Oh, do come in, come in!" And he pattered away, calling, "A moment, whiles I set the kettle to boiling and fetch some cakes!"

"Cakes?" Gregory was all ears.

"Remember thy manners." Gwen marched in, never at a loss. Rod let the younger contingent pass, then brought up the rear.

The room was a delight, with a circular rug, an intricately carved chair near the window, and a table with three straight chairs near a brick stove. Rod eyed it warily; it looked almost Russian. He found himself braced for the house to lurch; if it rose up on three chicken legs, he was tossing the kids out the nearest window.

"Let me aid," Gwen said, all sweetness and light, and fixed the little pot with an unwavering gaze. It began to bubble; then steam poured out the top.

The plump man stared. "Why, how is this?" He turned to Gwen, smiling. "Gramercy, lady! 'Tis so much quicker thus!"

"I delight in aiding." But Gwen seemed a little discomfited that he had taken it so easily.

He turned back, pouring the hot water into earthenware mugs. "Thou art a witch, then? Nay, of a certainty thou art; none else could do thus! I have another witch who doth visit me from time to time."

"Do you indeed?" Suddenly, he had Rod's total attention.

"Oh, aye!" The man started bringing mugs to the table. "I fear there are no chairs for the young ones; much though I delight in company, I've rarely more than two who come together."

"They're used to it," Rod assured him. "You were saying, about this other witch?"

"Two, though to be sure, one's a warlock. I am, too—did I tell thee that? Oh, 'tis so good to have other witchfolk to natter with! I am hight Ari, Ari the Crafter, as my neighbors do call me. Aye, neighbors, though they'd not have me live in their town. Still, 'tis enough for me to live near a stream, and with birds and small furry creatures for friends, oh yes, it is enough. Wilt thou have honey with thy brew?"

A delicious fragrance rose from the mug. "Uh, no thanks," Rod declined. "Gwen?"

"Nay, though I think the children might." Gwen was off-balance, too, disconcerted by the man's friendliness.

"Nay, certes," he chuckled, handing a honey-pot down

to Cordelia. "Was there ever a youngling had no taste for honey?"

"I," said Magnus.

"Well, so, but thou'rt a young man now, art thou not? No longer a child, no. Ah, I do wish I could offer chairs to thee and thy sister! I must make some." He went to the window, lips pursed. "Aye, there is a patch of witch-moss large enough. I think . . ."

"I would not trouble thee," Magnus said quickly.

"Oh, 'tis no trouble." Ari frowned for a moment.

Rod took the opportunity to lean close to Gwen. "Can this really be the man who made those metallic rocks we've been hearing?"

"Who else could it be?" she responded. "He hath the skill. Yet how are we to set him to talking of it?"

"There! 'Twill be along shortly." Ari stepped over to open the door, then bustled back to the stove. "Now, the cakes. Ah, they're warmed!" He set a platter of biscuits in front of Rod and Gwen, then handed another down to Gregory, with a chuckle of delight.

"Did you make everything in this room?" Rod asked, trying not to stare.

"Each and every. Do taste of my cakes, goodman!"

"Uh, no thanks. Things of witch-moss don't agree with me."

Magnus spluttered into his tea.

"Oh, the cakes are not of witch-moss, no! My neighbors do bring me flour and eggs and such from time to time, yes, in thanks for my crafting small things for them, aye!"

"I don't doubt it," Rod said.

He turned at a knocking sound, just in time to see the door swing open a little farther as a brand new chair came walking into the room.

"Oh, come, come!" Ari clucked his tongue. "Knowest thou not better than to leave a door ajar?"

Rod could have sworn the chair blushed. At any rate, it turned around and knocked the door shut with a leg.

"'Tis such a trial to teach them not to slam it." Ari sighed. "Nay, little chair, find one who needs service." He nodded at Magnus, and the chair scuttled over to the eldest.

Magnus edged away. "Oh, I could never take a chair when a lady hath need of a seat!"

The chair turned toward Cordelia.

"Nay, brother, I'll yield it to thee," she said quickly. "I am quite settled now."

"Magnus," Gwen said, with a tone of dire warning.

The eldest sighed, rose from the floor, and sat in the chair. It settled contentedly under his weight.

"It will stay still now," Ari assured them.

"Desirable," Rod admitted. "And now you have one more, in case your witch-friends bring company."

"Aye, though I doubt that they will. There have never come more than two of them, though Ubu Mare hath not come this half-year and more."

Rod could feel his whole family tensing. "Ubu Mare?"

"Aye. She . . ." Ari bit his lip, then glanced about him as though to make sure no one was listening, and leaned closer to Rod and Gwen with a conspiratorial whisper. "She is ever polite and well-spoken, mind, but the poor woman is burdened with a hideous countenance."

"Is that so?" Rod eyed Gwen.

"The poor woman, indeed," she murmured.

"Aye," Ari sighed. "She must be the ugliest witch in the whole of the land. Yet she is civil, and did give me gold for things I made! Couldst thou credit it? Gold!"

"Somehow, I don't doubt it." Rod had a nasty suspicion of where the witch was getting the money. "You built the house, too?"

"Nay, for I've no skill as a carpenter. The goodmen from the village did that for me; they were happy to, when I gave them gold for it."

"I should think they would have been," Gwen said. "And dost thou pay one to clip thy lawn?"

"Only a lad from the village, who doth bring his sheep. 'Tis no great sum, and I can craft aught else I need, or trade for it. I scarce know what to do with all the gold they give me."

"In truth?" Magnus asked, disbelieving.

"Aye." Ari threw up his hands. "I could think of naught else—so I give each month's gold piece to the folk of the village, that they may buy food for the needy, and clothing."

"Dost thou indeed!" Gregory was incredulous, too, and Geoffrey was shaking his head slowly, in wonder.

"Oh, aye! And all this from the generosity of Ubu Mare! Is it not wondrous?"

"Amazing," Rod said, feeling a chill envelop his back.

"It is, in truth! Yet she hath not come these six months, no, but doth send Yaga and Axon in her place. I've no doubt 'tis still her gold they bring, for they, too, buy of me rocks that make music."

"Oh." The tension was winding tighter. "You crafted those wonderful stones that made the enchanting sounds we heard in your front yard?"

"Aye, they are mine!" Ari beamed. "These are my latest, look you. I essay new musics each time; I delight in inventing new forms." He frowned. "Yet not of the sort Ubu Mare doth wish me to make, no. 'Tis hideous stuff with a scratching and wailing to it, and words that make no sense. And they do not even rhyme!"

"Horrible," Rod agreed. "I think we've heard a few like that. Where did they come up with the sound?"

Ari shrugged. "Belike whence I found mine—in my heart."

"What manner of heart must they have!" Cordelia exclaimed.

Ari turned to her, saddened. "Lass, lass! Is it for us to judge our neighbors? Nay, nay! If their taste and fashion differ from mine, who am I to say theirs is wrong and mine is right?"

"The one who actually makes the rocks," Rod said.

Ari looked up, astonished. "Assuredly that doth not give me the right to judge!"

"It doth," Gwen said, "and it doth give thee also the duty."

"Duty?" Ari stared at her, totally at a loss.

"Responsibility," Rod explained. "You do have to bear

in mind what they want to do with the things you've made."

"Why, these music-rocks are but entertainment!"

"I'm beginning to develop a definite suspicion that nothing can be 'just entertainment,'" Rod said. "You must consider, Goodman Ari, what effects your wonderful inventions can have."

"But what effects *could* music have?" Ari asked, pole-axed.

Rod took a deep breath. "We've seen young people walk away from their parents, and from their chores, to do nothing but listen to the rocks' music."

"Aye," said Gregory, "and to float down the river with thy rocks, to do naught but eat lotus and lie dreaming."

"Folk of our age are ever mired in confusion, though we hide it," Cordelia said gently. "We have seen folk in whom that confusion has been steadily worsened by the words that accompany this music."

"But how can that be!"

Then, one by one, they told him of the things they had seen as they came across the country from Runnymede. He was shocked to hear of the wakened dead, but he was horrified to hear of the flagellants. Finally, when they were done, he sat, gray-faced and whispering, "No more. What horrid things have I wrought? Nay, never again must I make music-rocks!"

"Nay, thou must needs make more," Gwen said, with that tone of motherly sternness that evoked total attention from any listener. "What thou hast broke, thou must needs mend."

"But how can I mend music?"

"Why, with harmony!" Gregory offered.

"Aye!" Magnus's eyes lighted. "Take the words of greatest beauty thou dost know, and set them to the clearest melodies thou canst make!"

But Ari shook his head. "How can sweet music heal a ruptured soul?"

"How can it not?" Cordelia countered, and Gwen laid her hand on Ari's. "If dissonance hath sickened their hearts, may not harmony cure them?"

Ari's eyes lost focus. "It may be. . . ."

"But it must not!"

They whirled. Two forms stood black against the twilight that filled the doorway, and the shorter, a woman, cried, "Who are you, who would twist our Ari against our bidding?"

Gwen stood, and only Rod could see the mantle of rage building about her. "Why, who art thou who dost seek to claim this good and gentle man as thy slave?"

"We are Yaga and Axon," the hag shrilled, "and we have bought him!"

Rod noticed Magnus sidling around behind the taller intruder, pushing Gregory behind him, and Geoffrey slipping around on the far side.

"Oh, nay!" Ari cried, shocked. "Thou hast bought my music, aye, but never myself!"

"Thyself, body and soul!" The old woman stumped forward into the light, eyes filled with malevolence. "Thou art ours, Ari, bought and paid for! Who is this that doth seek to rend thee from us!"

"I am Gwendolyn Gallowglass," Gwen said, in glacial tones, "and I have come to consign thee to the doom thou hast made for others!"

Before she even finished the sentence, Yaga's form erupted into flame.

The children glared, and Axon, the tall warlock, was immersed in a globe of inwardly stabbing light. He screamed, then slumped unconscious as one of the spears found his spinal cord.

But Yaga only cackled with glee as the flames drew in, swallowed up by her person. "Fools! Dost thou not know 'tis this, even this, I have sought all my life? To be as wrapped in throes of anguish as I am filled with them? Nay, have at *thee!*"

Gwen screamed and twisted as something flamed inside of her. Yaga crowed with delight and turned on Rod. A current seethed through him, jolting him with pain, immobilizing him with spasms.

But Yaga howled, hands clutching at her head, and spun

to face Magnus's unrelenting glare. She stumbled toward him, screaming, "Stop! Make it stop!"

Magnus twisted, and his lip trembled; but he clung more tightly to Gregory's hand, and his gaze held steady.

Cordelia's eyes narrowed and, quite calmly, she walked over to the witch and touched her temple. Yaga froze, and the pain inside Rod and Gwen was gone, as though their daughter had turned a switch. They staggered, clutching at one another, striving to rally their senses to attack. . . .

But Ari came up to Yaga, his hands twisting and molding something, then held it up to her forehead.

It was a rock.

The witch's eyes lost focus; her face unclenched, looking startled.

Then she slumped.

Geoffrey reached up and caught her, lowering her to lie beside the warlock he had been guarding.

"Are they dead?" Ari asked anxiously.

"Nay," Geoffrey assured him, "though they ought to be."

"Oh, nay! For if thou hast the right of it, I have cured them!"

Geoffrey could only stare at him as though he were mad.

"Thank *Heaven* you kids were on the ball!" Rod staggered up to them.

"We would not have been," Magnus returned, "hadst though not drawn her anger first, to show us the manner of her attack."

"Believe me, I wasn't trying." Rod shook his head. "Where did she ever get that kind of power?"

"From a hundred and more of her kind." Gwen was kneeling by the unconscious witch, fingers against the base of her skull. "I read it in her memories. . . ." She shuddered. "Faugh! What a twisted mass of vileness is there! Yct in it I see that she and many others have been gathered into a coven by this Ubu Mare."

"For what purpose?" Ari asked, white-faced.

Gwen shook her head. "To yield up their power to her in some fashion, and to bear hers, vastly magnified by all of theirs united—but it doth make of Yaga only a tool, an extension of that vile witch."

"And in that," Rod guessed, "she was content—as long as she could be part of something bigger than herself?"

Gwen nodded. "Yet now, by a wonder, the twisting and turnings within her that made her easy prey to this Ubu Mare, all that bitter confusion and hatred, is straightened to the beginnings of harmony!" She looked up at Ari. "How didst thou achieve it?"

The crafter relaxed, and his smile returned. "Why, even as thou didst say, good folk—I crafted a rock that would make music with all the lightheartedness, harmony, and order that is in me."

And he was, of course, an unusually tranquil, optimistic person. Rod looked up at Magnus. "But what did *you* do, that stopped her in her tracks?"

"Much the same," Magnus answered. "I had seen her swallow the flames of Mother's anger, so I sought to fill her with peace and goodwill. I enwrapped it in those strains of Bach that Fess hath taught us, and projected it into her mind."

"Yet surely she struck back at thee!"

"Aye, most horribly," Gregory said, and shuddered, squeezing his eyes shut.

"And thou wast my shield." Magnus turned to hug his little brother against his hip. "I am sorry, Gregory—but I could not unravel her hideousness *and* think Bach at her, both at once."

"I was glad to aid," Gregory said, pale-faced, "and I sought to loosen the knot of anger and bitterness as quickly as she sought to tie it within thee—but oh, brother! May I never have to again!"

"Amen to that," said Cordelia, "but that must needs be why she could not repel my hand."

"And what didst thou?" Gwen looked up, worried.

"I thought of May mornings, and my delight in the dawn and the songs of the birds. Naught more—but blended toward music, as Papa did say of the rocks without this house."

"So." Ari was filled with wonder. "She succumbed to my music, only because thine had prepared her for it!" He turned to Gwen, uncertain. "Cannot my music, then, heal ripped souls?"

Gwen pulled herself together and managed a smile, rising to her feet. "It can, oh! Assuredly, it can! Yet as thou hast seen, good crafter, it will take not one melody, but many—and not one hearing, but an hundred."

Ari stared at her.

Then he turned away, with decision. "I must set to crafting them! An hundred, a thousand! I will make them and spread them throughout the length and breadth of this land, though I have to walk it myself!"

"In that, at least, I think thou wilt have aid." Gwen turned to her children. As one, they nodded.

A few minutes later, as they walked away from Ari's house into the gathering dusk, they could hear, rising from the cottage behind them, strains of melody that told of sheer delight in the beauty of the world—but all underscored by a beat, a repetitive rhythm that, no matter how light, could only be termed characteristic of rock music.

# 24

They hadn't gone very far the next morning before the music began to be physically painful. It wasn't just the volume of the sound—it was the total cacophony of a dozen different tunes and beats all going at once. They were all oddly similar, but contrasted just enough to set Rod's teeth on edge. He remembered what the young folk near the rocks' meadow had said, that the sounds had to be so loud that they could feel them in their bodies, and wondered once again how impoverished their souls must be, if the only way they could have any feeling was through the impact of sound waves.

Gregory walked with his hands over his ears, looking miserable. Gwen and Geoffrey stumbled along, determined to be brave and stoic about it, but even Magnus was beginning to look a little dazzled, and Cordelia was glassy-eyed and twitching three ways at once. As for Rod, he had a humdinger of a headache building, which he could swear was working its way up to a migraine.

Finally, Gwen had had enough. Rod saw her halt, standing firm with resolution; he saw her hands clap together, he saw her mouth move; but he didn't hear the clap, or a single word. He frowned, shaking his head, and pointed toward his ear. Gwen sighed, and her words echoed inside all their heads: *We cannot abide this. We must halt and find some way to block out these sounds.*

The children stopped and gathered round her. *Mayhap as the peasants did,* Gregory suggested.

*Well thought,* Gwen approved. *Find wax.*

It didn't take long to find, or much doing to get—the bees were limp on the floor of the hive, stunned by the sonic booms. The boys did think it odd that the markings grew in the shape of a G on their abdomens, but dismissed the oddity and brought the wax to their mother—and found their sister busy stitching together strips of bark into a little pot. They knew better than to ask why.

Gwen took the wax and molded it in her hands, staring at it intently the while. For his part, Rod was astonished at her fortitude, as always—softening the wax by telekinesis took concentration, and being able to concentrate in the midst of this racket took incredible strength of mind.

As Gwen finished each pair of covers, she handed them to the child whom they fit. Rod took a spare blanket from his saddlebag, tore it into strips, and helped tie the make-shift bandages over the earcovers. Each relaxed visibly as he or she tied the knot. Then Rod set his own into place, and the worst of the racket dimmed amazingly—except for the thumping and growling of the bass notes. He turned to explain this to Gwen, but she was wearing her own earcovers now, and was busily at work, stirring herbs into the bark pot Cordelia had made. Steam rose from it; she had heated the water without fire, by speeding up molecular motion. She finished, lifted the pot to her lips, swallowed, then handed it to Cordelia, who sipped and passed it on. When it came round to Rod, he drained what was left—and found that the thumping rhythms dwindled to a bearable level. He turned to Gwen, amazed. *How'd you do that?*

*I brewed a potion,* she thought simply. *Our minds can shut out aught we do not wish to heed; I have only aided and directed them.*

A perceptual screen, Rod realized—and more a matter of persuasion than of medicine. The potion had done what they wanted it to do; he suspected sugar pills would have done just as well, provided it had been Gwen who had made them.

Whatever the method, the goal was accomplished— Gwen had brewed an excellent rumble phyltre.

He faced her and moved his mouth slowly as he said, "Of course, now we can't talk to each other without mind-reading."

But surprisingly, he could hear her answer. Her voice sounded muffled, but it was there. "It would seem we can, my lord. What magic is this, that the music is muted but our voices are not?"

"Your speaking voices are in the middle of the range of pitches human ears can hear," Fess explained. "The waxen covers seem to block out the higher frequencies, while the potion dampens the lower ones."

"So they're filters, more than silencers?"

"Yes, Rod. They screen out the noise and preserve the information."

"I guess we can manage with that. Thank you, wonderful woman." Rod offered his arm. "Shall we promenade?"

They strode off into the worst that music could do. The good part was that Rod's headache began to fade. The bad part was that Cordelia and Magnus were tapping their toes again.

Then they followed the road around a curve and saw the priest sitting by the roadside.

Instantly, Rod distrusted him—he wasn't wearing ear-muffs. He also wasn't wearing the habit of the Order of St. Vidicon, and they were the only legitimate Order in Gramarye. No, this man was wearing a robe of plain black broadcloth, and his tonsure was definitely the work of an amateur. Needed a shave, too. The man was obviously self-ordained—one of the new crop of hedge-priests he and Tuan had been worrying about lately.

But the priest was, at least on the surface, all affability.

He looked up with a smile of welcome. "Godspeed, goodfolk! Whither art thou bound?"

"North," Rod said, forcing a smile. "We're trying to find out where this plague of noise is coming from."

"So small a thing as that?" The priest said, surprised. "Why, I myself have been to its center and back again!"

Rod was astonished—and while he was trying to figure it out, his daughter, with the full friendliness of innocence, was pleading, "Lead us to it, then! For we shall be forever on the road, without thy guidance!"

Rod caught his breath for a blistering tirade, but Gwen's fingers touched his lips, and he just barely managed to bite it down. Probably wouldn't have been heard, anyway. "If thou wilt, holy man," Gwen said. "We would cry thy mercy."

They needed somebody's mercy, that was for sure—but the priest was nodding with a happy smile. "Come, then, come! Be assured, there's naught to fear!" And he turned away, striding north with the aid of his staff.

They followed, with Rod thinking at Gwen, *You know I don't trust him, of course.*

*Neither do I*, she answered, *but I'd sooner be at his back than have him at mine. Yet we are proof against ambush whiles our senses are not dazed by this pandemonium.*

*Full vigilance, Fess.* Rod directed the message by thought, knowing the robot would have his audio gain turned down again. *Why don't you trust him, Gwen?*

*For that he wears no covers to his ears, yet seems to scarcely notice all this clamor*, she answered. *Thy reason?*

*Just the look of him—and the fact that he hasn't told us his name.*

Rod set himself to the journey, feeling a bit more confident—but scrutinizing every outcrop of rock and every smallest shrub on the road ahead.

"I am Reverend Iago," the black-robed priest said over his shoulder.

"I am Rod." He hurried to catch up with Iago, wondering why he didn't prefix his name with the more usual "father" or "brother." He decided the man was just a little stuffy and asked, "Anything we should be careful about when we get there?"

Iago shrugged. "We must cope when we must. It is confusing, I will own, yet I find little enough danger in it."

Rod noted the qualifications; his adrenaline started flowing. "How far is it?"

"Yon it begins." Iago pointed to a lofty castle towering above the forest trees.

"Strange—I hadn't noticed that before," Rod said.

The turrets seemed to soften around the edges, then to melt, flowing together into a mountain.

The children gasped, and Gwen demanded, "What witchery is this?"

"Further," Iago urged. "There is more to see." He went forward another few steps, then looked back, frowning. "Do not delay—oh, come! You must hasten to see! See such wonders as thou never hast aforetime!"

Rod glanced at Gwen, but her face had hardened, and she nodded slowly. "Okay," Rod said, "we're coming."

The children followed, subdued, Magnus's glance flicking from his mother to his father and back, then on to the priest.

Above them, the mountain seemed to melt, like a dish of ice cream left in the sun—revealing a glittering diamond tower at its core.

Iago pushed through a stand of tall grass. The Gallowglasses followed him—and came out into a broad plain. They stopped, and gasped.

The plain was filled with impossible forms, all in pastel colors. Behind them, the sky was all glowing mist, wreathing and curling in continually shifting shapes. The forms themselves weren't all that stable, either—here a giant clock stood in the form of a zero with nine hands, each a number, all revolving at different rates with two turning backward; there a giant beetle crawled before a towering obelisk that had an opaque, multicolored cloud churning about its top. Nearer and to their right, two knights jousted, never touching one another but forever wheeling and charging again. Here the plain suddenly bulged, the mound growing and swelling until it had become a hill, with skids sliding down it; then its northern face began to slump. Down its side a wheel rolled by itself, but as it rolled, it elongated into a cam, flipping along with an eccentric motion; then even the cam slowly changed, warping and squeezing into a long, slender track, then melting on down to disappear into the floor of the plain. But the line of it rose up again in an undulating form, until a hydra writhed where the wheel had melted—but the flailing arms grew heads, and the heads grew bodies and tails, and six snakes crawled away from the place where the hydra had been. As they crawled, though, they changed, one becoming a tapir, another a salamander, a third a raven, and so on.

In fact, all the forms on the plain were constantly in flux, the knights becoming dragons, the clock turning into a windmill, the cloud flowing down over the obelisk and forming a giant beehive. Behind and above all towered the diamond tower, though its surface was hardening and dulling now, beginning to show the mortar lines of masonry.

Over it, and under it and through it, ran the heavy, pulsing beat of the metal stones, snarling and whining back and forth across the plain, audible even through their filters.

Rod clutched at his wife. "Gwen! I'm hallucinating again!"

"Thou art not," she said, clinging to him just as tightly. "I see them too."

"And I," said Magnus, staring, and the other children chorused their agreement.

"Tell me," Rod demanded of Iago, "are any of these things real?"

Iago shrugged. "What is reality?"

"Oh, not again!" Geoffrey groaned. "Wilt thou answer him, Fess?"

Iago looked up, startled.

*He cannot hear me*, Fess reminded them.

"Reality is not a matter of opinion," Gregory informed the priest.

Rod and Gwen stared at their youngest, taken aback. Rod turned to give Fess a narrow glare. But Iago only grinned, and his smile wasn't entirely pleasant. "Then thou shouldst not fear to walk among these dreams."

"Nay, not so," Geoffrey contradicted, "for though these things may not be what they seem, they may nonetheless be summat fearsome."

"*These* things shall not harm you," Iago insisted, "but if you seek to find the center of all this music, you must needs come within." He turned away, walked a few paces, then looked back, as though to ask them whether or not they were coming.

Magnus gazed out over the plain, frowning, but the younger children looked up at Rod and Gwen, who looked at each other; then Gwen said, reluctantly, "We are proof against it."

"So far," Rod agreed. "Fess, what do you see?"

*Only a plain, Rod, with rocky outcrops here and there, and occasionally a grove.*

"You're our touchstone, then. Okay, family, it's psionic—which means we can probably counter everything it can throw. Just remember, kids, that anything you're seeing isn't really there. Stay alert to your mother, and do whatever she does."

"Gramercy for thy confidence," Gwen said sourly. "How wilt thou guard?"

"As you do, of course—and with this." Rod drew his sword. "Just in case."

Steel slickered as Magnus and Geoffrey drew.

"Psi first, boys," Rod cautioned. "Don't start fencing unless I say to—I have a hunch our enemies here aren't going to be soldiers. Fess, tell us if you see anything armed."

*Of course, Rod.*

"After Iago, then. Let's go."

They stepped out onto the plain, and waded into the morass of illusion.

* * *

When they were in the center of the plain, surrounded by strange, transforming shapes, Rod suddenly stopped. "Wait!"

Iago turned back, still smiling but with glittering eyes. "Aye?"

"That—big thing!" Rod pointed. "It was a castle when we first saw it, and then it was a mountain, then a diamond tower, which turned to masonry—but now it's something huge and amorphous."

Iago turned to look. Sure enough, the masonry tower had melted into a sort of bulging obelisk that tapered at the top into a hyperbola. It was a mélange of shifting colors, streaked through with melting bands of various hues, reminding Rod of a silken moiré.

"It doth seem like to a giant chrysalis," Gregory said.

"If that is the chrysalis, brother, Heaven defend me from the butterfly!"

"Is that what you see, Fess?" Rod asked.

*Yes, Rod. It has been coming into view gradually, as the fog has been dispersing.*

Interesting. Whatever it was, was perceptible to visual senses, as well as to psionic.

Iago turned back to them. " 'Tis an odd form, true, but only its latest—and like as not in mid-shift between two forms."

Well, at least now Rod *knew* the man was as befuddled by glamours as they were—or was a liar.

At the base of the giant cocoon, two jets of flame flared.

Rod frowned. "What was that?"

"Let us go see," the priest suggested.

He turned away, and the children started to follow, but Gwen held out a hand to bar their path. "Nay! We shall not move till that changeling mount doth settle to a form!"

"Why, then, let us rest."

The younger boys plumped down cross-legged. Cordelia and Magnus were a bit more graceful about it, but Rod located a stump and a boulder for himself and his wife and sat carefully, hoping they wouldn't melt away beneath him. He looked up to see that Iago had joined the youngsters on the grass, and felt a stab of apprehension at the man's thus identifying himself with the young, virtually declaring that *he* was not a grown-up—he was one of them, and was therefore to be trusted.

His first words weren't exactly encouraging, either. "Wherefore dost thou encumber thyselves with these bulky headgears?"

"So that the music doth not drive us to distraction," Gwen answered.

"Be assured, thou canst accustom thyself to it! Walk among these sounds awhile, and thou wilt scarcely notice them!"

Cordelia began to look uncertain, but Rod said, "That may have been true fifty miles back. Now, though, it's so loud and discordant that we can't possibly block it out."

"Nay, surely! 'Tis merely a matter of learning the joy of it!"

Magnus glanced at Rod, but asked, "Wherefore should we learn to enjoy music that we dislike?"

"Why, for that it will give thee pleasure if thou dost!"

Magnus eyed the man warily, but made no answer.

"That may be true of music that requires knowledge to appreciate," Rod said, "but it doesn't mean you should try to overcome an innate dislike for music that grates on your nerves."

"Oh, nay! 'Tis only a matter of what we are accustomed to," the priest protested. "If you had heard such strains from your cradle, you would love them!"

Cordelia was following the debate, eyes switching from her father to the black-robed priest and back, her face uncertain.

"Somehow, I doubt that," Rod said. "It's not just a matter of music that seems strange—it's a manner of music that's poorly done."

"I assure thee, within its style, it is most expertly made!"

"Thou speakest too kindly, husband," Gwen said, eyes hardening as she watched the priest. "It is not 'poorly done'—it is bad music."

The priest's smile became a little wider, as though it

needed forcing. He swept them all with a glance, then focused his argument on the one who was weakening. "Come, pretty maid! Thou dost know that all thine age do revel in these sounds! Remove thy filters, and immerse thyself in music!"

Slowly, Cordelia reached up to her ears.

"No!" Gwen snapped. "Leave them!"

Cordelia yanked her hands away. "But Mama, all young folk do heed these strains!"

"What 'all'?" Gwen demanded. "I have seen many fond of gentler music, but only a handful here! What reason hast thou to think that they were more than a few who had gathered all together?"

"Why . . . the priest doth say so."

"Thou hast it, pretty maid!" the priest pressed. "Do not let them command thy soul! Think for thyself!"

"Think for yourself, by doing what he says?" Rod let the sarcasm drip. "Who's thinking for you, then?"

"Hearken not to the voices of age, who ken not the virtues of the new!" The priest rallied her.

"Actually, it isn't all that new," Rod said. "It's the same stuff we heard back near Runnymede, only bigger and louder—and not as well done. Maybe they figure that if they make it big enough and bad enough and tell you it's good, you'll believe them."

"But how am I to refute what he doth say?" Cordelia wailed.

"You don't need to! Just say 'No!' "

"But he is a priest!"

"Is he so?" Gwen's eyes narrowed. "Any can pull on a monk's robe and shave a tonsure."

"How durst thou question my vocation!"

"If they will not, I shall," declared an iron voice.

They all looked up, startled, and Geoffrey leaped to his feet, hand going to his sword, mortified—for strangers had come upon them unnoticed, in the midst of the clamor.

Not that they were strangers to worry about—at least, by their looks. They were monks, wearing the plain brown habit of the Order of St. Vidicon, with gentle, smiling faces. One was young, gaunt, and blond, but the other was in his fifties, plump, grizzled, and black.

The children stared, and Gregory sank back against Gwen's skirts.

"Avaunt thee!" the black-robed priest screamed. He leaped up and away, face contorted in loathing, pointing a trembling finger. "They are false monks, they are limbs of Satan! Folk, be not misled—here are demons in the shapes of men!"

"Why, what lies are these?" said the older monk sternly. "We are of St. Vidicon! But thou—what habit's this? What Order dost thou claim!"

"I will not submit to any's orders!" the black-robe screeched. "I am free in heart and mind! I will not suffer those who bow to idols!" He snatched a vial out of his robe, pulled its cork, and snapped it toward the monks. Gray-green droplets spattered, and the Gallowglasses instinctively pulled back.

As did the monks, though a droplet hit the younger one's habit, and burned through it. He gasped with pain, but glared at his shin, and the skin healed where the liquid had burned it.

"See!" the black-robe cried. "Evil burns where the blessed water doth touch!"

"That is not holy water, but corrupted ichor," the elder monk snapped. "What creature are you, who would seek to lead the innocent astray!"

"Lead us astray?" Cordelia was totally confounded. "But he is a priest!"

"Nay," the younger monk told her. "He is a false monk, a Vice, whose purpose is to tempt and corrupt. He is a Judas priest."

"Do not believe him!" the Judas priest screamed. "He speaks with the voice of they who wish no change!"

"We wish all folk to change by kinder conduct, each toward each," the elder monk said, "yet thou wouldst have them debase one another." He pulled on a chain around his neck, drawing a locket from his robe and thumbing open its cover. "Stare within this jewel, and seek to work thine evil if thou canst!"

The Judas priest stared, fascinated. His lips pulled back from his teeth in a hideous grin, emitting a grating whine.

The jewel seemed to come alive, beginning to glow—and the Gallowglasses began to feel it pulse with psi energy.

The Judas priest started to tremble in time to that throbbing. Then the elder monk snapped, "Begone!" and the air cracked in a sudden implosion, kicking up dust. When it settled, the Judas priest had vanished.

The monks relaxed, and the elder closed the locket.

Cordelia stared. "What magic's this?"

"The magic of the jewel within that amulet," the younger monk explained. "It doth transform whatever power a witch or warlock doth use. This Judas priest was the sort of warlock who can bemuse good folk and make them to believe things that they would know for lies if their minds were clear."

"The jewel did take that energy and change it to another form," the elder monk explained, "yet it was for me to choose that form."

"What manner of jewel is this?" Gregory asked in wonder.

"One made by the High Warlock of Gramarye, little one."

"*Thy* rock?" Magnus looked up at his father in surprise.

The elder monk paused in the act of closing the locket. "Art thou the High Warlock, then?"

"I am Rod Gallowglass," Rod acknowledged, "and this is my wife, the Lady Gwendolyn."

"Lady Gallowglass!" The elder monk inclined his head. "I am Father Thelonius, and this is Brother Dorian."

The younger monk also bowed.

Gwen returned the gesture, saying, "And these are my children—Magnus, Cordelia, Geoffrey, and Gregory."

"We wondered how four young ones had stayed safe within this vortex of corruption," the younger monk said, "yet if they came under thy protection, we are answered."

Gwen smiled, but said, "'Tis more that we are their parents, I think, than that we are magical."

But Father Thelonius disagreed. "Would it were so—yet many are the young folk we have seen led astray by just such as this Judas priest, whether their folk were by them or no. They are canny malefactors who do seek to use these music-rocks for their own purposes, look you, and that purpose is to fill their lust for power, and drain the vitalities of a generation. They are cynical, and have learned the worst of human impulses, then have used that knowledge to mislead and warp. Most parents lack such knowledge; they cannot hope to oppose ones who devote their whole attention to beguiling youth."

Magnus and Cordelia shared a horrified glance.

"Yet how knew you this false priest for what he was?" Geoffrey asked.

"Because he did not preach the word of Christ, and His Eucharist," Brother Dorian explained.

Geoffrey eyed them with suspicion. "Yet how may we know that thou art true monks? For surely, having been misled by one friar, I hesitate to trust another!"

"I profess the Christ, and His miracles," Father Thelonius answered, "but most especially His miracle of giving us Himself, in the forms of bread and wine. Will that satisfy thee?"

"No, not quite, I'm afraid," Rod said. "You'll pardon me, good monks, but I find I share some of my son's skepticism, at the moment."

"Then test us as thou wilt," said Brother Dorian.

*Cloistered members of the Order of St. Vidicon,* said Fess's voice inside Rod's head, *are taught at least the rudiments of modern science.*

Rod nodded. "I believe your profession of faith, Father—but can you tell me the Laws of Thermodynamics?"

Brother Dorian stared, but Father Thelonius smiled and said, "*Primus,* that the amount of energy within a closed system is a constant."

"Which is to say," said Brother Dorian, "that human folk

cannot create or destroy energy, only change it from one form to another—as thy rock hath done."

Father Thelonius beamed with approval, then went on. "*Secundus*, that in any flow of energy, entropy will ever increase."

"We must ever strive to maintain harmony and order," Brother Dorian said softly, "but the universe will someday end—and Christ will come again."

*Scientifically, they are accurate,* Fess's voice said, *though I question their theological inferences.*

"We're satisfied," Rod said. "You're real. Sorry about the testing, Reverends."

"Nay, do not be," Father Thelonius said.

And Brother Dorian murmured, "Would the young folk so test those to whose words they hearken. We should always question authority before we accept it."

"But we should listen to the answer," Father Thelonius amended, "and sieve its worth."

Gregory was puzzled. "Please tell, Father, how thou didst govern the action of Papa's jewel."

"Aye," Magnus chimed in, "for he could not."

Rod gave him a gimlet glance, but Gregory pressed, "Didst thou have but to say, 'Begone'?"

"In a manner, yes—but the saying of that word did focus my will, giving an imperative to the forces molded by the jewel. I am a projective myself, though not greatly endowed; if I were, I'd need but the impulse-thought, and would not have to speak the word aloud. Still, I've strength enough to direct the operation of this crystal."

"Why could not the Judas priest have taken its direction from thee?"

"Because he held it not. We have found that whosoever doth touch the jewel doth direct its action."

"Anyone?" Gregory exclaimed, saucer-eyed.

"Anyone who doth know the manner of using it, aye."

"Then where is thy squadron of knights, to protect thee?" Geoffrey cried. "Where is thine army of guardians? For surely, if that Rock did fall into the hands of one who wished to exploit others for his own use, he could wreak great havoc!"

"Aye, we know," Father Thelonius said, his face grim. "Yet there was no time to send for guardsmen, for our Abbot did heed the words of his thought-sentinels, who did say that there was a hideous force building on this West Coast, seeking to capture and twist the power of the music-rocks to enslave the folk."

Rod found it interesting that the new Abbot had monks mentally scanning the island for trouble. That could be a blessing—or a curse. "So there was no time to send to the King for aid?"

"Aye; he could only send out teams of us to counsel and advise, and myself—with Brother Dorian to watch o'er me—to find the evil soul that doth seek to misdirect the power of music, then to wield the Warlock Rock against him."

"Yet if thou wert taken . . ." Geoffrey protested.

"None other could wield the Rock, for they know not the manner of it," Father Thelonius assured him.

"Yet if they chanced to discover it . . . !"

"They won't." Rod clasped his son's shoulder. "Because as of now, they've got the best guardians they could ask for, haven't they?"

Geoffrey turned to him, startled, then drew himself up, eyes alight. "Aye, sir!" He turned back to the two monks. "Thou shalt not take a step that we shall not shadow!"

Father Thelonius inclined his head gravely, to hide his smile. "We shall walk in thy debt."

"Nay, for thou hast banished that false priest that might have swayed us." Geoffrey's glance lit on Magnus and Cordelia.

"What mistrust is this?" Magnus demanded, and Cordelia said hotly, "We were tempted, aye—yet now our eyes are cleared, and we will no longer be misled!"

"Yes." Rod smiled. "As long as you keep your ear mufflers on."

"Then let us go forward in company." Father Thelonius held out a hand, and Geoffrey fell into step beside him.

So they strode onward into the world of illusion, a family led by a boy and a middle-aged monk. The melting forms rose and fell about them—but, strangely, seemed to part and make way for the two monks.

As they went, Rod stepped up beside Father Thelonius and murmured, "A word with you apart, Reverend, if you would."

The holy man looked up with a smile—and without surprise. "Surely." He turned to Brother Dorian and murmured a few words, then turned back to Rod. "At your disposal, Lord Warlock."

"I hope not—I wasn't planning to be disposed of, yet." Rod lengthened his stride, to put a little space between himself and the rest of the family.

"But I had heard you were a man of excellent disposition," Father Thelonius protested.

Rod winced. "Whoever told you that, don't believe him—but I *am* predisposed in favor of your Order."

"I rejoice to hear it," the monk said softly. "But what did you wish to discuss, Lord Warlock?"

"Just wanted to know how things are on Terra."

The monk took it without batting an eyelash. "They are well at the moment, Lord Warlock. Are there so few Blacks on Gramarye that you could tell me for a foreigner at one glance?"

"Right on the first guess, Father. There's the occasional folk tale, from which I gather that the chromosomes link up now and then—but I've never met anyone who wasn't Caucasian, here."

That startled the monk. "Really! Well, that explains your children's reaction on seeing me. I would have thought the original colonists would have included a few people of my race."

"They probably did—but after five hundred years of intermarriage, I would expect their genes to be so thoroughly dispersed among the population that they wouldn't show much. May I ask why Father Al didn't come himself?"

"Because there was no cause for concern."

"No *cause* . . . !"

"None that we knew of at the time." The monk raised a hand, palm out. "It was simply good luck that I happened to arrive at a time when I could be of use. Father Aloysius Uwell sends his regards, of course, but didn't know there was any particular reason for him to come himself."

"Well, I'm glad to hear he's well, at least," Rod sighed. "So he didn't have a hunch about things going wrong here on Gramarye?"

"Not in this case. I am not here in response to any emergency, Commander Gallowglass. . . ."

It had been long years since anyone had called Rod by his military title. It felt odd, somehow—strangely ill-fitting.

". . . nor to any concern of the Vatican's. I am only here out of scholarly interest."

Rod couldn't dispute anyone else's right to visit the planet—after all, it wasn't his personal property. Nonetheless, he said, "I would have appreciated your checking in with me, Father—just as a matter of courtesy, if nothing else. I do have some concern about who's visiting and who isn't."

"I understand, Lord Warlock—and my apologies for not having contacted you immediately. I had intended to, but had scarcely acclimatized myself before the Abbot asked me to attend to this little problem that has come up."

"Scarcely 'little'—it's one of the larger threats I've seen. I hope that means you'll be able to take care of it easily?"

"Sadly, no—I am an excellent scholar, but not terribly able as an engineer."

Rod had heard the same thing before, from men who had moved mountains with little help—or asteroids, at least, which could be classified as flying mountains. "How are you on R&D?"

"Research and development? Oh, I'm quite able—as long as I have a laboratory assistant." He nodded toward Brother Dorian. "This young fellow seems very competent. He's Gramarye-born, by the way."

"That's reassuring. Should I interpret this to mean that

the Abbot gave you a local guide, but expects you to solve the problem?"

"Oh, no! Brother Dorian is much more than a guide. He is quite talented, and very skilled for so young a man."

Rod noticed who was left solving the problem, though. "Skilled in what area?"

"As a musician. And a projective."

"Oh." Rod left his lips in the form of the letter. He glanced at the younger monk, chatting amiably with Gregory and Cordelia. "Isn't music a little—odd, for an engineer?"

"Not entirely, when you consider that he is continually trying to learn more about the interrelationships between psionic powers and music."

Insight exploded in Rod's mind. "Perfect combination, in light of the current crisis. But everybody thought what he was doing was pure research, without any practical application?"

"Oh, it was—until now."

"Yes, of course." Rod nodded. "As soon as you find some use for it, you stop calling it pure research. Might I infer, Father, that his interest is in some way allied to your own?"

"Quite accurately." The black man smiled. "I trained as an electrical engineer and managed to make a living designing musical intruments. But the more heavily involved I became, the more I realized that the computer programs involved might bear some resemblance to the musician's mental processes—and the more deeply I delved into that, the more I became convinced that musical talent had some kinship to psionic talent. Then, of course, I began speculating on the nature of talent—which led me to my vocation, and the Order."

"Of course." Actually, Rod didn't really see any link between talent and religion, but he wasn't about to open that topic just then. "So your research led you to Gramarye."

"To the only pool of operant espers in known space, yes—and I seem to have arrived at the ideal time for my researches."

"Ideal for us, too. When this is all over, I'll have to introduce you to Ari the Crafter—but only if you promise not to try to lock him up in a laboratory."

"The man who made these musical rocks? Excellent! But in the meantime, I think we have to deal with people whose talents may be exceptional, but are devoted to using music rather than making it."

"You mean they want to make a living from music, but don't want to go to the trouble of learning how to play?"

"I see you're familiar with the syndrome. Yes, the idea seems to be that if you have the talent, you don't need to learn anything—it will all come naturally, without any effort. It doesn't, of course—and in their disappointment, the young hopefuls become cynics, seeking to exploit those who have taken the time and trouble to learn how to play."

"And you think we're facing such a person?"

"It is possible. Certainly the young woman—excuse me, she might not be young, might she?—the woman, this Ubu Mare I've heard of, seeks to use music to gain power and status, not for the sheer exhilaration of it."

"She's getting something out of it, that's for certain—and doesn't mind who gets hurt in the process."

"Ever the way of them." Father Thelonius sighed, shaking his head. "We have known them for a long time, Lord Warlock—the vampires who batten on people's souls, who drain the joys and hopes of youth as Dracula drained the heart's blood, leaving only dessicated carcasses behind. We have fought them, they who seek to grow rich from works that should be freegiven, since Philip the Deacon turned the people of Samaria away from the sorcerer. We have protected the weak and gullible from these wolves for three millenia and more, and we will protect them now."

"Then we'd better hurry," Rod told him, "because the wolves are coming in packs these days."

"Haven't they always?" Father Thelonius flashed him a smile. "Be of good cheer, Lord Warlock—vampires thrive by night, but we bring the sun."

# 25

Brother Dorian said, "It cannot be much farther now, for I do sense such a morass of psi power about me that I feel as though I wade."

"Morass of psi?" Rod looked up in surprise. "I thought it was the music!"

"Mayhap 'tis psi power reflected through the music-rocks," Gregory suggested.

Rod stared at him. "A field of psi power that's active even though it's separated from the crafter who began it? I never heard of such a thing!"

"That will not prevent it from being invented, Papa," Cordelia pointed out.

"No, apparently not," Rod said, feeling numb.

"What are these music-rocks, if not just such an invention, husband?" Gwen said gently.

"Yes," Rod acknowledged. "It does make sense, doesn't it? Sorry to be the slow one in the family."

"Thou art not." Gwen squeezed his arm. "None of us could have seen it, plain though it was, had it not been for these good friars."

"And for thy bauble, Papa," Gregory piped up.

"Why, yes," Rod said, feeling stunned, "that was kind of the main clue, wasn't it?" Then he snapped out of his mental fog. "No, it wasn't! That's technology, not magic!"

Gwen only raised her eyebrows.

"I know, I know," Rod conceded. "Don't say it."

"Father," Cordelia said to Thelonius, "if the Judas priest sought to mislead us—where was't he sought to mislead us to?"

"Aye," added Magnus, "and wherefore?"

Father Thelonius shook his head. "I can but conjecture, children."

"Then do," Gregory urged.

The monk sighed. "I fear he meant to lead thee into bondage, to enslave thee to the sorcerer who hath gained dominion over this fall of rock."

"For what purpose?" Cordelia asked.

"I cannot tell," Father Thelonius said, with a dark frown. "Mayhap to be a sacrifice to his fell purpose."

"What is a sacrifice?" Gregory asked.

"Never mind, little brother," Magnus put in quickly. "In any event, 'tis but conjecture."

"It is," Father Thelonius agreed. "I cannot tell to what purpose he would have warped thee—nor do I wish to."

"Nor," said Magnus, "do we."

"Rod," Fess said, "whatever that amorphous shape before us may be, it bodes ill. Perhaps you should leave the younger children behind under my care."

"Good idea," Rod said, but Geoffrey whirled. "Nay! Assuredly thou shalt not bid me bide when the fighting hath at last begun!"

Father Thelonius looked up in mild surprise. "Truly, good folk, there is no great danger yet."

"Let us at least discern what perils lurk, ere we dispose our forces," Brother Dorian urged.

Geoffrey looked up, amazed. "Thou speakest well, for a monk!"

"And thou," Brother Dorian returned, "dost speak well, for an aspiring warrior. Shall we not go see, then?"

"No." Gwen spoke with decision, unlimbering her broom. "Prithee, friars, let us go no farther till I have seen what I may, from above."

The monks exchanged a quick glance, but Rod said, "Let's try it her way, if you don't mind, Father. She's almost never wrong."

Gwen halted in the act of leaping on her broomstick, staring at him. "Almost?"

"Well," Rod said, "there was that time you tried putting saffron in the . . ."

"It matters naught," she said quickly. "Be ready, husband!" Her broomstick shot up into the air.

The two friars started, then watched after her, wide-eyed.

"I take it you've never seen a witch ride a broomstick before?" Rod inquired gently.

"Nay," Brother Dorian answered. "We dwell in a monastery, seest thou, and 'tis a female's talent. . . ."

"What did she bid thee be ready for?" Father Thelonius asked.

"Just in case she runs into trouble—which we both doubt. But just in case."

"She had no need to say it," Magnus protested.

"No, but it made us both feel better."

"Papa," said Cordelia, "in what did she put the saffron?"

Rod took a deep breath, thinking fast, but he was saved, because suddenly Gwen's broomstick shot upward, then back and to the side, as though some huge hand had slapped her away—and, for a moment, she was falling.

Rod didn't even remember taking off; all he knew was that he was halfway to her, and she was halfway to the ground, when the broomstick pulled out of its tumble and came swooping back toward him.

*I am well*, Gwen assured him, even before she came into earshot. *Yet there is danger there that will take greater preparation than we have made.*

Rod went limp with relief, which is not entirely safe in midair. He hovered till she was alongside, then flew next to her. "What did you see?" But Gwen was nosing her broomstick up for a landing, and he had to jump down beside her.

"Most amazing!" Brother Dorian was shaking his head in admiration. "Few of our monks can fly so well, and none so quickly!"

"Oh, Mama!" Cordelia flung her arms around her mother and squeezed. "We feared for thee!"

And her boys were around her, too, with shaky grins and sweaty brows.

She embraced Cordelia, allowing herself a little smile. "Peace, sweet chuck. 'Twill take more than a wall unseen to best me."

"An invisible wall?" Brother Dorian looked up sharply.

Gwen nodded. "I had just come close enough to begin to see what stood at the base of the tower, when I jolted into a barrier that gave, then hurled me back. But in that time, I had seen a mass of people, and a dais with flaring torches."

"That hath an ominous sound." Father Thelonius scowled. "Canst say more clearly?"

"Nay," Gwen said, "for I had but glimpsed it ere I fell."

"We must see more," the priest said, rubbing his chin, "but how?"

*I have a surveillance device, Rod,* Fess advised silently.

"Come to think of it, you do." Rod turned to the robot, eyes lighting.

"Be not concerned—he is well," Gwen assured the two monks. " 'Tis only that his horse can talk to him when none others can hear."

Now it was *her* they were looking at as though she were crazy. Then they smiled apologetically and turned away, taking it on faith.

The metal egg popped out of Fess's saddle again. Rod saw the monks' faces, and smiled. "The horse is a robot, Reverends."

Their heads lifted; they smiled. They did, at least, know the basics of technology.

So they weren't too surprised when the sphere drifted up

into the air, then winged away toward the giant cocoon. "It will seek out what sight lieth there?" Father Thelonius asked.

"Yes," Rod said, "and show it to us on a built-in screen."

"So many of us shall see little on so small a screen," Geoffrey said plaintively.

"Well, let me see." Rod frowned.

*I can monitor the video in progress, Rod,* Fess contributed.

"Yeah." Rod's face lit up. "And we can all monitor Fess. He's telepathic with the family, Reverends. If you can read *our* minds, you can see it, too."

Brother Dorian smiled and closed his eyes, concentrating.

"My talent is weak," Father Thelonius lamented, "yet we are so close that mayhap I shall see summat." He closed his eyes, too.

Rod kept his open, just in case, so that the image relayed through Fess was superimposed dimly over his surroundings, like a vacation remembered during a conversation.

The viewpoint was high, looking down on the plain as the spy-eye skimmed toward the cocoon. Then Rod saw the mob at the tower's base, and the slab flanked by flares of fire. The image grew larger; the spy-eye was swooping lower. Whatever barrier had stopped Gwen had no power over Cold Iron, or even an aluminum alloy. The image became larger, clearer . . .

And Rod saw an altar flanked by huge, oily torches, all set down in a pit, a sort of amphitheater, jammed full of people who seemed to have absolutely nothing in common except dirt and disorder. They wore all manner of clothing, in a range of colors that was guaranteed only to clash—but they achieved consensus in voice and motion. They chanted and swayed in time to a dimly heard beat, overlaid with snarling tones. Before the altar, facing them, stood a woman in a robe that was all flashes of metallic light against dark cloth, moving in some arcane ritual involving a huge knife and a staff—but her movements were abrupt, random, almost palsied.

The giant cocoon that overshadowed them all drew Rod's attention, as it must have drawn the attention of anyone looking upon the scene—for it was, very clearly, a vast stationary whirlwind. What could have held it in place, what could have enclosed it to prevent it doing damage, Rod could scarcely imagine—perhaps some new and immensely powerful form of psi. Even its noise was muted and distant, as though shut away—a constant roar that was only a background for the grating music of the ceremony before it.

The picture abruptly filled with flames. The children cried out, pressing their hands over their eyes and turning away. Gwen's head snapped up as she and Rod broke their connection with Fess instantly. They were all silent for a moment, staring at one another.

Then Father Thelonius said, " 'Tis well we did watch through thy robot, whiles we could."

"Yes," Rod said, feeling numb. "Not much question about it, is there? The sorceress saw we were watching, and blew that spy-eye to bits." Almost involuntarily, he reached out and caught Gwen's hand. She returned the pressure, knowing his panic at the notion that it could have been she who was so destroyed, reassuring him that she was still there, still alive and vibrant.

*We can make another surveillance device, Rod.*

"Glad to hear it. Uh, I don't suppose there's any chance you recorded that episode, is there?"

*Of course I did, Rod—that is standard operating procedure. Do you wish to review it?*

"Yes, it's recorded," Rod informed the monks. "Anyone want to see it again?"

"Aye." There was a sudden grim intensity about Father Thelonius. "An we can, I must study that sight, Lord Warlock."

"And its sounds," Brother Dorian added, scowling.

They closed their eyes, concentrating on the link with Rod's mind.

He saw it again, the flight over the plain, the crowd in the amphitheater, the torches. . . .

"There is a cross inverted betwixt the flames," Father Thelonius said.

The children looked up, shocked.

In the image, the sorceress before the altar suddenly threw off her robe and danced naked.

She didn't have the body for it.

Then the flames came, and instantly, the scene disappeared.

"The sound is wrong." Brother Dorian's eyebrows drew down. "Canst review it backwards?"

"Backwards?" Rod asked in surprise. "Well, I guess . . ."

*Surely,* Fess said, and the picture disappeared. Then, a moment later, came the sound of the chanting—and Rod broke out of the playback, looking up, startled. "Latin!"

"Aye." Brother Dorian had turned grim. "Latin, chanted backwards."

"Inversion, reversion, perversion . . ." Father Thelonius' face twisted with disgust. "They seek to enact the Black Sabbath."

"Trying to worship the *devil?*"

Gwen was horrified, and the younger children, shaken by the thought, crowded closer to her almost without realizing it. Magnus stepped a little nearer to Rod.

"That is what they attempt," Father Thelonius said. "All they achieve is the sacrificing of what little power of psi they have to the hag."

"But what can have led them to this?" Cordelia protested.

Father Thelonius' eyes met Rod's and Gwen's.

Magnus saw the look, and knew its meaning. "Thou canst not mean 'twas the music!"

Father Thelonius nodded heavily. "I do so mean. This woman before the altar—'tis she who hath beguiled the crafter into twisting the music of his rocks, who hath gathered and dispersed them, to win herself followers and gain some measure of worldly power."

"And she gains it," Rod asked, "by combining the minimal talents of ordinary people?"

"Aye, and strengthens them by the basest of their emotions—which, though less powerful than love or compassion, are more easily evoked."

"And that tower of wind behind her," said Gwen, "is the repository of their powers."

"Gathered and compressed, aye, and churning the air into a maelstrom."

"But what can hold it bound?" Gregory asked.

"She doth hold the churning winds within the envelope of her own mind's force—for she, at least, is an esper of genuine power."

"A psi-made tornado," Rod breathed, "held in a cell of pure force—a cysted twister."

But Gwen shook her head. "It cannot be her mind unaided. If she were so powerful a witch, I'd ha' heard of her ere now."

"There could be aids," Rod said slowly, thinking of high-tech devices.

"But what hath led her to so foul an end?" Cordelia exclaimed.

Father Thelonius shook his head. "I can but conjecture."

"So can I," Magnus said darkly. "This much we know—that she is the ugliest witch in the land."

Cordelia glared at him, incensed, but before she could argue, Rod asked, "Now that she has managed to gather some power, what does she intend to do with it?"

"To gather more, of course. That is ever the way of power," Brother Dorian said, and Father Thelonius nodded.

Rod caught at Fess's saddle for support, staggered by a sudden vision of witch-moss rocks imbued with hate, greed, and lust, flying out from this plain of delusion, sped onward with all the power of the chained minds of the mob, gaining more and more converts to the worst of human nature—and the worst of the new fanatics finding their way back here, to contribute their own hatred and self-contempt to the swelling power of the emotional sink. "It could be the end of all that's good in Gramarye," he whispered.

He was aware of a strong hand on his arm and opened his eyes to see his wife's face, taut with concern. He forced a weak smile, managed to stand away from Fess, and turned to the monks.

Father Thelonius met him with a steady, grave gaze, nodding slowly. "Therefore can we not allow this obscenity to continue."

"But how can we stop it?"

"We have powers of our own." Father Thelonius touched the amulet. "Yet even without this jewel, there is great virtue in the yearning for right. We shall focus that—the aching for goodness and order, for love and compassion, gentleness and understanding, that is locked away in the hearts of us all. We shall focus and condense it, and pit it against that hideous chaos."

"Well said." Rod frowned. "Now, how about the engineering?"

Brother Dorian smiled and drew a long leather case out of his robe.

The children stepped forward, curiosity swelling.

Brother Dorian untied the case, and drew out . . .

An artifact of advanced technology.

Rod's eyes widened. "You *made* that?"

Brother Dorian shook his head, and Father Thelonius said softly, "We do remember the arts that the rest of humankind do own, mind—yet in this case, 'twas sent us from Terra."

It was a keyboard, with a full set of built-in visual synthesizers and subsonic modulators.

"You really know how to *use* that?" Rod asked skeptically, but Brother Dorian answered with a very serene smile. He extended the legs of the keyboard and set it up for playing.

"What is it?" Magnus asked.

"Listen," Brother Dorian said, "and watch."

His fingers moved over the keys, and a lilting melody arose. It wasn't nearly as loud as the rock music around them, but somehow it compelled attention, making the snarling and whining seem to recede into the background.

The children were transfixed.

A mist of glowing mauve formed in the air above Brother Dorian. Then, moving in synchronization with the music, it thickened, swirling, and churned itself into the form of a drooping flower bud. As the music built, the flower quickened, blooming and opening, lifting its face to the sun. It faded as the music swept down to a hush—and now, where the melody had been, a series of squeaks and chirps began. The children knelt hushed, recognizing the sounds of small woodland animals and birds—but what were they doing here on a plain?

Then they appeared, off to the side of the keyboard—foxes, badgers, mice, pheasants, hedgehogs—gathered in a semicircle, staring spellbound.

"What do they see?" Gwen whispered.

It was almost as though the music shaped itself to answer, swirling and settling into physical form—the figure of a small man with blue skin, clad only in a fur loincloth, a wreath of flowers in his hair and a flute at his lips. They could hear his piping, clear and flowing, and as he played, a small dancing shape appeared between him and the small furry creatures, a tiny elfin being, whose pirouettes whirled it so fast that it became a spot of light.

Then it dimmed as the music faded—and the small man and his creatures faded with it, disappearing, gone. The music took on a bittersweet, nostalgic quality, that both regretted and promised renewal—and ended.

The children were silent for a few breaths, and it seemed that even the music-rocks held their peace.

Then Rod realized the twanging and bonging was still going on around them, and the children released their breaths in a concerted sigh. "Wondrous!" Cordelia said, and Geoffrey added, "Thou art a magician!"

"Aye, certes," said Magnus, his eyes on the monk, "for thou art of the cloister of St. Vidicon, not of a parish. Thou art a wizard, art thou not?"

"Only in this," Brother Dorian demurred, "only in my music."

"Yet that is his magic," said Father Thelonius, "not the instrument alone."

"Yes, there is psi power in that, isn't there?" Rod mused. "You're a genius, Brother Dorian."

"Not I," the monk protested, though he flushed with pleasure. "Not I, but he who composed this piece."

"I could almost believe that such magic as this could counter the power of that fell maelstrom," Gwen said.

"It can! I assure thee, it can!" Brother Dorian said, his eyes bright. "Yet not alone."

"No, not alone," Father Thelonius agreed, "but with other instruments to aid it, and the power of a sacred ceremony to counter the vicious impulses drawn by the sorceress's profane ritual, we may hope to build a strength of psi power that will stand against it."

"Not just us eight," Rod protested.

"Aye, not we alone," Father Thelonius agreed, "for there are twelve-score monks in the monastery who shall sing and play, and shall link their upwelling of hope and serenity to ours."

"Why, how shall this be?" asked Gregory.

"It is the talent of our choirmaster, little one—the blending of musics, and the sharing of their power with those who have need of it, no matter how far removed—for he is a man for distances."

"A tele-man?" Rod asked. "And you'll be linked to him?"

"Aye, and he to all of us. We must have a meeting of minds, seest thou, a concert indeed."

"But how shall we aid?" Cordelia wondered.

Brother Dorian smiled and came around the keyboard, taking small instruments from hiding places within his robe. "Why, thou shalt play with me, as the spirt moves thee. Youngest one, a pipe for thee." He gave Gregory a wooden flute. "And a harp for the lass."

Cordelia took the wooden frame, gazing at it, caressing it. "But I have not the time to learn to play!"

"Thou hast but to sweep the strings, for they are tuned in harmony. A tambour for the warrior-lad." Brother Dorian handed Geoffrey a sort of shallow drum, a tambourine without the bangles, and a stick with a head on each end. "Strike the skin in time to the lowest notes I shall sound. And thou, O eldest son, shalt have an heir's portion." He held out a flat slab as long as his forearm and as wide, with four inset plates for the right hand and and six pressure-pads for the left. Magnus took it, frowning, and pressed one plate. A chord sounded, seeming to come from the air before his face. He almost dropped the instrument. "But how shall I know when to press which?"

"Thou shalt feel the impulse from me, for I have just such plates and pads upon my board."

"Yet wherefore should we play," Cordelia asked, "if we know not how?"

"Because," said Brother Dorian, "there is great power for good in the innocence of youth."

Father Thelonius nodded. "That is why such innocence is so great a threat to those who wreak evil—and why they are so eager to corrupt it."

Rod gave the monk a measuring gaze. "You seem to have this awfully well planned out, Father."

"Aye." Father Thelonius looked up with a smile from where he was gathering brushwood. " 'Tis for this we were sent, Lord Warlock—to keep the domain of vengeful music from increasing, and to push it back if we may."

Rod watched him silently for a minute. Then he said, "No wonder you found us."

"Aye." Brother Dorian smiled. "No wonder at all."

Rod was tempted to ask why Father Thelonius was gathering sticks, but decided he didn't want to know.

Brother Dorian turned back to the junior Gallowglasses. "Thou must attune thyselves to me, young ones, so that we may make sound together—and that blending of musics will increase the linking of our minds."

"Then we must be linked with thee, too," Gwen stated.

"Thou must indeed." Father Thelonius locked gazes with them—and, suddenly, the atmosphere was grim. "Thou must needs be at one with all of us—thy children, ourselves, and the monks in the monastery."

Rod was almost afraid to ask: "And how shall we make music?"

"Thou shalt not."

They stared at him in silence for a long moment. Then Gwen asked, "What shall we do?"

"Thou shalt fly sped by melody," said Father Thelonius, "for someone must bear the Warlock's Rock into that unholy place, to turn the witch's power back upon herself."

They were very quiet, the children stock-still, chilled with dread.

Rod wasn't exactly feeling warmed himself, but he swallowed and nodded. "Okay, Father. Give it to me. Someone has to stop her."

"Nay," Gwen snapped. "Whither thou goest, I will go. 'Twas into my keeping thou didst give the jewel, husband." And she stepped forward, bowing her head.

Father Thelonius nodded, slipping the chain over his head and holding it out.

"No!" Rod protested. "One of us at risk is enough!"

"Yet life would never be enough for me without thee," Gwen returned. "I beg thee, Father."

He slipped the chain over her head.

Gwen straightened, then turned to her eldest. She rested a hand lightly on his shoulder. "If we should miscarry, do thou care for thy sister and brothers."

Eyes huge, Magnus nodded.

"And thou." Gwen gave the other three her sternest look. "Do thou heed and obey him."

Wide-eyed, they nodded slowly.

"Take care of them, Fess," Rod said softly.

"I will at need, Rod—yet I hope that need shall not come."

"Yes." Rod smiled, and broke the spell. "What's a mere coven, against a cloister-ful of psionic monks and a family of espers? Even if they *are* reinforced by the more depraved emotions of an eighth of the souls of Gramarye." He turned to Father Thelonius. "What ceremony is this you'll be performing to the music, Father?"

The monk turned back from draping a linen cover over a table improvised out of stones and scrub. "It will be the Mass of Light."

# 26

It was the Missa Lubba, actually, blending the traditional meolodies of the Latin Mass with African rhythms, and coupling the highest aspirations of both cultures. The *Kyrie* rang in Rod's head as he strode beside his wife into the domain of a warped witch. The landscape about him seemed dim and remote; all his attention was on channelling his psi powers now. He was forgetting himself, becoming aware only of his anxiety for his wife, and the power filling him; he didn't really notice that Fess was following them.

Nightmare shapes grew, collapsed, and flowed on every side, for they went on foot to escape detection, detouring around newly risen forms of distorted dancing bodies, hideous faces with leering grins, and monstrous forms that comprised parts of three or four animals; but the illusions were only that, and seemed unaware of their passage. Their nature finally became clear to Rod, with the impact of insight—they were the nightmares of the souls before him, warped and twisted by their own depravity, images of foulness called up out of the depths of the subconcious by the perversion of an art form that had begun as a vivacious celebration of youth and life, but had been twisted to the titillation of the jaded and vicious, corrupted into a medium for the evoking of cruelty and degradation.

Then they were through, quite suddenly, on the lip of the amphitheater. Only a hundred feet away, the naked witch cavorted in an obscene and insulting dance, beating time for the chanting that focused the sickened hungers of a thousand souls, drawing tenfold psychic energy from the raw emotions of bemused and baffled young.

They paused on the brink to clasp hands; then they plunged into the mass of people, driving straight toward the witch.

Fess followed, immune to illusion and relentless in purpose.

Rod's ears were filled with the *Gloria;* only dimly, in the distance, could he hear the roaring and thumping of the metallic music. As if by coincidence, the people before them shifted aside, or turned away with the force of the wind, so that they seemed to move in a spreading path, a furrow through the human mass. But neighbors looked up, rouged and whitened faces stared, arms in patchwork sleeves raised up pointing fingers. Suddenly they were surrounded by tunics that glittered but were quartered with dun, by hands lifting cutlasses and sabres and scythes and spindles. Pitchforks and rusty swords speared at them; rouged and chapped lips stretched over rotted teeth in howling glee.

But Rod and Gwen couldn't hear them, for a choir filled their world with harmony, and the blades rebounded inches away from them, whiplashes slashed but did not touch them, and the ragtag horde rolled back from them like a bow wave as they plowed through the sorceress's motley crew on wings of unseen song.

The witch saw them, though, and had time to ready herself, reaching behind her to draw on the power of the storm, gathering in and drawing up the strength of sickened souls, then lashing out an arm, a taloned finger pointing at them. They could almost see the bolt of thought that rocked them, made their heads ring. For a moment, Rod could see only a wash of red, hear only a roaring. He shook his head, cried out, strove to hear again the sound of song, then looked up to see the sorceress's minions pulling themselves up off the rocky floor, dazed by crashing blows from steel hooves—and a steel horse, legs stiff, head swinging, beset by too many enemies, too many sights and sounds, seized by unconsciousness.

Then Rod saw Gwen go down, too, and his anger erupted. He dropped to one knee, cradling his wife in his arms, and all the rage that he had ever felt, all the buried angers, leaped up and shot out from him in white-hot fury.

The sorceress staggered back and would have fallen—but his mental blow slammed her against the side of her immense reservoir of vice. She straightened slowly, seeming to swell up larger than human, eyes widening into moons, filling with corrupted power, becoming a channel for her own creation.

Then she released all her hatred toward him, all her sickened fury for the world that had disdained her, aimed at the High Warlock.

But Gwen had pulled herself up, supported by Rod's chest and shoulder, and held up the amulet as a barrier between themselves and the witch.

The sorceress's eyes bulged; her skin seemed to go taut as the hatred she'd released rebounded on her. There was no bolt of energy, no explosion, no flare of all-consuming fire—only a sudden slackness as she slumped and went limp, her eyes rolling up.

A wave of nausea swept Rod as he felt her memories fleet through him and past him; then she was gone, and only an empty hulk fell off from the giant cocoon behind her.

Dimly, Rod could hear the snarling music halt as, all around them, a despairing moan rose up to a wail. Then it slackened and died—but eyes kindled with glee, crooked teeth gleamed in gloating grins, and the grinding music rose up again, to decorate the whirlwind's roar.

"She set up a feedback circuit!" Rod shouted. "She started something she couldn't control—she could only be a conduit for it! It was burning her out—but it became self-sustaining, it's still going!"

With a howl, the sorceress's minions fell on them.

But a choir of voices lifted in exultation within Rod and Gwen; incense seemed to wreathe them, and Gwen spread her hands in an open fan. Inches away, the human jetsam jarred to a halt, then shrank back with howls of fright.

Gwen didn't notice; she was concentrating on the huge cocoon, her eyes narrowed. "Husband, 'tis no power of mind that doth hold that force of minds chained."

Rod's eyes were fixed on his wife.

Then, cradling her in his arm, he rose to his feet, lifting her, and moved, step by step, toward the altar.

"What dost thou?" Gwen cried.

"If it isn't psi, it's tech," he answered, "and if it's built, the builders put in controls."

Gwen stared; then her eyes lost focus as her mind sought out electron paths. "The altar," she said. "There is a reactor buried in it, and a valve to hold it."

The miasma of evil surrounding the altar was enough to make Rod dizzy—and nauseous; he wondered what deeds had been done there. He clung to Gwen, who wasn't in much better shape—but together they held each other up as they rounded the huge stone block.

The coven saw and moaned with sick horror, but were too weakened to do much. A few clambered toward them, but far too slowly.

Rod and Gwen tottered in the shadow of the huge cocoon; its roaring drowned out the sound of the choir. That was scary enough, but the true fear was in realizing what might happen when the force that chained the whirlwind was released. *If this is it, my only,* Rod thought, *know that I love you.*

It almost melted her. *And I thee, my love—forever!*

Then Gwen's hand found the patch, and pressed.

Then universe erupted in an explosion that surpassed their ability to hear. Roaring filled the world, roaring and a tumbling whirl of light that sent them spinning off into the void, still clinging tightly to one another in overwhelming, all-consuming fear.

Then the world steadied and clarified—above them. Rod realized they were out of whatever had happened, were out but still flying away, up. He longed for the earth with sudden, frantic hope of survival, then with a surge of fear for his children. The world rocked about them, sideslipped, and swung beneath them. They looked down, and found that same world rushing up at them.

A world devoid of an amphitheater now—only a huge, ragged hole in the rock. The plain about it was blasted raw for half a mile in every direction, but a handful of ants well beyond that had to be his children and the two monks. Then Rod could feel it through Gwen, the frantic fear and hope borne on the tranquility of the chant, and knew his children were alive and safe.

Finally, he could look for the psi storm.

*We fall,* Gwen reminded him, panic controlled now.

Somewhere, she'd lost her broomstick. Rod thought about the earth, and their descent slowed and stopped. They hovered a thousand feet above the ground, watching the whirlwind move around and about in a widening spiral.

"It could do some damage that way," Rod called into Gwen's ear. "Let's give it a little push, shall we?"

She nodded, and he knew again the sweetness of her mind joined with his, as they stared at the churning cloud, freed from its chrysalis now. Slowly, it began to move out of its circle, farther and farther, in a lengthening arc.

"Lift," she called, and the storm ascended, high enough to roar over the distant hills that stood between the plain and the coast.

Beyond glittered the sea.

Concentrating all their energy, they pushed and kept pushing and, slowly, the maelstrom moved away, over the shore, over the waves, until it was only a smudge on the horizon—a smudge that spread, and widened, and dissipated.

"The trade winds," Rod called. "The winds that follow

the current from the mainland. They tore it apart, shredded it."

Gwen nodded. "And the evil powers with it. They are tattered, and have lost their strength."

"We won," Rod said, marvelling. "The good guys."

Then he remembered where they were. "Can I collapse now?"

She looked up at him with a weary smile. "Not quite yet, prithee. Set me first upon the earth."

# 27

They came back to find Brother Dorian still at his keyboard, and the children, caught up in his music, still with their instruments. Rod paused to watch, astonished—the sound of the pipe and tambour, the sweeps of the harp and the doubled pure-tone chords, all fitted perfectly with Brother Dorian's melody, punctuating and underscoring it as though they, too, were parts of his instrument.

All about them, angels danced.

At least, if angels could really be seen, they might have looked like this—no wings or long white robes, but abstract glowing forms, fluxing and shifting in time to the music. The pillars of a cathedral soared up around them, pillars that seemed real even though Rod could see through them, supporting a dome inlaid with abstract designs that somehow blended tranquility with excitement.

Around them wreathed the aroma of incense.

Father Thelonius finished veiling the chalice and looked up to give them a taut smile. He started toward them, but Rod could see his strain and held up a palm. The monk stopped, nodding his thanks, then stilled as his eyes lost focus.

Rod glanced at Gwen; she nodded, and the two of them opened their minds to the concert Brother Dorian led.

It was glorious—a heavenly choir singing to the tones of massed strings, with trumpets now and again gliding high above. The tones of the children's instruments were there, though subtle, and nowhere nearly as vivid as their delight. Rod sensed a hundred souls or more, all welcoming, all exalted with the beauty of the music and the glory of their praising; the beneficence of their purpose was still there, but less important than the wonder of the experience itself.

Gwen's mind blended with his own, and they saw together why the choir still sang, felt the waves of dissonance and the clashing chaos of interference arising from the turmoil of despairing, angered minds all across Gramarye—from youth led into confusion by the sorceress, seduced into the nightmare disorientation that made them malleable and would have brought them eventually to her coven, to swell her power.

But the harmonies of the choir of linked minds rolled out over the land now, welling from the monastery in the southeast and this small fountain in the northwest, to soothe and calm and reassure, lifting souls from despair and giving them the inspiration of a fundamental certainty that there was some sort of sense to existence somewhere, that harmony and hope still existed, though the troubled young might not yet perceive them—but could eventually find them, and the peace and, perhaps, even the happiness they sought.

Finally, Rod could feel exhaustion dimming Brother Dorian's music, could feel the choir weakening—but they had lasted long enough. The worst of the standing waves of confusion and chaos spreading outward from the psychic storm had decayed; physical entropy had subsumed emotional entropy. The energy input was gone, and the nightmares it had generated had begun to die.

Slowly, Brother Dorian began to soften his tones. The glowing forms around him dimmed, then faded. Finally, his chords were silenced, and only a single melodic line held sway. One by one, the Gallowglasses laid down their instruments as the single tune resolved the whole symphony, was met with a final chord, and was done. Brother Dorian stood, face uplifted, exhausted but exalted, immobile.

" 'Twas miraculous," Cordelia said softly.

"A miracle of thine own making, then." Brother Dorian's voice seemed to come from far away.

"Nay, Brother," Father Thelonius demurred. "Miracles come from God alone—we can but hope that they flow through us."

Still, Brother Dorian's voice was not of this world. "There are more miracles than we realize, then, for they are all about us, and need not be great and mighty. Grace comes to all who are open to it; miracles hap in places far removed from fame. 'Tis only the few that catch the eye of mighty folk that do astound us all."

"Thy work this day hath astounded me," Geoffrey said, and that was enough to make Rod marvel.

"I believe more strongly in Heaven, for having been a part of this upwelling of souls," Cordelia said. "Can we never be of it again?"

"Mayhap thou canst." Finally, Brother Dorian's gaze met theirs, and he came back to the present. "You have but to learn to make music yourselves, and play it together—and, now and again, when all is true and right, this feeling may come upon you. Not in such intensity, no, for such as this is rare, that so many souls be conjoined—but enough, enough."

"Then I will anticipate it," Magnus murmured.

Gwen turned to Father Thelonius. "What form of Mass was this, that had every form of sense involved, and made so many folk a channel for the common greatness?"

"Each one of us was a medium for the goodness in the hearts of all others," Father Thelonius answered, "and for a while, we were able to put aside our jealousies and spites, our shadows' hungers and desires. For some brief time, we learned again that what is good in us is of greater moment than what is fell."

That wasn't much of an answer, Rod decided, but it was enough.

"Yet what of thee?" Father Thelonius' tone sharpened with anxiety. "How didst thou fare, who took the brunt of peril upon thee?"

The children looked up, suddenly aware again of the potential for horror. "Oh, Mama!" Cordelia fled to embrace Gwen, and the boys crowded round.

"Nay, child, I am well." Gwen caressed Cordelia's hair. " 'Twas harrowing, I will own, but 'tis done, and though thy father and I had some pain in the doing of it, we emerge unscathed."

"What pain?" Magnus cried, but Gwen said, "Hush. 'Twas of the passing moment, and is gone."

"Forgive me, then, when thou art so wearied." Father Thelonius wasn't looking too spruce himself. "But I must know, if I can—didst thou discover aught more of the way in which this blasphemy came to be? I must forestall its recurrence, if I can."

Rod shuddered at the thought. "I'm afraid we had a good summary of that, Father."

Gwen nodded, gaze fixed on Thelonius' eyes. "As the sorceress died, her memories sped through our minds. We know more of her than we wish."

"Say, then—what manner of thing was she?"

"Only another peasant with a modicum of talent of the mind," Gwen explained. "Partly for this, and partly for her misshapen features, she was scorned and shunned by her fellows, till their contempt did fester within her soul and yield conviction that she was far better than any, though her qualities were hidden. Yet she was certain that they would one day burst forth to bring her power and glory—and scope for revenge."

Father Thelonius nodded sadly. " 'Tis an old tale and a sad one, told out aye many times. Its only cures are grace and faith, and devotion to charity. Yet lacking these, she was fertile ground for those who sought to make a tool of her."

Rod nodded. "You have it. That was no psionic construct

that held that tornado in check—it was a force field, set up by electronic devices and maintained by the power of a nuclear reactor."

"Ah." Father Thelonius lifted his head. "It was an agent from off-planet, then, who played her tempter."

"He was indeed," Gwen said, "though she knew it not. He came to her in the guise of a devil, pleading for her sympathy and offering her the satisfaction of her lust. If she would worship him, he said, he would give her power—power to destroy. He gave her a mission—to reduce the land of Gramarye to anarchy. And he showed her the way to it—told her of the peasant who did make the witch-moss stones, and how to entice him to make rocks that would bend to her will the common folk who have no witch-talent of their own. Then did he show her how, once bent, she could bring them to her, could use music to entice them into blending what little mind-power they had with her own talent, thus shaping a stronger power to bend more folk and bring them in. Thus did she gather a 'coven' of deluded mortals who, like herself, did think themselves great because, in their hidden hearts, they believed themselves diminished. She promised them the power of the devil who had appeared to her, and aided them in deluding themselves to believe they had witch-powers."

"But they truly had no talent of any kind?" Father Thelonius asked.

"None, save perhaps the great-heartedness that might have been, had they not killed it aborning with their own poisoned pain. Some among these she sent out to the crafter, to pay him and tell him what new forms of music she wished to have come from his next rocks. Others she sent out to spread those first rocks broadcast, and bring in more folk like them."

"That's why the music took such an unpleasant turn," Rod explained.

"Aye," Father Thelonius agreed, "there was something of a poisoned mind underlying it. But what of the strange beings that did seem to accompany this music as it spread?"

Rod shook his head. "No one person's doing. But the

music itself did start to suggest strange things. My own guess is that they came into existence the way the elves did—from the vivid imaginations of people who didn't know they were projectives. Only this time, instead of old folk-tales suggesting forms for witch-moss constructs, it was music."

Father Thelonius nodded. "And did this agent in a devil's guise give her the thought of worship of him?"

"There are men who would enjoy such a thing," Rod admitted. Magnus glanced sharply at him.

"Even so," Gwen agreed. " 'Twas he who built her the altar that hid her devices of power, he who told her how to make of it a reservoir of minds' energies. Yet not being psionic, he could not tell her the manner of using that resource; she discovered that herself, and this opened a channel she could not close, directly from the reservoir to her mind."

"And it destroyed her mind?" the monk asked.

Gwen nodded. "As her music gathered in more and more deluded folk to yield what little power they could, and channel the far greater amount that came from others stirred by her grating sounds, the power from the reservoir overwhelmed her brain. She began to lose control; the disminding noises she herself had made beat most strongly on the brain that had engendered them, making her to think of sounds more strongly bent. These did she make to sound in the minds of those about her, and her agents took the memory of those sounds to the crafter, to make rocks that would emit such noise."

"And the reservoir would distort the new sound into a grosser sound, and the agents would take that out to the crafter," Rod added. "So the whole cycle would begin again, swelling the reservoir from the power of the people it absorbed, with no one directing it."

"A regenerative cycle," Father Thelonius said, "a vicious circle."

"A feedback loop by any other name," Rod agreed. "The more it fed back, the more it warped the brain that had begun it—and the more power that the coven brought in, the more it seared its single path through her neurons, numbing what intellect she had."

"The power she used burned her out," Gwen agreed. "She may have harnessed the whirlwind, but she had little mind left with which to direct it."

Rod nodded. "She turned the whole assemblage—herself, her adherents, and the reservoir—into a runaway engine, out of control."

"But thus they sought to be," Gwen protested. "They sought to lose control, all—even, toward the end, the sorceress herself!"

Father Thelonius shook his head. " 'Tis the instinct in the social animal, to yield itself up and become a part of something greater than itself."

"That is the impulse that should start us on the road to Heaven," Brother Dorian murmured.

"But can be used to turn us onto the path to Hell." Father Thelonius scowled. "Thus can we be misled—oh, so easily misled! And the younger we are, the more easily 'tis done."

The junior Gallowglasses exchanged glances.

Then they turned, as one, to Brother Dorian.

He was packing up his keyboard.

"What!" Cordelia protested. "Wilt thou leave us lorn?"

The monk paused in the act of slipping his keyboard away under his robe. "Nay, I think not," he said with a smile. "I shall return to the monastery, aye—but I think there shall be some new songs in the land ere long."

# STEVEN BRUST

### __JHEREG  0-441-38554-0/$3.95
There are many ways for a young man with quick wits and a quick
sword to advance in the world. Vlad Taltos chose the route of the
assassin and the constant companionship of a young jhereg.

### __YENDI  0-441-94460-4/$3.50
Vlad Taltos and his jhereg companion learn how the love of a good
woman can turn a cold-blooded killer into a _real_ mean S.O.B...

### __TECKLA  0-441-79977-9/$3.50
The Teckla were revolting. Vlad Taltos always knew they were lazy,
stupid, cowardly peasants...revolting. But now they were revolting
against the empire. No joke.

### __TALTOS 0-441-18200/$3.50
Journey to the land of the dead. All expenses paid! Not Vlad Taltos'
idea of an ideal vacation, but this was work. After all, even an
assassin has to earn a living.

### __COWBOY FENG'S SPACE BAR AND GRILLE
### 0-441-11816-X/$3.95
Cowboy Feng's is a great place to visit, but it tends to move around
a bit—from Earth to the Moon to Mars to another solar system—
and always just one step ahead of whatever mysterious conspiracy is
reducing whole worlds to radioactive ash.

# MULTI-MILLION COPY
# BESTSELLING AUTHOR OF DUNE!

---

# FRANK
# HERBERT

---